LET ME GO

EVA RAE THOMAS MYSTERY - BOOK 5

WILLOW ROSE

Books by the Author

HARRY HUNTER MYSTERY SERIES

- All The Good Girls
- Run Girl Run
- No Other Way
- Never Walk Alone

MARY MILLS MYSTERY SERIES

- What Hurts the Most
- You Can Run
- You Can't Hide
- Careful Little Eyes

EVA RAE THOMAS MYSTERY SERIES

- Don't Lie to me
- What you did
- Never Ever
- Say You Love me
- Let Me Go
- It's Not Over
- Not Dead yet

EMMA FROST SERIES

- Itsy Bitsy Spider
- Miss Dolly had a Dolly
- Run, Run as Fast as You Can
- Cross Your Heart and Hope to Die
- Peek-a-Boo I See You
- Tweedledum and Tweedledee

- EASY AS ONE, TWO, THREE
- THERE'S NO PLACE LIKE HOME
- SLENDERMAN
- WHERE THE WILD ROSES GROW
- WALTZING MATHILDA
- DRIP DROP DEAD
- BLACK FROST

JACK RYDER SERIES

- HIT THE ROAD JACK
- SLIP OUT THE BACK JACK
- THE HOUSE THAT JACK BUILT
- BLACK JACK
- GIRL NEXT DOOR
- HER FINAL WORD
- DON'T TELL

REBEKKA FRANCK SERIES

- ONE, TWO...HE IS COMING FOR YOU
- THREE, FOUR...BETTER LOCK YOUR DOOR
- FIVE, SIX...GRAB YOUR CRUCIFIX
- SEVEN, EIGHT...GONNA STAY UP LATE
- NINE, TEN...NEVER SLEEP AGAIN
- ELEVEN, TWELVE...DIG AND DELVE
- THIRTEEN, FOURTEEN...LITTLE BOY UNSEEN
- BETTER NOT CRY
- TEN LITTLE GIRLS
- IT ENDS HERE

MYSTERY/THRILLER/HORROR NOVELS

- SORRY CAN'T SAVE YOU
- IN ONE FELL SWOOP
- UMBRELLA MAN

- Blackbird Fly
- To Hell in a Handbasket
- Edwina

HORROR SHORT-STORIES

- Mommy Dearest
- The Bird
- Better watch out
- Eenie, Meenie
- Rock-a-Bye Baby
- Nibble, Nibble, Crunch
- Humpty Dumpty
- Chain Letter

PARANORMAL SUSPENSE/ROMANCE NOVELS

- In Cold Blood
- The Surge
- Girl Divided

THE VAMPIRES OF SHADOW HILLS SERIES

- Flesh and Blood
- Blood and Fire
- Fire and Beauty
- Beauty and Beasts
- Beasts and Magic
- Magic and Witchcraft
- Witchcraft and War
- War and Order
- Order and Chaos
- Chaos and Courage

THE AFTERLIFE SERIES

Cover design by Juan Villar Padron,
https://www.juanjpadron.com

Special thanks to my editor Janell Parque
http://janellparque.blogspot.com/

To be the first to hear about new releases and bargains from Willow Rose, sign up below to be on the VIP List. (I promise not to share your email with anyone else, and I won't clutter your inbox.)

- GO HERE TO SIGN UP TO BE ON THE VIP LIST :
http://readerlinks.com/l/415254

Tired of too many emails? Text the word: "willowrose" to 31996 to sign up to Willow's VIP text List to get a text alert with news about New Releases, Giveaways, Bargains and Free books from Willow.

FOLLOW WILLOW ROSE ON BOOKBUB:
https://www.bookbub.com/authors/willow-rose

Connect with Willow online:
https://www.amazon.com/Willow-Rose/e/B004X2WHBQ
https://www.facebook.com/willowredrose/
https://twitter.com/madamwillowrose
http://www.goodreads.com/author/show/4804769.Willow_Rose
Http://www.willow-rose.net
madamewillowrose@gmail.com

Prologue
NEW ORLEANS, LOUISIANA

Prologue

"WE'VE SET up the perimeter, boss. Team's ready. They're just waiting for your go."

Reed nodded. His pulse was pounding in his ears as the adrenaline rushed through him. His hands felt clammy, and he had to wipe them on his shirt to get them dry enough. He couldn't let slippery hands interfere with what was about to go down. He really didn't want to have to do this.

"I just shot my dad in the head."

That was the message that dispatch had received and passed on. A hostage situation, they said. A young kid who told them his name was Peter was in there, in that two-story house in front of Reed. With him were his mom and younger sister.

An argument had made the boy shoot his father. The boy had then called nine-one-one. He said he was standing inside the house with the firearm and that his mom and sister were hiding in the bathroom, that he had poured gasoline all over the house, and that he'd kill himself and what was left of his family.

"Please, don't do that," Dispatch had told him. "There's no need. Stay on the phone with me."

But the boy had hung up. Reed and his men were sent out to prevent a tragedy from happening. Reed wasn't going to lose any more lives tonight.

Not on his watch.

The boy had told dispatch that it was an accident, that he didn't mean to kill his dad, but Reed also knew that the guy was desperate and capable of anything if he was capable of killing his own father.

Reed wasn't taking any chances. In his fifteen years as leader of the SWAT unit, he had seen his share of desperate young men. And one thing was certain; you never knew what they might do next. The fact that the boy had poured gasoline all over the house showed him that they had to be very careful with this one.

"I see movement behind one of the windows," Harris said to him.

Harris had been with Reed's team for almost ten years now. The two of them had been through hostage situations like this many times.

Not all of them ended well.

"Is there any way of getting in contact with the boy?" Reed asked and looked through his binoculars.

"Negative," Harris said. "There's no landline, and we don't have any cell phone numbers. It's gonna take a while to get them. Too long if you ask me. We don't have time. We need to act now before he lights a match or shoots any more of his family members."

Reed sighed deeply, but he agreed.

"All right." He grabbed the radio and spoke into it: "Team is a go."

Reed saw the silhouette of a person bobbing up and down in the window and wondered if the kid was performing CPR on his father. On the call, he had said that his dad was lifeless and not breathing. Was he trying to resuscitate him?

The shadow disappeared.

A pack of officers was creeping up toward the front porch. Three others came from the east side. Reed grabbed his PA, ready to try and address the boy, ask him to come out and surrender himself, giving him a last chance to end this peacefully.

But before Reed could place the PA against his lips, the door to the house cracked open. A figure appeared and emerged through the screen door and walked onto the porch.

Prologue

PETER JAMES WAS in the living room when he heard the noise coming from outside his windows. Thinking it was just some of the neighborhood's kids, he chose to ignore it at first.

He stared at the computer screen in front of him, where he was making a new gaming video for his seven-hundred-thousand followers who tuned in every week to see him play. He was in the middle of a huge battle when the noise disturbed him again.

"Give me a second," he said to his viewers. "I have to go and see what's going on. I'll be right back. Probably just some neighborhood kids messing around."

He let the video run and paused the game, then rushed to the front door and opened it. A white and extremely bright light met him outside the screen door, and he had to use his hand to cover his eyes. He did so while taking a step onto the porch. Suddenly, he was met with loud voices yelling from multiple angles.

Desperate and frantic yelling.

"Don't move. Put your hands in the air."

Peter froze. The yelling continued.

"Hands where we can see them!"

Peter felt confused. The light was still blinding him, and it was like a surreal dream. What was happening?

"Raise your hands!"

"Excuse me?" Peter turned his head very slowly to the left and realized that there were about half a dozen police cars, lights flashing, and more officers pointing firearms in his direction, including a shotgun and a semi-automatic rifle.

"Raise your hands NOW!"

Peter did as he was told. His arms shot straight up, his heart pounding.

"Face the house, back down your front steps, and walk backward toward us."

Peter blinked, trying to get the information right and not make a wrong move. As he did his turn, the light blinded him so much he instinctively lowered one hand toward his waist.

That would prove to be fatal.

The shot came from behind the white light and blasted through his chest with such force his body was slung backward, back through the screened door. The bullet ripped through his heart and killed him instantly.

He didn't even hear his mother's terrified screams coming from inside the house.

ONE YEAR LATER
BOOKS-A-MILLION, NEW JERSEY

Chapter 1

"HE REFUSES TO DO IT."

"Let me talk to him."

Liam overheard them talking and smiled secretively as his agent, Ben, came toward him. He could see Ben was grinding his teeth as he walked. Liam pretended to be listening to the dolled-up woman in her high stilettos and pretended to not feel sick from her overpowering perfume or her thick layer of make-up. He considered commenting on it, putting a little insult into some sarcasm or a joke and seeing how she reacted.

Just for fun.

Here comes the smile. Come on, Ben; put on the smile.

And there it was. Ben clenched his fists one more time, then looked up, and as his eyes met Liam's, he smiled.

A smile so phony that Hollywood should be calling soon.

Liam chuckled and shook his head. Sensing that she was being ignored, the dolled-up woman slipped away quietly.

"You do know that a genuine smile doesn't show the bottom teeth, right?" Liam said and sipped his champagne. The bookstore had provided it for him as he had demanded they did like he demanded every bookstore did if they wanted him to come to their insignificant place and attract a crowd.

"You're a son-of-a-gun, you know that, right?" Ben said, speaking with a low voice.

"I do," Liam answered as he lifted his glass at a woman who made eyes at him while passing by. "It's part of my charm, remember? It's why they love me so much."

"Don't sleep with anyone here," Ben said. "And please…for Christ sakes, just do what they expect you to. The publishing house wants you to do this tour, and it's the last God darn book signing. We've been all over the country for the past several weeks. Just sit in the stupid chair, smile at the nice housewives, flirt a little, and sign their books. It's as simple as that."

"I won't do it," Liam said.

Ben sighed resignedly and threw out his arms. "And why the heck not?"

Liam nodded at the area where they had put his chair and table. It was surrounded by his books on both sides. A full-body-sized cardboard figure of Liam stood next to it, and a poster was hanging behind it, showing a picture of him in his chef's uniform with a big knife in his hand. He looked ridiculous. But that wasn't anything new. Everything about this entire charade was absurd. It was, however, his life now, and he had made an image and a career of it. They expected him to cause trouble, to act like a diva. That's why they called him the Rockstar of Cooking.

"What's wrong with it this time?" Ben asked. "Is the chair too low again because I can get you a new one. I know you don't like to look small in front of people."

"Look to the right of the table," Liam said. "Look at what they have placed next to me. On the wall behind me. I refuse to sit there with his books glaring down on me."

Ben took an extra look, then nodded. "All right. I get it."

"You know how I feel about that imposter."

"I do know that, but still, don't you think you're overreacting a little here? The guy did say he was sorry for the things he said about your food."

"I just can't stand him," Liam said. "And don't let me get started on his use of truffle oil. It's preposterous."

Ben exhaled. "All right. I'll have them remove his books from the shelf behind you, but then…then you promise me you'll go ahead and sign the books, right? Because people have been waiting for hours now. We all want this done so we can go home after a long book tour, right?"

Liam nodded and finished his glass. He was looking forward to going home more than anything, even if it was to a teenage son who hated his guts and hadn't spoken to him in months.

Chapter 2

I HAD BEEN WAITING for hours in the line outside in the freezing cold and finally made it inside the warm store. I was surrounded by housewives wearing heavy makeup and low-cut shirts, puffing themselves up to meet him. They were all waiting to have fifteen seconds with the guy who had written the book under every arm in the line in front of me. The closer we got to him, the more mouths were pouting and hair was being corrected.

I felt like an outsider in my flat white sneakers, jeans, and a leather jacket. My red hair was in a ponytail, and I was wearing absolutely no make-up whatsoever. I saw no need. I wasn't here to flirt with the guy or even to see him because I had read his book. To be honest, up until now, I had thought it was just a cookbook. But, apparently, it was a book about him and his childhood growing up in the streets of Philadelphia before making it as a famous TV chef and household name. The first African American to have made it in the world that was mostly dominated by British and French chefs.

If I stood on my tippy toes and stretched my neck, I could see him. There he was, smiling at a woman in a tight red dress, then glaring at her behind as she turned around and walked on.

The Rockstar of Cooking all right.

"What am I even doing here?" I mumbled as the line moved forward.

But I knew very well why I was there, and it wasn't a social call. This was important enough to embarrass myself if I had to.

As soon as it was my turn, I slid my book across the table to him.

Liam Berkeley looked first at my fingers, holding the book, then up at me.

"You bite your nails," he said.

I shrugged. "So? Is that illegal?"

That made him chuckle.

I gave him a fake smile. That made his chuckle turn into a laugh. "You do realize that a genuine smile doesn't involve showing your bottom teeth, right?"

"Whatever," I said and dropped the smile. "I don't usually smile a lot."

"Oh? Why is that?"

I shrugged again. "Because I don't think there is a lot to smile about."

"What do you mean?"

I threw out my arms. "Have you seen the world we live in?"

"You're fun," he said and pointed at me with the pen. "Now, who should I make this out to?"

He opened the page to sign it, and I bit my lip. This was it. This was the moment that I had waited hours in a line for, freezing outside those doors, knowing it was the only way I could get my message to a guy like him.

He read the message I had scribbled on the blank page, then looked up at me, eyes suddenly serious.

"What is this?"

"Just do as it says. You'll know more when you get there."

And after that, I ran out, elbowing my way through flocks of ladies in high heels and cocktail dresses who were making Books-A-Million seem a heck of a lot more glamorous than usual on a Tuesday night.

Chapter 3

THEN:

"Nine-One-One, what's your emergency?"

"Yeah, hi…uhm, my name is Brady. I just want to say that there is a…uhm bomb."

"There's a what?"

"A bomb."

"A bomb? Where?"

"At Lincoln High School."

"There's a bomb at the high school, you say?"

"Yes."

"And how do you know this?"

"I placed them there."

"Them. So there is more than one bomb at the high school?"

"Yes."

"How many?"

"Uhm…seven."

"Seven bombs at the high school?"

"Yes. They're scattered all over the school in backpacks. I placed them there myself. There's a timer on them. They'll go off in ten minutes."

Chapter 4

THE SMALL LEBANESE restaurant Suraya in Fishtown in Philadelphia was turned into a café and market during the day while there was a full-service restaurant and a bar for dinnertime. The beans were Stumptown, and their Middle Eastern and French pastries weren't to be missed, or so it said in the online review I had read when looking for a good place to meet.

I wasn't there for the food, even though I had already gulped down two cups of coffee and two pieces of greasy yet yummy pastry by the time he was supposed to be there. I had chosen a place in Philadelphia because that's where he had lived all his life. If I wanted him to come, then I needed it to be convenient for him.

The décor was not fancy, and that was part of what I liked about this place. Just a few wooden chairs and tables scattered about in what looked like the lobby of a boutique hotel.

I stared into my oversized mug as someone approached my table. I lifted my glance and saw him.

"This is not something I usually do," he said. "It better be good."

A few other guests recognized Liam Berkeley, and a woman beamed in his direction but left it at that. I had hoped that no one would bother us in this place since it wasn't one of the trendier cafes where young people went to get their coffee.

"Me either," I said. "Sit down, please. Do you want some coffee? It's good, and so are the pastries."

Liam didn't even smile. He did sit down, however, and that made me relax slightly.

"Do you know how many messages like this I get every time I do a book signing?" he asked. "Asking to meet up or even if I want to have sex?"

I chuckled lightly. "I bet it happens a lot. But that's not why I did it."

"I kind of got that. Yours was different. How did you know it would work?"

"I didn't. But I had a feeling it might."

The waitress arrived with coffee for Liam and a refill for me. It was obvious that she had recognized him in the way she looked at him and then at me before rushing off.

He stirred sugar into his coffee. I readied myself for what I was about to tell him. I knew it might not go over too well.

He sipped from his cup. I expected him to make a ruckus about how awful the coffee was, but he didn't. This wasn't his TV show. We weren't on set, and he was off duty. Maybe he wasn't as nasty as they all said he was, as he was made out to be on his TV show. Sitting there in front of me, he seemed like a surprisingly normal guy in his mid-forties, if you didn't count all the stares and giggling coming from women behind his back, that was. He had lost his wife to pancreatic cancer five years ago and was alone with his teenage son, I had read. Since then, he became known worldwide as the angry chef who was impossible to satisfy. It wasn't a pleasant image, and I, for one, couldn't stand watching it, but his show had sky-high ratings, especially among young people.

"So, how do you know my son's gaming username?" he asked. "You wrote it in the message? When you asked me to meet you here? You said it had to do with him? BOOTERS4U?"

I cleared my throat. This was the hard part.

"It does."

"So, what's going on? Is he in some kind of trouble?"

I sipped my coffee, bracing myself, then nodded. "You could say that."

Liam Berkeley groaned, annoyed, and I assumed this wasn't the first time his son had been the center of a conversation like this.

"What kind of trouble?"

I leaned forward, took a deep breath, then said:

"I have reason to believe that someone wants to kill him."

Chapter 5

"EXCUSE ME?"

Liam raised both his eyebrows. I wondered how he had managed to become such a big TV star. He had a crooked nose, floppy ears, and narrow-set eyes. On top of that, he had this angry energy to him that I found appalling. He was far from likable, in my opinion.

I cleared my throat. "I am sorry to have to be the one…"

"Did you just seriously say that you believed someone wanted to kill my son?" he asked, narrowing his eyes so they almost disappeared.

"Yes, that is what I said."

Liam scoffed. "And just who might you be?"

"Eva Rae Thomas," I said. "Former FBI-profiler."

He lifted his eyebrows again and gave me a look. "Former, as in *used to be?*"

"Yes. I used to be."

"So, you're not with the bureau anymore?" he asked, sounding more and more condescending. I had a clear feeling of where this was heading.

"I am not, no. I quit a year ago to be with my family."

Liam leaned back in his chair and crossed his arms in front of his chest. "And why exactly are you here and not with them now?"

A very good question, indeed. I should be with my children. But instead, I am here, far away from home, trying to save the life of someone I don't even know.

I paused too long, and he continued without waiting for my answer.

"If my boy's life is in danger, then why am I not sitting with someone who's actually working for the FBI or the local police?"

Another very good question.

"Because they don't know what I know," I said, trying to keep it simple. I didn't want to have to explain to him how the local police and FBI didn't believe me when I told them. That wouldn't exactly help my credibility with this guy.

He gave me another look that told me I was losing him. I exhaled deeply while feeling him slip between my fingers.

"Listen, I need you to take this very seriously. If you could just give me a chance to explain…"

He rose to his feet and took out his wallet. "It's too bad. I had really thought you weren't a lunatic. I liked you from the moment I saw you, with your unpolished, raw, bitten-down nails and your no makeup and feisty red hair. You have this spark in your eyes that I enjoyed, and you were…different. I really believed you weren't one of the crazy ones. Maybe it was just wishful thinking. I should have known that no good ever comes from responding to a message like that. But I am sad to prove myself wrong. It's sad, really," he said as he pulled out a twenty-dollar bill and placed it on the table.

"This should cover the cost of the utterly despicable coffee they serve here. I want to say it was nice to meet you, but it really wasn't."

I opened my mouth to protest, to tell him that if he left now his son would be killed within twenty-four hours, but before I could get the words across my lips, he was out the glass door and gone.

"Dang it," I said a little too loudly and slammed my fist on the table, causing everyone else in the restaurant to turn their heads and look at me. I didn't even care if any of them posted about this meeting on social media and humiliated me publicly. All I cared about was his son and whether or not he would live to see the next day.

The way it looked now, he wouldn't.

Chapter 6

"DO you want me to throw this old chair out too?"

Matt's mother grabbed the back of the chair and pulled it out so he could better see it.

"There's nothing wrong with it," she continued.

Matt nodded.

"It's old, and Eva Rae doesn't have that much space."

"But it's such a good chair," she said and gave him that look again, the one that said *is she going to let you bring anything that is yours?*

"You can have it," Matt said and turned his back on her. He grabbed a lamp, then looked at it, wondering if it was of any use, then decided it wasn't. It had gotten an ugly spot on it by being left in his mother's garage for years. Most of his stuff was worthless, really, and needed to go. It wasn't just because he knew Eva Rae didn't want him to bring too much stuff when he and Elijah moved in with her and her three kids, it was also that he didn't want to bring crap. Eva Rae had nice things, and she was good at decorating. She wouldn't want old worn out chairs or spotted lamps in her house.

"But what will you take then?" his mother asked. "If none of this is any good?"

"I'll bring my personal stuff, clothes, and so on."

"And what about all your trophies?" she asked and glanced up at the shelf on the wall where all his running trophies were standing, gathering dust.

He chuckled. "I can't bring those. That was back in high school, Mom. I'm forty-two now."

She shrugged. "So, what do you want to do with them?"

"Can I leave them here? You don't use the space anyway."

She forced a smile. Matt knew she wasn't too pleased about him and Elijah moving out. It was only natural. They had lived with her for quite a while now since Elijah's mom died, and she had taken care of the boy. But now it was time for Matt to take matters into his own hands. He had never managed to forge a good relationship with the boy since he blamed him for his mother's death, and if Matt was honest, he hadn't tried very hard. He had barely known the boy when his mother was still alive, and he had no idea how to go about it. Not until now, that was. Now, he wanted to. He wanted to be the dad he knew he could be, and it was time for him to take care of the stuff, the day-to-day things that his mom had done for him up until now. He wanted to be the one who packed Elijah's lunches and picked him up after school. If other dads could do it, then so could he. He was a detective at the local police station, and Chief Annie was fine with him taking care of his own hours as long as he was there for the important meetings and solved his cases in a timely manner. Plus, he didn't want to be a burden to his mother anymore, either. She shouldn't spend her life taking care of her grandchild. It was his job. He wanted to move on with his life and take his relationship with Eva Rae to the next level.

It was time he grew up.

Elijah came out to him, holding his backpack in his hand. The boy was angry that he was going to move and hadn't spoken a word to Matt since he announced it. It didn't make that big of a change since he hardly ever spoke a word to Matt before either.

"You ready, buddy?" he asked, smiling.

The boy didn't say anything. He just stared at him, holding his backpack tightly. If Matt knew him at all, he knew that it probably contained only his iPad and Xbox…maybe a shirt and a tooth-brush, but that was probably all. Matt had packed the rest of his things earlier, and they were already in the truck.

Matt grabbed a box and walked it out to the driveway, then placed it in the back of the truck where there was still a little room. He had borrowed his mother's truck for the move, and it could fit almost all their stuff, except for two boxes. Elijah got into the front and slammed the door shut. Matt kissed his mother's cheek.

"I'll be back tomorrow for the rest."

His mother answered with a sniffle, then tightened her lips.

"Take good care of our boy, will you?"

Matt sighed, then nodded. "It's not like you won't see him."

"I just don't like the idea of him being in aftercare now when he could be with his grandmother."

"I know, Mom, but I'm trying to take care of him myself now. If he's with you all the time, there's no need for him to attach himself to me. I think this will be good for us, Mom. I really do."

She nodded and kissed him back. "All right, kiddo. Just remember that I'm right here in case you need anything."

Matt nodded and stifled his tears. It felt like he was moving away for the first time. He waved at his mom, then got into the truck and drove off, Elijah playing the music in his air buds so loud that Matt could hear every beat of it.

Chapter 7

I COULDN'T SIT STILL. I was pacing back and forth in my hotel room in Philadelphia, flipping through the TV channels for news broadcasts, only stopping to bite my nails. Still, there was no breaking news about the son of a famous TV chef being killed, but I knew it was only a matter of time.

And it was about to destroy me.

I had tried to call his publicist to get the man to listen to me. I had even called the local police and told them to be aware, but they wouldn't give me the time of day. And since I didn't really know exactly where Liam Berkeley lived, and since he kept his address very private as most celebrities did, I couldn't drive there and try to stop it from happening.

At seven, Matt called me. I picked it up, heart in my throat.

"I thought you were coming home tonight?" he asked.

"I wanted to; I really did, but...well, the meeting took longer than planned and..."

Matt exhaled. "I'm here at the house. Your house, or rather our house. I moved most of our stuff today, and you weren't even there when we got here. Your mom and Olivia had to help us carry the stuff inside. I thought you'd be here, and we could celebrate that we are officially moved in together? I bought champagne?"

I closed my eyes. I had completely forgotten. I was supposed to drive home this afternoon and be there when he and Elijah arrived.

"I…I'm so sorry, Matt."

"You forgot, didn't you?" he asked, sounding more than disappointed.

"I…I…"

What could I say? There was no excuse. Yes, I had forgotten it completely. I had been so immersed in getting to Liam Berkeley to warn him, and for what? It didn't make any difference. He wouldn't even hear me out. And now Matt was mad at me?

I felt embarrassed.

"I'm coming home tomorrow," I said. "I promise."

"Okay. But you better keep that promise. It's kind of lonely here without you."

"Did my family at least treat you well?" I asked. "Did the kids behave?"

Matt sighed. "They did. Your mom made cauliflower steaks with Chimichurri sauce. It was quite good."

"How's Elijah coping?" I asked.

"Well, he didn't eat any of the food tonight. He normally likes a burger or hot dog, but I'm sure he'll come around."

Matt, the eternal optimist. He refused to give up on the boy even though he had barely said five words to his father since his mother died. He didn't even look at him when he spoke to him. Still, Matt believed he'd come around. Eventually, he would.

I could only be impressed with his will to constantly remain optimistic.

"How's he doing with my kids?" I asked.

"Well, so far, they haven't really spoken or had any interaction. Elijah stayed in his room all afternoon and evening. I don't think he and Alex are talking yet, though."

Alex had been thrilled by the idea of sharing a bedroom with Elijah since he thought the boy was so cool. I wasn't sure Elijah shared the enthusiasm to have to share a bedroom with a seven-year-old boy when he was nine. But it would have to do for now, at least while my mom was still living with us. I had asked her about it cautiously, suggesting that she at least sell the old house, but she wouldn't hear talk of it. Every time I as much as mentioned it, she'd just turn her back on me and walk away. I guess I just had to give her the time she needed, and I didn't want her to feel like I wanted her out of the house, so I had stopped bringing it up.

"So, when are you going to tell me what you're up to?" Matt asked. "Why you had to leave so suddenly?"

I sighed and stared at the TV screen in front of me, my stomach in knots when thinking about Liam Berkeley and his son.

"You wouldn't believe me."

"Try me," he said.

"It's something I've been working on for a few months now. I'll tell you everything when I get back."

Chapter 8

"HOW WAS YOUR DAY?"

Liam stood on the threshold of Tim's room. The boy was sitting at his screen—as usual—playing Fortnite or Call of Duty. Liam never knew the difference, and he didn't care either.

They had drifted apart when Anna got sick six years ago and died a year later. Tim was still angry with Liam for not being there…for traveling and taking care of his career.

And he was right. The boy had been absolutely right. Liam had beat himself up for not prioritizing Anna more back then. But his career had just taken off, and if he was brutally honest, Anna's sickness was unbearable. He couldn't stand watching her wither and die. It broke his heart. So, he threw himself into work and said yes to any assignment that came his way, hoping it could take his mind off the many worries and the sadness that engulfed him.

Losing her had almost crushed him. He had barely been able to pull himself up from the dark hole he had ended up in. But working had helped. When he filmed his TV show, he wasn't Liam, the sad father who had lost his wife. He wasn't lonely. It was a part he played like an actor in a play, a mask he put on. While doing the show, he could get as angry as he wanted. He could yell at the contestants and act as crazy as he needed to. It became his outlet for his many frustrations…for his helplessness when seeing the woman he loved die while he stood by and could do nothing.

Tim couldn't forgive Liam for not being there in the weeks that followed when he needed him the most. But Liam had been such a mess. He didn't think he could have been there for anyone.

"What's it to you?" Tim answered without turning around.

"Just asking. Out of curiosity and genuine interest in your life," Liam said.

Tim didn't say anything; he kept playing. The boy was fifteen now. Five years had passed since then, and it wasn't getting better between them.

Liam stood for a few minutes, staring at his back. He was wearing the old gray hoodie that his mom had bought for him when he was nine, but had been a couple of sizes too big back then. Now it was tight in the shoulders and the sleeves were a little short. Still, he refused to wear anything else. He would only take it off when Juanita, their housekeeper, scolded him and said that it was a dirty rag that needed to be washed.

Poor kid.

Liam thought about the meeting with the crazy lady earlier in the day. Thinking about her made him angry again. Where did she get off telling him something like that? Was it just to taunt him? Did she just want him in pain; was that it?

I believe someone wants to kill your son.

Why would she say something like that? Had everyone in this world gone completely mad?

Liam chuckled, then walked down the hallway and checked the alarm. His house was among the best-secured homes in the area. Even if she was right and someone tried, there was no way they could get in.

Chapter 9

I STARED AT MY WATCH, heart pounding harder and harder in my chest. I still had the TV on when it struck eight-thirty. I was just staring at the screen, at the twenty-four-hour news channel, not really listening to what was being said. From what I could make out, the news anchor talked about a story of a teen being charged after driving around with his sister on the hood of the car. After that followed the story of how a university doctor from a local university allegedly had inappropriate relationships with his students and is now being investigated.

All were ordinary stories on an ordinary Wednesday night.

I exhaled and rubbed the bridge of my nose, closing my eyes and trying to calm myself.

Just for this one time, Lord, let me be wrong. Let me have misinterpreted the messages; let me just be crazy enough to read things into what I see that aren't really there. Just for this once.

I looked at my watch again. Eight-forty-one. We were getting closer. I tried to think about something else and went to the window to look out at the city in front of me. I had taken a small bottle of white wine from the minibar and poured it into one of the glasses in the room. It didn't taste very good. It was kind of bitter, and I grimaced after every sip, but I still drank it.

The city with its sea of lights seemed so peaceful. I couldn't even hear sirens or anyone yelling.

Calm before the storm.

I had chosen one of the cheap hotels where a night's stay cost only eighty-five bucks. It was called Red Roof Inn and was pretty nice for the price. I couldn't complain. I wasn't exactly rich like my sister, the Hollywood actress, so it was what I could afford for the time being.

Eight-forty-eight.

I bit my lip, trying to think about something pleasant instead. I pictured my children back at the house, hanging out with Matt and my mother, eating dinner. Gosh, I suddenly missed them. Things hadn't been easy for them since their dad died two months ago. Both of the girls had struggled with getting back to daily life after the funeral. Chad had been their everything when growing up, espe-cially since I hadn't been around much, and he had taken care of them while I climbed the career ladder within the FBI. And now, he was gone. I was a single mom of three children. Luckily, I had Matt in my life. We had known each other since early childhood. We were dating before Chad was shot and killed. But right before it happened, Chad had asked me to get back together again, and I had almost accepted. Matt didn't know this, and I wasn't going to tell him. But the fact was, I had thought we'd be a family again. Just for a few seconds, I had believed we could.

And then it was taken away once more. With the snap of a finger. Just like that. My children would never have a real family again.

I cursed myself for not having been there when Matt and Elijah moved in today. I could have been if I hadn't been so preoccupied with saving Liam Berkeley's son. The kids all loved Matt, but still. I should have been there. Now, it was too late. The damage was done, and I still hadn't managed to save Tim Berkeley.

I turned my head to look at the screen just as the numbers showed eight-fifty-six on the clock beneath it.

Chapter 10

HE HAD JUST FALLEN into a deep sleep, dreaming about Anna and the life they used to have when he heard the ruckus, and it woke him up. Liam opened his eyes with a gasp and felt his heart begin to race in his chest. He shot up and looked at the clock.

It was only a little past nine.

He had only been in bed a few minutes as he always went to bed at nine because he had to get up at four-thirty. Had he been dreaming? Was it because of her that he had woken up? Or was it something else?

What's that noise?

Liam hurried to the window and pulled the curtain aside. He glanced down into the driveway but could hardly believe what he was seeing. There were about a dozen police cars parked outside, their red and blue lights blinking and lighting up the trees in his front yard.

Liam mumbled under his breath, "What the heck is going on?"

Confused and with his heart pounding, he stared down at the police activity when he saw officers in protective clothing, body armor, helmets, and who were heavily armed run up toward the house. A chopper circled the house from the sky, lighting up the ground below.

"Tim!"

Liam ran for the door and into the hallway just as the front door was kicked in. Heart racing in his chest, Liam rushed toward his son's room when there were rapid footsteps on the stairs, and seconds later, he was surrounded by black boots, guns pointed at him. The officers were yelling commands at him loudly while pushing him down and blocking his way so that he couldn't get to his son.

"Hands where we can see them. Raise your hands NOW!"

Liam fell to his knees; arms lifted high above his head. His body was shaking when he felt the guns pointed at him.

"Please," he said. "This is my house. I live here."

"Keep your hands where we can see them!" one of them yelled. "Don't make a single move, or we'll shoot!"

Liam could hear the anxiousness and deep fear in the officer's voice. He didn't dare to do anything but what he was being told. Meanwhile, boots were moving across the floors, and he heard someone yell *Clear* before more boots tramped around and then stopped. A door was opened, and Liam realized it was the one leading to Tim's room.

"Please, my son's in there!" he yelled, but no one listened. There was so much yelling that he couldn't be heard. Shaking in fear, Liam began to cry and scream Tim's name, just as he heard Tim's voice say something that he couldn't make out, but he sounded scared and desperate.

"Please," Liam tried. "Please."

And that was when someone yelled the word that no one wants to hear, especially not coming from an officer's mouth:

"Gun! He's got a gun!"

The shot that followed might as well have hit Liam straight in the heart. It hurt just as much as if he was the one who had been shot. Liam felt himself frozen in a scream as he fell to the ground, face first, while his hands were being cuffed behind his back.

TWO WEEKS LATER

Chapter 11

MATT LOOKED into one of his boxes, then pulled out an old snow globe that he had gotten from his dad before he died. He turned to look at Eva Rae, who was hunched over her computer in the living room.

"Where can I put this?" he asked.

She didn't look up. He exhaled, then placed it on the shelf above the fireplace. He grabbed a wooden sculpture that he had bought on one of his surfing trips to Bali when he was younger.

"How about this one?"

It was Saturday, and they both finally had some time off. During the week, Matt was busy with his detective work, and Eva Rae was writing her next book on profiling, which she had a contract for. He wasn't so sure that she was actually working on it and not on this new obsession of hers, though. She still hadn't told him much about what she was doing or why she had been in Philadelphia two weeks ago. She hadn't told him where he could put his stuff either, so now he had begun simply placing it where he could find room.

"Eva Rae?"

She finally looked up from her screen. "I'm sorry?"

He smiled. "Where can I put this? It can't fit on a shelf. It's too big and should stand on the floor. It would look good over here; don't you think?"

He placed it in the corner by the recliner. Eva Rae didn't look like she agreed. She just smiled like she had no idea what he was talking about.

"You don't think it looks good over here?" he asked. "Maybe it'll be better by the fireplace?"

"It's probably fine," she said.

"I don't want it to be *probably fine*," Matt said. "I want us to agree on these things. If you don't like it there, then I'll find somewhere else for it."

"No, it's fine."

His shoulders slumped as her eyes returned to the screen. Could she not spend just a few minutes on him?

"No," he said. "Something is wrong. What is it?"

She looked up again. "It's just…well. We don't really have much room in the house for all this extra stuff. Do we really need to have an old wooden…*thingy*…in the middle of the living room?"

Matt looked at the sculpture in his hand, then nodded. "I see what's going on. You don't want any of my stuff in your house."

"That's not what I said," Eva Rae said. "You're twisting my words. I'm just asking how important this thing is to you. We are a lot of people living in this small house, and frankly, it's getting a little cramped."

"Well, it wouldn't be if your children would pick up some of their toys," Matt said as he put the sculpture back in the box.

"Excuse me?" Eva Rae said. "Isn't Alex allowed to play with his toys anymore?"

"Well, you don't' see Elijah leaving his toys everywhere."

"Because your kid only sits in his room, playing on his iPad. My kid likes to play with real toys," Eva Rae said.

Matt glared at her. "And it's your house, right? So, your son is more entitled to make a mess than Elijah and I are. I get it."

Matt grabbed the box and lifted it, then carried it out in the garage, where he found a shelf for it. He closed it up with tape, wondering how long it would be before he'd be using his boxes again. Living with Eva Rae hadn't exactly been the treat he had thought it would be. She barely gave him the time of day, always so busy on her computer, and he wasn't getting any closer to having Elijah opening up to him. He was always in his room, playing on his iPad or Xbox, never saying a word to anyone.

Two weeks, Matt. It's been two weeks. Give them time to get used to the new arrangements. It'll get better. Eventually, it will.

Matt felt the tension building inside of him and decided he'd take a walk. It wasn't like Eva Rae or Elijah would miss him anyway.

Chapter 12

DeVilSQuaD666: Did you see me clear out that high school?

FanTAUstic345: You did that?

DeVilSQuaD666: Yeah. It was on the news and all. Pretty sweet. They searched for those bombs for hours, giving the kids the entire day off.

FanTAUstic345: Police are looking for the guy who called in the bomb threat. You might get in trouble.

DeVilSQuaD666: No way. They'll never know it was me. I'm too good.

FanTAUstic345: You done this before?

DeVilSQuaD666: About 10 now.

FanTAUstic345: You do anything else?

DeVilSQuaD666: Sure. Did local TV station in CA twice. It was all over the news too. They had to evacuate during live broadcast Bahahaha.

FanTAUstic345: Cool. You do anything else?

DeVilSQuaD666: I am about to.

FanTAUstic345: Like what?

DeVilSQuaD666: Watch me clear out that comic conference next weekend. Look out for the news.

FanTAUstic345: Wizard World Comic Con in Chicago?

DeVilSQuaD666: That's the one.

FanTAUstic345: You wouldn't dare.

DeVilSQuaD666: Watch me.

FanTAUstic345: I sure will. I'll be watching every second of it.

Chapter 13

I GLARED at the door to the garage where Matt had disappeared. I wondered if I should go out there and talk to him. I couldn't stand seeing that look in his eyes. I didn't mean to hurt him; I really didn't, but it just happened.

The thing was, I was frustrated. Not with Matt, but with the case. I had watched every news clip I could find about the police raiding Liam Berkeley's house and shooting his son, and it got to me every time. I knew this could have been avoided if only the guy would have given me a chance to explain.

Or maybe if you hadn't given up so easily…if you had run after him as he left the restaurant.

I hid my face in my hands, then shook my head. I had to stop doing this to myself, blaming myself. It was just so darn hard not to.

I rose to my feet and walked toward the door. "Matt…I'm…"

I didn't get to open it before, out of the corner of my eye, I spotted a car driving up into my street. It wasn't just any car, and that was why it grabbed my attention. It was a big black limo, not a car often seen in Cocoa Beach on a Saturday afternoon. It drove up and parked in front of my house.

For a second, I wondered if it was Sydney coming home. She

was filming a movie in Canada these days, so we hadn't seen her in four weeks. But she would at least have called first if I knew her right. She wasn't big on surprises.

As someone stepped out, I realized I was right. It wasn't Sydney. It was someone else, just as famous, if not even more so.

"Oh, no," I mumbled.

"Who is that?" Olivia asked, coming up behind me as I was staring at the Rockstar of the Cooking World, striding up toward my front door, wearing black sunglasses and a tight white T-shirt that showed his abs.

"Isn't that…?"

I nodded. "Yes."

"Oh, my God… What is he doing here?" Olivia asked, her voice growing shrill with excitement.

I exhaled. "My best guess is he's coming to talk to me."

She wrinkled her forehead. "You? Why would he come and see you? Don't you think he's here for Sydney?"

I gave her a look. "I know a few people in this world, too, you know."

"Okay, sorry. I just didn't know that you knew…him?"

"Because he's too cool for someone like your mom?"

"Actually, I think he acts like an idiot on that show of his. But I know a lot of kids from my school who love to watch it and who idolize him. It's not my thing, though."

I sighed happily, thinking I had to have done something right with this child, at least. I stroked her cheek gently, wondering how I got to be so lucky when there was a rapid *ra-ta-ta-da* on my door.

Olivia gave me a taunting look. "You better open that."

I grimaced, then took in a deep breath and braced myself for what awaited on the other side of the door. Him coming here after what had happened could hardly be a good thing.

Chapter 14

"LIAM BERKELEY?"

I bit my lip as our eyes met. His had changed drastically. He had also lost weight and seemed to be a shadow of the man I had met in Philadelphia two weeks earlier. His red-rimmed eyes looked down at me. The words seemed like they wouldn't leave his lips. Seeing him like this made my heart ache. He spoke through gritted teeth, fighting to get it out.

"You…knew. You knew. How?"

I exhaled deeply. "Maybe we should go inside. I'll make us some coffee. Or maybe something stronger? Wine? Whiskey?"

I stepped aside and let him into the living room, where he sat on the couch. The way he placed his hands in his lap with a resigned gesture and slumped his shoulders made him suddenly seem like an old man.

I rushed to the kitchen and put on a pot of coffee, then pulled out the bottle of whiskey that I had gotten as a birthday present from a friend whom I suspected had hoped I'd open it and he'd get to drink himself at my party.

I poured coffee in the cups and returned to Liam with glasses and cups and placed it all in front of him.

"I have some cake too if you like?" I asked.

He lifted his hand to stop me. "I don't want anything. Except for you to sit down and explain this to me. Because ever since...*that* night, I haven't been able to understand anything that's going on. I need you to explain it to me; I need you to make sense of all this because I can't."

I nodded. "First of all, I am so sorry for what happened to your son..."

Liam closed his eyes briefly. "Tim."

"Tim, yes. I am so sorry for what happened to him. I can't even begin to imagine..."

Liam lifted his hand to stop me again. "I don't want to hear it. Everyone says the same things, and it makes me want to puke, to be honest. No, you can't imagine what it is like to lose your son. And why would you want to? Nothing could be worse in this world. Why would you want to know what it feels like?"

"I think people are just trying to be nice," I said and grabbed a cup of coffee. My hands were shaking, and I poured a little whiskey into my coffee, thinking I needed it. Sitting in front of Liam under these circumstances, I needed something to keep me strong.

"I don't want people to be nice to me," he said. "I want them to talk to me like I'm a normal human being and not some fragile woman who might break into pieces any second."

"Not a fan of women, I take it?" I said and took a deep sip from my cup.

He sighed. "That's not what I meant. What I meant to say is, I need you to treat me the way you would have before this happened. You came to me. You told me my boy was going to die. You hold the answers, and now I want to hear them because I can't stand all these questions in my head, all these things I can't explain. Put me out of my misery and tell me why my son had to die. Please."

I took another deep sip before I put the cup down while gathering my strength. "All right. I'll tell you what I know. But first, I need you to tell me exactly what happened on the night Tim was killed."

Chapter 15

"THEY SAY they got an emergency call from someone claiming to be Tim who said that he was inside our house and that he had just shot his mom and dad and that he was going to shoot himself. He told them he was armed and that he would shoot anyone who came to the house if they tried to stop him from killing himself."

Liam leaned back in my old couch that I bought off Craigslist and took a moment to gather himself.

"I know they're not lying since I heard the recordings, but the voice on that tape wasn't Tim's."

"But the police had no way of knowing that," I said. "I'm guessing it looked like the call came from your house, right? When they traced it?"

Liam nodded. "You're right about that. I don't know how that is even possible."

"It's not that hard today, using spoofing technology," I said. "It can be an app or computer software."

"I saw them from my window right before they stormed the house. You've probably heard it all on the news or read it in those magazines that are all writing about it. A hashtag with my name in it on Twitter exploded when it happened, or so I've heard."

"They thought he was armed, right?" I asked. "When they came to your house? Because the caller had said he was and then your son made one wrong move and…well, they assumed he was going for his gun?"

Liam rubbed his stubble and nodded. "Yes. That's exactly what happened. I wasn't in the room, so I don't know what he reached for, but he reached for something, and the police claim they were convinced it was a gun. It could have been his phone or maybe nothing at all. They're still investigating it, though. I hope the officer who shot him will rot in jail."

"In their defense, there had been a shooting just a week before where six officers got shot when approaching an armed guy in his home. It shakes them up and makes them anxious."

"That's what they keep telling me," Liam said, breathing heavily. "They were only doing their job."

"But, of course, your son wasn't armed, am I right?"

"No! He's never owned a gun."

"But do you?" I asked.

He nodded. "Sure. We have a gun in the house. I have a permit."

"If there is a gun registered to the address, it will have made the officers even more anxious, thinking the boy got ahold of your gun and shot his parents. That's any uniformed man's worst nightmare right there. They're tense and scared even before they get there, and, of course, they'll shoot if they have the slightest fear that he is carrying a weapon, and for all they know, he is, and he *will* shoot because that's what he told them on the phone."

"So, now it's my fault?"

"That's not what I said."

"Okay, I'm not getting anywhere here," Liam said, shaking his head violently. "I know you're a cop or used to be, or whatever, so, of course, you'll defend them, I kind of expected that. But what I came here to ask you is how you knew. How did you know something would happen to Tim? You said someone wanted him killed? Who and how did you know?"

I grabbed my cup and sipped more of the spiked coffee, then

looked at him intently. "All right. But I'm going to need you to keep an open mind here."

"I am as open as I can be," he said. "Full-blown open."

"And you're sure you want to know? It's not going to be pleasant."

He nodded. "Yes. Absolutely certain."

Chapter 16

AMAL BUKHARI LOOKED at her phone as she boarded flight 456 from Atlanta to New York. She rechecked her email for the fifth time in the past ten minutes—still nothing.

Amal was waiting for an email from her agent. NBC wanted her for a big new live talk show, and she was awaiting the final confirmation. It was down to her and another famous YouTuber who had seventeen million followers, whereas Amal or *IWondergirl*, had eighteen million. According to her agent, she was in the lead and best suited for this job. But he was supposed to say that, wasn't he? It was his job to make her feel confident and cheer her on.

Come on. Just say, yes.

Amal sat down in her seat and placed her bag with her computer under the seat in front of her. She was going to work on her bits during the plane ride. She was doing a stand-up show tomorrow night.

Amal checked her email again. Still nothing.

The road to success had been long for Amal, but it had been her own. Her Pakistani background didn't make it easier, especially not when her family didn't approve of what she did. They had cut all their ties to her except for her brother, Samir, who still called now and then when he wasn't near any other family member.

Come on. I need that email before I have to shut off my phone.

The guy who was going to sit in the seat next to her arrived, and she got up to make room for him to get into the window seat. Amal had asked for a window seat because she hated sitting on the aisle, but apparently, there had been none available.

Amal checked her email again as the plane filled up around her. Her stomach was lurching, and it didn't feel good. Shouldn't they have decided by now? What was taking them so long?

I'm not getting it, am I? It's because of my skin color; I just know it is.

The door was closed, and the flight attendant checked that their seatbelts were fastened. Amal stared at the phone, touching the screen lightly with her finger. The flight attendant came to her seat and spoke from behind a toothy smile.

"Please, turn off your cellphone now."

Amal felt like making a snappy joke about phones and planes and why people had to shut them off, but she refrained. She didn't feel like it. Instead, she nodded and returned the smile, then pretended to be shutting off the phone as the plane slowly rolled out on the runway.

As the flight attendant moved away, she checked her email once again, frantically tapping on the screen.

And there it was.

Heart in her throat, Amal opened the email and read through it, skimming it as fast as she could.

I got it. I can't believe it. I actually got it!

Smiling widely, Amal shut off the phone and leaned back in her seat, just as the plane accelerated down the runway and, seconds later, soared into the air. Amal couldn't help comparing the feeling to her career literally taking off, and she broke into cheerful laughter as they reached their cruising altitude.

Chapter 17

"IT'S CALLED SWATTING."

I looked up at Liam's face. I had poured us a second cup of coffee, and he was holding his between his hands.

"Swatting?"

I nodded. "It's a criminal act in which the perpetrators call or message a target's local nine-one-one operators, claiming a fake hostage situation or a bomb threat in progress with the expectation that the local police may respond to the target's address or whereabouts with deadly force, more than often sending in a SWAT team, hence the name."

Liam blinked. He stared at me for several seconds before sipping his coffee. "You mean to tell me that's what happened to us? To my...to Tim? Someone called in and told them to go to my address...deliberately?"

"Yes. I'm afraid so. It's something that has been going on for the past year or so. I've been trying to tell the local police about this; in your case, I even telephoned all the departments in Philadelphia and warned them that this would happen, that someone would call in a false incident. But..." I paused and shook my head.

Liam leaned back in his chair, rubbing his forehead. I could tell he was fighting his tears. He started biting his nails vigorously.

"So, you mean to tell me that my…my *Tim*…died because of some…prank?" he asked, his eyes gleaming in anger.

I cleared my throat. "I'm not sure I'd call it that exactly. I think this guy is very serious and extremely brilliant."

"What do you mean?"

"I believe what we're facing is a serial swatter…someone who's responsible for a series of these calls and many of them with deaths to follow. I believe this guy is responsible for eleven deaths so far all over the country. Not all are fatal, and I have traced him to other swatting attempts where no one died. But so far, eleven have. And those are just the ones I've detected. But there could be more."

Liam looked at me, puzzled. "How do you know it's the same guy who's behind all those calls?"

"There's a pattern that I have detected. First of all, many of them are called in at the same time of day. At exactly 8:56 p.m. is when dispatch usually receives the call. That's the case in most of the incidents I've found. Second, I've found that he leaves clues as to who he'll strike next. He seems to be choosing rich and famous people, YouTubers, gamers, or in your case, a famous cook's sons. My guess is that he chooses celebrities to gain attention. He wants to make sure the story gets on the news. Why? I don't know. Maybe it makes him feel proud like when some killers take a trophy from their victims, or maybe he feels stronger when the world knows what he's doing and fears him. That's one of the characteristics in his pattern that I still need to establish."

"And you think it was the same guy who called in the emergency that ended up killing Tim?"

"I do. In my opinion, he's a serial killer like any other. I think this is a murderer who is so clever that he has found a way not to have to do the actual killing and take responsibility."

"It's the perfect murder," he said

"Exactly," I said. "Because it doesn't look like murder. He can sit anywhere in the country and do this. The police usually think it's a prankster and may try to find the caller, via tracking the number it was called from, but when they can't find him, they give up. The majority of the time, they don't even try to find out who called it in since they simply don't have the resources for such an investigation. They call it an accident or an unfortunate incident, and only the event itself is investigated. Last month, there was a similar event in Utah where a woman was shot in her home because the officer thought she had a gun when it was, in fact, a glittery cell phone. The public demanded that the officer stand trial. He did and was sentenced to ten years in prison. So, it's not like it's not taken seriously; they're just not seeing the real issue. The problem is that the investigators in these cases usually focus their investigation on the event itself. They almost never dig really deep into what started the event, who the caller was because they can't find him and don't know that this person is not just a prankster. And they don't talk to one another across state lines about this. That's why they don't realize they have a serial killer on their hands. But they do. He's a killer who has swatted and killed more than eleven times."

"But you did. You dug deeper and found a connection between these calls. Why?"

I exhaled and sipped my coffee. "Let's just say I'm not like most detectives."

Chapter 18

LIAM WAS BACK to biting his nails again. I wanted to tell him to stop, that there was barely anything left to bite, but then I remembered I did it myself when I was agitated or even scared. I bit my lip or my nails.

I rose to my feet, then walked to the counter and found a folder. I opened it and pulled out a sheet of paper.

"This is the earliest case I have found so far. I call him victim zero. His name was Peter James. His gaming name was EvilPeter-Pan, and he had more than six million followers on YouTube. On November 4, 2018, at exactly 8:56 p.m., the emergency operators in New Orleans received a call from a guy who called himself Peter James. He said that he had shot his father in the head and was holding his sister and mother as hostages, that he was armed and going to kill them, that he had poured gasoline all around the house and was going to light them on fire. The police arrived at the scene and shot him on his front porch. It didn't help that he was African American. Police claimed he was armed, but that was later proven to be wrong by investigators. He's the earliest one I've found so far. But there might be others. I just don't have enough time in the day to find them."

"What made you realize that it was the same guy?" Liam asked and leaned forward. "And why did you start looking into it in the first place? I mean, it looked like ordinary police activity, right?"

I paused and took in a deep breath. "I know someone it happened to."

"Really? Who?"

I pulled out another sheet of paper from my folder. "This one. Victim six."

"Let me guess. He's also a gamer, right?"

"That has been the pattern so far, yes. They all stream on Twitch, a live video streaming service that primarily focuses on video game live streaming."

"Just like Tim," Liam said. "It was all he ever did."

"And they're all celebrities either from YouTube, or they have a famous parent like your son had. Something to make sure the story reaches the news."

"How did you know him? Victim six?"

I swallowed. "It was a she. *KittyWolfGamer* was her online name. In real life, she was Stacy. She was also my old neighbor and best friend, Priscilla's daughter. She was twenty-two when she died."

"Next-door neighbor here?"

I shook my head. "Back when I lived in D.C. Stacy was killed two months ago, and her mom called me crying the next day and told me everything. I've known Stacy since she was eight. I loved that kid. I promised her I'd take a closer look at exactly what happened and why Stacy's condo was raided. By then, Stacy was still in ICU, and they thought she might survive, but she died three days later. I contacted everyone I knew up there in law enforcement and had every paper and file in the case sent to me. I went through it and just couldn't believe what had happened. I then started to search through the Internet and found similar stories all over the country. And some of them had more than a lot in common, among them the time of receiving the call."

"What else? What else do they have in common?" Liam asked.

"Well, as I said, they're all gamers, which tells me the killer is one himself. And, as I said, they're all celebrities in some form, enough to make headlines."

"What else? I have a feeling there's more?"

"Well…he sort of tells us who will be the next victim. This, I found out later."

"I see. And that's how you found out that my Tim would be next?"

I nodded. "Yes. I didn't know this until his last victim, and that's why I rushed to tell you. You were the first one I knew beforehand."

He sighed and slumped his shoulders. "So, it *is* all my fault. Because I didn't listen."

I looked away. I knew it had to be eating the guy up, and I certainly didn't want to rub salt in an open wound. It had to be killing him. But I guess he was right, even though I couldn't blame him for not believing me. I was, after all, a stranger, and as a celebrity, he had to have met his share of crazy people.

"So, what is it? How does he tell you?"

Chapter 19

AMAL DIDN'T EVEN REALIZE that she had fallen asleep until she woke up. She blinked a few times when she realized that the lights had been turned on in the cabin, and the flight attendants were walking up and down the aisle, telling people to put their seats up and make sure their seatbelts were fastened.

Are we there already?

Amal looked at her watch. They had only been in the air for an hour. It was a four-hour flight. What was going on? Were they about to enter heavy turbulence?

Amal turned to look at the flight attendants. Their faces were strained. They were smiling and talking in a calming manner, but still, there was an uneasy nervousness behind it. A female flight attendant who walked past her mumbled under her breath. It sounded like a small prayer.

What the heck is this?

Amal had never been keen on flying and hated turbulence like nothing else in this world. She pushed her head back in the seat and closed her eyes to calm herself, mumbling the phrases she knew to be true.

"No plane has ever fallen due to turbulence. It's just wind and bad weather on the ground. It's not dangerous. You will not die from this."

Amal exhaled and opened her eyes again, then met the eyes of the man sitting next to her. He, too, seemed confused. She was trying to smile, but then she spotted something out of the corner of her eye that just about made her heart stop.

"Is that…Is that an…?"

Amal leaned toward the guy by the window who turned his head to look at the F-16 that flew by their window.

That was when panic erupted both inside and outside of Amal. She turned to look at the other side, where another F-16 fighter jet pulled up and seemed to be escorting them.

Around her, all the passengers sat up straight and started to talk. People looked around them, casting nervous glances around the cabin. Tension was thick in the air, lots of furrowed brows and frowns. Some pulled out their phones and began to film. Amal decided to do the same. If nothing else, then to document her last hours in case the phone survived.

Finally, an announcement was made by the captain.

"Ladies and gentlemen. We are preparing to make an emergency landing in a few minutes. Please make sure you are all in position. Seats are up, seatbelts fastened. I need all of you to remain calm."

"Kind of hard when you don't sound calm," Amal said to the camera. She felt terrified as she stared out at the F-16 escorting the airplane, then spoke with a low voice to her camera.

"What I'm asking myself right now, just like probably most of the people here, is if they will shoot us down if necessary? I mean, that's why they're there, right? That's what I heard, at least. To protect the people on the ground. Why else would they send out military planes?"

The man sitting next to Amal whimpered slightly. Amal couldn't blame him. She was terrified, too, and she was beginning to wonder if she'd make it out alive. The cabin crew tried to keep their cool, but Amal could see how anxious they were. Amal felt claustrophobic. The cabin suddenly seemed so small. People were chatting nervously to one another. A child was crying and asking her mother if they'd make it home alive.

"I heard there was a bomb on the plane," someone turned her head and said. "Someone further up heard the cabin crew talking to one another, mentioning the word bomb."

That confirmed Amal's deepest fear. That was why the F-16 planes were there. If the person who brought the bomb threatened to explode it, they'd shoot them all down.

The thought wasn't exactly calming.

"Why isn't the pilot saying anything?" the guy sitting next to her asked. "He hasn't said a word since he told us we're going to make an emergency landing."

Amal nodded. He was onto something. Usually, when there was bad weather, he'd give updates regularly to calm the passengers, but now—when there was actual danger—he remained silent.

Was it because he was scared too?

The thought didn't feel reassuring to Amal. Yet, she continued to film with her phone. Not because she thought it would make her even more famous or because she thought about her millions of YouTube followers who might want to watch it.

No, it was all she knew how to do in a situation where she felt utterly helpless.

Chapter 20

I GRABBED a book from the shelf and put it on the table in front of him. He took it into his hands and looked at it, front and back.

"You wrote this?"

I nodded. "I'm not showing you this to brag, but just to tell you that I've been studying serial killers for many years, and I'm considered to be somewhat of an expert. What I wrote about in this particular book is that, after studying more than two hundred serial killers, I concluded that most of them communicate in some way or another about their murders. Either during the murders or afterward. They talk about it somehow. Now, how they do it differs a lot. Some like to taunt the police, while others leave clues. A few try to explain their murders, while others try to justify their actions. Often, they leave messages at the crime scene, written on walls, or leave clues on the body or small notes at the crime scene. In my experience, when dealing with serial killers, as soon as you discover their means of communication, you can start tracking them down. That's the best way to go about it. So, that's what I did. I spent hours and hours researching the old cases, and I couldn't figure out how this killer was speaking to me. How was he trying to leave me clues? There were, of course, the similarities in the killings, the time of the call, the choice of victims, and that they all use the same live-stream platform Twitch, and so on, but I knew there had to be more. And that's when it hit me. It had been right in front of me all the time. The killer did inform me of the next victim; he even warned them."

"Really? How?"

"By meeting up with them in the game Call of Duty – WWII."

Liam wrinkled his forehead. "In the game?"

I nodded. "You'll understand why it took me so long to figure out because it's an online game. It wasn't until I realized that several of the victims were in the middle of playing that game when the police came to their house. The first one, Victim zero, Peter James..."

"EvilPeterPan," Liam said.

"Yes. He was playing the game when the police came to his house. It was all streamed live to his six million YouTube followers. You can't see what happens, but you can hear everything that takes place, including the moment he is shot out on his front porch. I later saw it from a different angle, from the officer's bodycam when it was made public."

"You're telling me this person, this serial killer or swatter or whatever you call him, meets with his next victims inside of Call of Duty, and then what? Like, how did you know that my Tim was going to be one of them?"

"I had to start playing it myself," I said, "in order to figure it out. I don't know how much you know about it, but it's a multiplayer game, a shooting game that simulates combat from a soldier's point of view during World War II. You play in teams and help each other out, fighting through events like D-day, and they've also added Nazi-zombies to make it even more creepy. Anyway, when I took a closer look into Peter James' case, I kept coming back to the fact that he was playing when it happened, and that was the case for others as well. Not all of them. But then I thought, who could he have been playing with? I called my dad, who is a very skilled computer geek, and asked him what to do. He hacked into Peter's account and found the players he had been playing within the twenty-four hours before it happened. Then he did the same with some of the other victims and managed to find one player profile that kept turning up. Under the name FaZeYourFeaRs."

"So, that's the guy?" Liam asked. "Can't he be tracked?"

"It's not that easy, I'm afraid. Not with this guy. He doesn't leave any trace when calling in the threats, and he makes it look like they actually come from the house they're about to swat, or a cell phone of the victim's. And he doesn't let himself be tracked either. We tried, but it led to an address in Singapore that, within minutes, changed to an address in South Africa. My dad says it's common for hackers to hide their whereabouts this way. This killer is a skilled hacker, and, so far, he's stayed under the radar. He knows his victim's identity and personal information before he teams up with them in the game. That's the only way I can see that he can do what he does. He chooses them carefully and does his research first before he makes his move, is my guess. I have naturally talked to the FBI about him and told them all I know, but they can't open a case with so little proof. I have been tracing him relentlessly in the game and tried to keep track of what he's up to, but it's easier said than done. I managed to see him team up with victim nine, and twenty-four hours later, he was dead. When I saw him team up with your son, I knew I had to try and warn you."

"How did you know it was Tim?" Liam asked.

"My dad tracked him down. I gave him his username, and he did his thing that I don't know how he does. But apparently, he found the credit card information of the person who had bought the game for the profile that your son was playing. I was so glad when I found out I actually had the possibility to warn one of the Swatter's victims."

Liam rubbed his face and sighed. "But I ruined that. Because I wouldn't listen. And now he's…"

Liam stopped to gather himself. I remained silent for quite a while to allow the information to sink in properly. That was when Matt walked in from the garage. He took one glance at Liam, then gave me a puzzled look.

"Who's this?"

Chapter 21

I ROSE to my feet and approached Matt, then pulled him into the kitchen. His confused eyes lingered on me.

"This is…"

"I know who it is," he interrupted me. "But what is he doing in your…*our* living room?"

I exhaled, feeling tired. It had been a long day. I realized it had gotten late and suddenly wondered where Matt had been all night while I was speaking to Liam.

"It's a long story," I said. "It's this thing I've been working on… you know when I went to Philadelphia. Well, Liam lost his son recently, and I believe that…he was killed."

Matt wrinkled his forehead. "He was shot by the police, as far as I've heard."

"Yes, but…I think he was killed."

"Wait, so that's what you did in Philadelphia? You met with this guy? That awful guy from TV?"

"Yes."

"Why?"

"If you must know, I knew what was going to happen to his son."

Matt shook his head. "I don't understand. You knew?"

"Yes. I didn't want to tell you because well…frankly, I didn't want you to know I was researching this thing since…I wanted to make sure I was right before I told you, okay? I can see it in your eyes already. You don't believe me and, frankly, it's killing me. I knew you wouldn't."

"What are you talking about? You haven't even told me what this is all about. How can I say if I believe you or not when I don't know anything?"

I sighed and rubbed my forehead. "I can't explain it right now. Just trust me on this. I am trying to stop a murderer."

"And him?" he said as he nodded toward the living room with an annoyed face. "What's his part in it?"

I gave him a look while wondering what was going on. What was this? Was Matt jealous?

"He came here because he had questions and believed I could answer them. My guess is that he wants justice for his son. Wouldn't you want that if it was Elijah?"

Matt exhaled. "I don't know the details, but yes. Probably."

"Of course, you would."

"But I would probably also trust that the police did their best to investigate it since I'm a detective myself."

"But that's exactly the problem. They don't realize this is happening. I tried Isabella Horne, you know my old supervisor at the FBI, and even she couldn't help me. I called all the local police stations in Philadelphia to warn them about what would happen, yet it happened anyway. This guy is winning."

"And you won't let him do that," Matt said with a deep exhale. He grabbed my neck, leaned over, and kissed me. "I will trust you. Just promise me you'll be careful, all right? We've had some scares this past year, and I don't want to have to worry about you again. I can't bear to lose you the way we lost Chad."

I stared into his eyes, feeling the knot in my stomach was about to burst. Chad, my ex-husband, the father of my three children. He had been killed when saving Matt's life of all people. I didn't want to think about him; it hurt too much, so instead, I pulled away and shook my head.

"I should get back to Liam."

"What? Because I mentioned Chad? Is it so terrible that you can't even hear his name? You haven't even cried over him, Eva Rae. Not even at his funeral did you shed one single tear. Why is that?"

I bit my lip while my hand lingered on the door handle, keeping my back turned toward him. I wanted to say something to explain myself, to justify my actions, but I couldn't. Simply because I didn't know. I just knew that if I allowed myself to think about Chad for even one second, the emotions were so overwhelming, I wouldn't be able to stand it.

"You blame me, don't you?" Matt asked. "I can see it in your eyes. You blame me because Chad took that bullet for me."

I closed my eyes for a brief second. I paused, then opened the door, and left. I would have answered him; I wanted to, but I couldn't. I simply didn't know what to say, and I didn't want to lie to him.

Chapter 22

THE FIGHTER JETS disappeared as the plane started to descend and soon landed in Houston, Texas. Amal had never in her life been more relieved than when she heard those tires hit the ground and felt the great push back in her seat as the plane came to a complete stop.

As everything inside the cabin quieted down, the passengers started to look at one another. The seatbelt sign was still on, and no one was making any announcements. The built-up tension was about to be released.

"Why aren't we at the gate?" someone yelled. "How long are you going to keep us in here?"

"What's going on?" someone else yelled.

"We want to get off this plane!"

Amal couldn't agree more. She found it hard to breathe properly and needed desperately to get out of this tin can. What if there really was a bomb on the plane? Couldn't it explode while they were sitting there? They weren't even out of danger yet, were they?

The sound of sirens blaring interrupted her train of thought. Out of her neighbor's window, she spotted firetrucks approaching, followed closely by so many police cars that they looked like stars in the sky.

Soon after, the door in the front was opened, and the police came in first. In full body armor and helmets, they stormed inside, holding their weapons in front of them. Passengers started to scream when they saw them. The men yelled at the flight attendants. One of them broke down crying.

Soon, they came running down the aisle, stomping their boots, and the passengers screamed anxiously. Amal filmed it all while it happened, wondering what they were doing; where they were going? Was someone on board the plane going to be arrested? Was it the same person who had the bomb? If so, then who was it?

As they all zoned in on her and soon stood in front of her, Amal at first thought it had to be the guy sitting next to her. But when a gun was pointed at her, and one of the officers yelled her name, Amal knew they hadn't come for him, but her.

"Arms in the air!" one yelled. "Keep 'em where I can see them!"

Amal stared at the man dressed in the Kevlar vest and black helmet in front of her. He was wearing complete combat gear. Was this some sort of joke? How could they think she—of all people—was dangerous?

"Excuse me…I think you've made…"

"Arms where I can see them at all times."

Scared half to death, Amal raised both of her arms high up in the air.

"What's that in her hand?" someone yelled.

"What's that in your hand?" the one standing in front of her yelled. "Put it down now!"

"It's just a phone," she answered. She lowered her arm and showed it to them, but that just made everything worse.

"Keep 'em up!"

"Keep your hands up!"

"Drop the phone!"

Amal felt like crying. Yet she did as they said. She let the phone fall to the floor with a thud, then stared at the uniformed men, tears springing to her terrified eyes.

"Rise to your feet, now! Slowly!"

"No sudden movements."

Amal did as she was told, as slowly as humanly possible. All eyes were on her in the cabin, and she fought her desire to scream in terror. She was so scared that they'd shoot her; she could barely keep her arms still.

"Walk," the officer said, making a movement with the gun. "Toward the door."

Amal swallowed. Thinking she'd have to grab her things, that she couldn't leave her computer under the seat, she reached down to grab it when they all yelled at once.

"She's going for a bag."

"It's the bomb!"

Amal barely managed to get her arm back up in the air when the shot was fired. As it tore through her skin, it was a surprise for her to realize that it didn't hurt at all. At least not when it entered her body. It wasn't until the bullet traveled through her body, cutting its way through her tissue, going upward and lodging itself just below her left ribcage that there was a sudden unbearable burning aggravated sensation. As she fell to the floor of the plane, she waited for there to be a bright light or at least a hand reaching out to welcome her to the next world.

But it never came. There was only deep darkness and the voices of people's terrified screaming around her.

Chapter 23

I WAS WATCHING the news while fighting my urge to cry. Liam was still there when I received the breaking news text about an airplane that had to make an emergency landing because of a bomb threat. I then turned on the news and saw that Amal Bukhari, the famous YouTuber, had been shot inside the plane because they believed she was carrying a bomb in her computer. Nine-one-one had received a phone call that same night as the plane was in the air, stating that there was a bomb on board and that Amal Bukhari was carrying it in her handbag, disguised as a computer.

"Son of a g…" I exclaimed as I threw the remote against the wall so hard it flew apart, and the batteries fell out.

"You knew she was next, didn't you?" Liam asked.

I stomped my feet angrily, then sat down before I rose up again and started pacing back and forth.

"I've only known since this morning and thought I had more time. I tried everything. I emailed her, but she never responded. I also tried to call her agent, but he just thought I was some weirdo and hung up on me. That's what they all think. It's not easy to get to famous people, you know? I even wrote several comments on her YouTube page, but I don't know if she's even seen any of them or my messages on Instagram. My guess is she hasn't. I thought I could get to her and warn her somehow first, but the Swatter probably saw the opportunity because she was going on a flight. What could be more spectacular, right?"

"It sure is something they'll be talking about for months. And you're sure it's him?" Liam asked.

"Positive. But how do I make the world understand it? To say that they played the same game isn't exactly proof."

"Let me get you another glass of that whiskey over there," Liam said and rose to his feet.

I stopped him. "It's okay. I don't really drink much hard alcohol. I think I'll just go to bed if you don't mind. It's been a long day."

Liam nodded and finished his third glass. I was happy that I knew he wasn't driving home.

"I'm staying at the Hilton downtown," he said and put the glass down. "I want more than anyone to catch this guy, and I believe you're the one who can do it. Let me know if I can help with anything."

"Unless you can turn back time, then I don't see how," I said and rubbed my temples frantically. I felt so frustrated I could scream.

Liam rose to his feet. I wondered about Matt and whether he had gone to bed or if he was still in the kitchen. I couldn't really face him right now, not after the talk we had in the kitchen. I didn't want to risk him bringing up Chad again, so I said goodbye to Liam, then hurried upstairs. I checked on the kids and told Olivia she needed to go to bed, too, before walking past our bedroom. The door was ajar, and I could see Matt was in there, asleep. I closed the door carefully, then ran back downstairs, where I sat by my computer and opened Call of Duty.

THREE WEEKS LATER

Chapter 24

"HEY, everyone. It's me, Amal again. Broadcasting live from my hospital bed, as you can see."

Amal lifted her phone to show her viewers the monitors next to her and the bed where she was laying. Then she returned to pointing it at her face again. She had lost a lot of weight and didn't really like the way she looked.

But at least she was alive.

She turned the camera toward her brother Samir, who was standing by the window looking worried. He had been with her since she woke up in the ICU, and every time he looked at her, he had that concerned look in his eyes.

It drove her crazy.

"Say hi to the viewers, Samir."

He waved at her to stop filming him, and she turned the camera to face herself again.

"The doctors are going to do another surgery today. Now, for those of you who haven't seen my earlier broadcasts and who are just tuning in, I can tell you that the bullet entered here in my side just above my right hip, then traveled upward and lodged itself just below my left rib cage. The bullet landed in a place that you usually don't survive when a bullet is caught there. I guess I was lucky. The bullet is still in there since they haven't dared to risk taking it out yet. So far, I have gone through seven surgeries; today will be number eight. I won't go into too many gory details, but one of the surgeries is one they normally perform on people with pancreatic cancer. Several organs were removed, and the remaining organs are reconnected so I can live. I no longer have a colon or a gallbladder; I've lost my left kidney and a third of my stomach. The bullet has, however, now moved closer to my skin's surface and is poking out under my rib cage, which makes it possible for them to remove it later today. Yay."

Amal tried to smile, but it was hard. She was still in a lot of pain, and the thought of having to go through yet another surgery was unbearable. She was sick of hospitals and of just lying there, doing nothing. She had begun updating her followers as soon as she was well enough to do so. The video from her being shot had gone viral as soon as her brother posted it when the police gave him the phone at the hospital, while she was fighting for her life. It had reached more than a hundred million views, and when Amal finally woke up, she had close to ninety million subscribers to her YouTube channel. A number that made her the second largest after PewDiePie, who had ninety-nine million.

"But that's not what I wanted to talk to you about today, dear friends," Amal said. "Today, I have a serious subject on my agenda, not that my surgeries aren't serious, but this is a matter that has an impact on us all. I don't recall a lot from the day I was shot inside that plane, but the more I learn, the more I realize that what happened to me wasn't an accident. It happened because of my skin color. I am more than convinced of this. The police received a fake call telling them that I was carrying a bomb. They took action as they should, no problem there. But then they entered the plane, took one look at my skin color, and decided I was dangerous. You saw the video. You all know that I wasn't armed and that I was doing what they told me to. I went for my bag, yes, because I thought I had to bring it, but as soon as they told me not to, I stopped. You can see it on camera; I raise my hands again after they yell at me, and that's when the guy decides to shoot. I could have died. I should have died, according to the surgeons here. It makes no sense that I am still alive. And that's why I believe it is my duty to address this matter. For years and years, we have been witnessing police brutality toward people of color. And we have been sitting on our hands. We have done nothing. Yes, Black Lives Matter. Brown Lives Too. I have decided to join the fight against police brutality. I am suing the police, filing a civil lawsuit against the police department in Houston. I believe in holding this man accountable for his actions. He didn't have to shoot me, and I don't think he should be allowed to hurt anyone else. He belongs behind bars like the rest of us would be if we shot an innocent person and almost killed them. And I ask you, my dear viewers, to come along with me on this road to justice. I am not stopping at the lawsuit. We need to wake up our politicians. So, I have decided to arrange a great protest in Washington, D.C., on January 15th. Let's see how many we can gather. If all of you come, then we will definitely make an impact. I will be there, no matter if they have to roll me there in a wheelchair. My brother will be in charge of all the arrangements since I will be busy with surgeries and recovery, but mark my words: They think they can do this to us; they think they can shoot us down in the street, in our own homes and even public places and get away with it. I say not this time. Not anymore."

Chapter 25

I TOOK THE ESCALATOR DOWN, my suitcase in my hand. I looked at my watch, annoyed. The plane was delayed half an hour, and the turbulence had been terrible as they prepared for landing. I still felt a little sick to my stomach from all the bumping. While the plane was in the air, I thought about Amal Bukhari, the YouTube sensation who had recently been the latest swatting victim and who was now stirring up a fight against the police. I couldn't imagine how terrified she'd have to have been when seeing those fighter jets outside the window and then learning that there was a bomb on the plane. I couldn't imagine the terror that had to have been going through her mind and the rest of the passengers for that matter. She had talked about it in her YouTube videos that she now made from her hospital bed. I had watched all of them, mostly because I was so thrilled that she was still alive, that the Swatter hadn't been able to get her killed after all. He had suffered a defeat, and it gave me hope.

The black limo waited for me outside the sliding doors, and I handed my suitcase to the driver, then got in.

"How was your flight?"

Liam looked at me from above his glasses. I didn't remember

ever seeing him wearing glasses before, but then again, I didn't know him that well.

"Bumpy," I said.

"Welcome to New Orleans," he said with a smile as the limo took off, leaving the airport behind.

"Yeah, well, I wish I was here on vacation or just to experience the town. That would have been more fun."

"You should at least get some crawfish or beignets while you're here," he said. "I know the right places to visit."

"Of course, you do," I said.

"So, what are we looking at here?" he asked. "You said you found the Swatter's next victim?"

I nodded and found the boy's profile on my phone. "FaZeYour-FeaRs hasn't been active for a very long time. My guess is that he felt such a setback from what happened to Amal Bukhari that he needed time to plan his next move. And I have been playing that silly game every day since. It's become an obsession almost. At least that's what my family thinks... That I'm just playing video games. My mom thinks I've lost my mind, while the teenagers find it kind of cool, yet a little embarrassing; they haven't really determined how they feel yet. Meanwhile, Alex, my seven-year-old son, is thrilled and wants to play it too. But I've told him no. He's not old enough. So now he's cross with me. But yesterday, FaZeYourFeaRs showed up again and entered a game with this guy here. My dad found his real name."

"Who is he?" Liam asked as he looked at the picture. "He seems awfully young."

"That was my reaction too. I just can't bear to see a young kid like him lose his life. Now, the kid is one of the top gamers on Fort-nite. He actually won the world championships last year, so he's quite good. But what scares me is that the Swatter is desperate now. After the setback at the airport, he's in dire need of a win. He wants to be sure that nothing goes wrong this time."

Liam nodded and took off his glasses. "Then we'll just have to make sure everything goes wrong this time."

Chapter 26

@MIsstressWolf: Welp! I can't believe it. Went to Chicago Comicon. The event just got evacuated. Standing outside now. Waiting.

@Legy: What's going on?

@MIsstressWolf: Apparently, there was a threat. Someone called 911 and said he was on meth and that he would shoot the place up. It was all evacuated. I was so confused as I ran out underneath the whir of choppers. Police are everywhere. It's so cold outside.

@ DeVilSQuaD666: Ha, ha, baby girl. I can just see you running for your life.

@MIsstressWolf: Excuse me @DeVilSQuaD666? You find this funny?

@DeVilSQuaD666: Sure do.

@MIsstressWolf: How? What could possibly be funny about me running for my life?

@ DeVilSQuaD666: It happens, baby girl. It happens.

@MIsstressWolf: I've been standing in the cold for three hours. I'm terrified and thought I was going to die. You still find that funny?

@ DeVilSQuaD666: Very.

@MIsstressWolf: There was a little girl who couldn't find her mother. She was crying because she thought she was dead. She kept clinging onto my arm while she called her mother's name. Is that funny too?

@ DeVilSQuaD666: Sure is. To me, at least.

@MIsstressWolf: How can you say that? What kind of a person says something like this?

@Legy: I can't believe you @DeVilSQuaD666. Why would you taunt her like that? Are you a Troll? Who are you?

@DeVilSQuaD666: Someone having fun, that's who.

@MIsstressWolf: You're sick. For all I know, you called it in.

@DeVilSQuaD666: Ha, ha. Maybe.

@MIsstressWolf: You're not well. Please stop commenting. I'll block you.

@DeVilSQuaD666: Will do. But I'm telling you. You ain't seen nothing yet.

Chapter 27

"LIAM BERKELEY. WELCOME."

A handsome man in an expensive suit opened his arms to welcome Liam. He couldn't be more than in his late twenties. He hadn't lost his hair yet but had a very obvious receding hairline. He laughed and hugged Liam, who seemed uncomfortable and pulled away quickly.

"So stoked that you're here. My client will be so thrilled to meet you. As soon as he heard you wanted to meet him, he got so excited. He's seen your show like...a gazillion times. And he loves it."

Liam nodded. He looked embarrassed and uneasy. It was one thing I had come to learn about this guy; he was nothing in real life like he was on TV. On-screen, he would yell and scream at everyone and say loads of offensive things. But in real life, he was actually quite humble and didn't seem very impressed with his own career. At times, I even got the feeling that he was a little embarrassed by it. I wondered if it was because it wasn't really him; it was a character he played. I also wondered how it had come about. When had it started? Did he used to be angrier, or had he always played a role? How many people knew his real self?

Jamal "Buddha" Robinson's manager barely noticed my presence with more than a nod, and we followed him into the Superior Seafood Restaurant, where they had set up the meeting with the young gamer and Fortnite world champ.

The teenager sat alone at a table, his fingers tapping on the screen of an iPhone when we entered. From a distance, he looked like any of Olivia's friends at school, with his cap and Nike sports jacket, except I had a feeling all his clothes were sponsored. His hair underneath the cap was dyed purple on one side and had been bleached on the other. His dark brown eyes lifted as he heard us, and he spotted Liam. They fist-bumped, shared an awkward half-hug, and we sat down. The waiter arrived and took one quick glance at Liam, then looked like he wanted to run away. Jamal ordered crawfish for all of us, while Liam told the waiter he'd like a good old-fashioned burger.

"I know it's not what you expect from me, but I like a little guilty pleasure now and then," he said when the waiter nodded, looking like he could cry. "And I promise not to criticize it. You have my word."

That made the waiter smile as he left, partly starstruck, partly terrified the restaurant might end up on TV, being mentioned as the worst restaurant and him the worst server. I knew Liam would keep his word. He had told me it was partly why he seldom went to restaurants anymore. People were terrified of him and his criticism. I had thought a guy like him didn't go out to eat because he could cook it better himself and because it would never be good enough for him, but that wasn't the case.

The agent left us, and Liam used the first twenty minutes to congratulate the boy on his big win and the three million dollars that came with it. He then went on to giving him advice on being suddenly famous and how to avoid being used, and he told him to make sure he invested his money properly, so he didn't spend it all. It was all to win the boy's trust and not scare him half to death.

"Why do I have the feeling this is not why you're here?" Jamal suddenly asked just as the food arrived. I had to admit, I was quite jealous of Liam's burger, but the crawfish was amazing too. Liam had told me I had to taste it here, and I was glad I got to.

"You're right," Liam said and glanced at me like it was my cue. I wiped my mouth and fingers, then looked seriously at the boy.

"This is FBI profiler, Eva Rae Thomas," he said. "She's here to warn you about something that we fear might happen to you."

"Technically, I'm not a profiler anymore," I said. "But that doesn't matter. What matters is your life, Jamal, and I believe you are in serious danger."

Chapter 28

"DO YOU KNOW FAZEYOURFEARS?" I asked. "Do you know who's behind that alias?"

Jamal shook his head. "No. I teamed up with him yesterday for like five hours, but then he left, real sudden, and I had to finish on my own."

"Did he threaten you in any way?"

"Not at all."

"Did he say anything to you in the chat?"

"We spoke, but only about the game."

I could tell Jamal was shaken up. The latest story of Amal Bukhari and how she was shot on board that plane was scary to everyone. The fact that Jamal was black didn't make it less frightening.

"So...what do I do?" Jamal asked. "If the police come to my house, I can't very well keep them from coming inside."

I bit my lip. "I'll warn the local departments that this might happen, and hopefully they'll listen to me. But I'm afraid it's no guarantee. I warned the police before they got the call involving Liam's son. Still, it went terribly wrong."

Jamal gave Liam a horrified look. "But…what do I do? I can't just sit at home and wait for the police to show up and kill me."

"If they do show up, at least make sure you keep your hands up. Get to your knees immediately and keep your hands over your head at all times," I said.

Liam leaned forward. "But the thing is, once it goes down, once those body-armored men enter your house, you're so terrified that you can't think. It all goes so incredibly fast. You don't know what you're doing in the moment," he said. He took a break to gather himself, and I felt a knot grow in my throat. "You don't really think. You just act, and it gets really easily mistaken for a threat."

Jamal whimpered and leaned back in his chair. His fingers were fiddling with his phone, turning it between them.

"But what do I do?"

"Do you have somewhere you can go?" I asked. "Somewhere where no one knows where you are? In that way, when the call comes, and the police come to your house, you won't be there."

"But my family will be. I live with my momma and sister."

"Take them. You just earned a lot of money, am I right? How about you take a trip for about a week or two? Go somewhere that you always wanted to. Or treat your mother to a nice trip. Maybe a cruise or something. I'm sure she deserves it."

Jamal's face lit up. "I could do that. She always wanted to go to Canada."

"There you go," I said. "Take the trip, and that way, when the police arrive, they'll find the house empty."

"But what about school?" he asked. "I've already been absent way too much due to the competition and all the things they've wanted me to do afterward."

"Deal with that once you get back," Liam said. "This is your life, and maybe even your mother's and sister's lives we're talking about. Get out of here, now. Deal with the consequences later. I'm sure you can find an excuse, or maybe Eva Rae can write them a letter telling them the FBI told you to go."

"I can't exactly do that," I said. "Since I am no longer technically FBI, but I can write a letter testifying to the threat on you. No matter what, I'm sure you'll get through it as long as you get out of this town immediately. Go home and pack, but tell no one where you're going; do you hear me? No one. Not that agent of yours or your best friend or even a neighbor. Don't tell your mother and sister where you're going either. Say that it's a surprise. And whatever you do, don't go online while you're there. No gaming and no live-streaming on Twitch. Stay low, go to the beach, enjoy your sister and mother. Survive this, Jamal, please."

Chapter 29

"ARE you sure you don't want to come downstairs and hang out with the rest of us?"

Matt stared at Elijah. The boy had come home from school, then run up to the room he shared with Eva Rae's son Alex. He was now sitting at his computer that Matt had just bought for him to make him feel better about the move. Matt knew he missed his grandmother, and he was angry about having to live with Eva Rae and her children. He had hoped the expensive computer would help.

So far, it hadn't. So far, it had only made him stay in his room longer, and Matt had soon regretted buying it for him. Elijah didn't even take off his headset or turn his head to look at Matt.

Matt closed the door with a deep exhale, then walked down the stairs where all of Eva Rae's three children were gathered eating snacks, fighting over who was supposed to feed the bunnies and who had played with them last, while Eva Rae's mother was in the kitchen, cooking tonight's dinner. Matt stood at the foot of the stairs, observing them all, then wondered what he was even doing there.

He didn't feel at home at all here, and Eva Rae wasn't home again.

"Where did she go this time?" her mother, Elizabeth, asked when Matt went in there and grabbed a beer from the fridge. It had been a calm day at the station, yet he felt exhausted. Maybe it was all that worrying about Eva Rae and what she was up to now. Was she with that Liam character?

He shrugged and took the cap off. "She didn't say. She just left a message on my voicemail and said she was so sorry, but she had to go. She hoped she'd be back before the weekend. She told me she'd explain everything to me later but that it was very urgent."

Her mother wrinkled her forehead. "She did the same to me. Told me she had to go for a couple of days, then asked me to take care of the children while she was gone, then she gave me the whole *I am so sorry you know I am, and I wouldn't do this to you if it weren't important* speech, and then she hung up before I could protest. She's got some nerve, that daughter of mine."

Matt shrugged again. "I guess it must be important. She's working on some case. She hasn't told me the details of it, but I'm sure she will later."

Elizabeth tilted her head. "Poor you. She's not exactly making things smooth for you, is she? The way she's always rushing off to something. You have, after all, just moved in, and she barely takes any time to be with you."

Matt sipped his beer then nodded. "My guess is she needs it."

"How so?"

"I think she has a strong need to save people. It feels more urgent than ever in her. Maybe because she couldn't save Chad."

Elizabeth sent him a smile while blending cauliflower and carrots. Once she stopped the blender, she gave him another look.

"You know, you could just tell him that he has to do it."

"Now, what are we talking about?"

She looked toward the ceiling. "Elijah. You're his dad. He's nine years old. You can give him orders, you know. It's your right and actually your duty to tell him what to do. It just might be what he needs."

"But he doesn't want to come down here," Matt said. "He just wants to play on that computer up there."

"Because no one tells him otherwise. You can't keep asking him for permission to be his father, Matt. You gotta just own up to it. Yes, he'll be upset with you, but isn't that better than being ignored? Plus, he'll get over it eventually. He'll make your life miserable for a little while, but then again, he's already doing that, so what do you have to lose? My guess is that he wants a family just as much as you do. He just doesn't know how to tell you. He's waiting for you to make a move. It might not be pleasant to have to do it, but it can hardly get worse from here, am I right?"

Matt drank from his beer again while Elizabeth put beets into the blender and turned it back on. While staring at her, pondering about what she had just told him and whether she could be right or not, he finished his beer. He put the empty bottle down and hurried upstairs, taking two steps at a time. He opened the door to Elijah's room without knocking, then walked straight to the boy and pulled off his headset. Elijah let out a whining sound, then turned to face Matt.

"Hey! I was using those."

Matt's eyes grew wide. That was the most the boy had spoken to him in all the time they had lived together. And he was actually looking at him, not ignoring him.

It was a start.

"That's right," Matt said. "You *were* using them. Now, you're not. Now, you're coming downstairs with me and hanging out with the rest of us. We can play cards or a board game if you want to, but no more computer or iPad. From now on, you have one hour of screen time each day after school. The rest, you spend downstairs with the rest of us."

Before the boy could answer or even protest, Matt walked to the wall and pulled out the plug.

"But...?" Elijah tried.

Matt shook his head. "Nope. I'm your dad, and I'm telling you to get downstairs now."

Elijah's eyes flickered back and forth, and there was obviously some struggle going on inside of him.

"That's not fair," he yelled, then stood to his feet and walked through the door. "You can't do this to me. You have no right."

"Oh, I have every right. Just you watch me."

Matt stood for a few seconds and stared at the cord in his hand, heart beating rapidly in his chest. Elizabeth had been right, much to his surprise. He wasn't winning any popularity contests due to this, and Elijah hated him more than ever, but he realized he hadn't felt this good in a very long time.

Chapter 30

"I'M sorry to have to bother you both at a time like this," I said.

I looked at Peter James's parents as they sat in front of me. We had come to them in their house outside of New Orleans in a small charming neighborhood called Elmwood. The house was a typical Victorian-style house with wrought-iron balconies and stained glass in the doorways and windows. It was beautiful on the outside, but inside, the air was thick with grief, and it saddened me deeply. Their son had been dead for more than a year, but time in here had stood still. It was December, and yet they had put no decorations up for Christmas.

"I'm just not sure how we can be of help?" His dad, Greg James, said.

His mother, Viviane, couldn't hold back her tears.

"I really don't like ripping up these old wounds," she said.

"We understand," Liam said. "But as we told you, it happened to my boy too. And we believe someone is doing this, is causing these episodes to happen."

"But...why?" Viviane asked. "Why would anyone do something like this?"

I swallowed and shook my head. "We don't know that yet. We

have no motive so far for these attacks. But we do know that he's not going to stop anytime soon. We came here straight from a meeting with another young boy whom we believe might be his next victim, had we not warned him."

"Oh, dear God," Viviane said and cupped her mouth.

"At least you could warn him," Greg said. "You said he lived around here?"

"Yes, but we've told him to go away for a little while," Liam said. "Just to make sure that he isn't at his house when the call comes in. Just in case."

"The thing is," I said, "that even if we warn them, the police have to go if they get a call. They have to take it seriously no matter what. We thought it was better that the boy got away."

"Good," Greg said, nodding. "Very good. Now, what can we do to help you find this guy?"

"I was wondering if we might be able to take a look at Peter's computer?" I asked.

Greg looked puzzled. "His computer? But…why?"

"There might be clues as to who this person might be. Peter is the first victim that I've found, so maybe the Swatter wrote something to him, or maybe he made a mistake of some sort that can guide us. Anything at this point would be a great help. We don't really have much the way it is."

"Do you still have his computer here in the house?" Liam asked.

Viviane nodded. "In his room. We haven't changed anything."

"Viviane hasn't been able to go in there yet," Greg said.

That was exactly what I had hoped when Liam had suggested we talk to this family; he had done so because he wanted them to know their son's death was no accident, that they deserved to know the truth. For me, it was just as much because I had a feeling his computer might have been left untouched. I remembered how it was in my home when my sister Sydney was kidnapped. My mom didn't dare to go into her room, and the door was simply closed like she was still in there sleeping or maybe playing peacefully. We just went on with our lives like she was still living there. I had a feeling the James family might have done the same thing. It was only natural when losing a child. There was no right time to remove his things, and it felt like removing the memory of him completely.

Just like you haven't gotten rid of Chad's things. They're still gathered in the garage in boxes. You haven't even looked inside of them.

I rose to my feet with an exhale, shaking the thought and reminding myself to call Matt before I went to bed at the hotel, then looked at the mother.

"Could you be so kind and show us the way?"

Chapter 31

"THEY GOT ON A LATE FLIGHT," Liam said and sat down in the bar of the hotel.

Liam had told me he'd pay for the entire trip since I had no money—at least none to spare—so he had booked us in at the Waldorf Astoria in New Orleans. It was a gorgeous old hotel, unlike anywhere I had ever stayed. The amount of marble and the huge chandeliers were enough to leave me breathless. We had rooms on the same floor and agreed to meet up for drinks downstairs. It had been a long day, going through Peter James' computer. Unfortunately, we hadn't found anything that could help us. His parents didn't know his passwords to any of his gaming profiles, so we couldn't get access to them. I then called my dad and asked for his help, and he gained access from his computer, but couldn't find anything extraordinary. All the chats were gone, and it would take months to go through all his private messages and comments on all the social media platforms. We concentrated our search around the days before he was killed and went through his emails but didn't find anything to help us.

It was a long shot anyway.

"To Montreal. Jamal called me as they arrived at the airport."

I ordered a glass of Chardonnay.

"I won't feel safe till I know he has landed in safety," I said. "I keep thinking of what happened to Amal Bukhari."

Liam placed a hand on my shoulder. The gesture felt a little awkward, and, realizing this, he pulled it away.

"He's going to be fine. As long as they haven't told anyone they're leaving and where they're going, they can't get to him."

I took a deep breath. "I still don't feel good about this."

My glass of white wine landed in front of me, and I sipped it. Liam had a whiskey that he turned a couple of times before tasting it. It looked almost like he washed his mouth with it.

"I don't understand you housewives," he said and looked at my Chardonnay. "Why you all drink that stuff. There are so many wonderful white wines out there that are way better than Chardonnay."

I stared at my glass, then drank some more. "I drink it because I like it. And please don't refer to me as a housewife again. I don't think I deserve that title, being as I'm never home in my house with my family."

That made him smile slyly. "Touché."

"You know what? You're actually a nice guy," I said. "Why do you act the way you do on your show?"

He smiled again. "Don't let my act fool you. I am not a nice guy. Believe me. I am anything but."

"So, you're telling me that you're acting now with me and not when you're on TV? That's your real personality? I don't buy it. You've been nice to me ever since you came to my house that day."

He shrugged and took a sip that was used as mouthwash once again. There was a point when I feared he'd spit it all out afterward like a fine wine tasting. But he didn't.

"Who's to tell, huh?"

I scoffed. "I, for one, think you should drop the act and just be you. People might like that even better."

"What? And no yelling at people anymore? No telling them what to do? No scolding them for the excessive use of garlic in their food? Are you crazy? I like that part. No, I love it. It makes me feel alive. Without it, I'd be more bored than your little friends out in suburbia drinking their Chardonnay, never doing anything with their lives. Look here. I'll send this whiskey back. It's only suited for use on your Christmas pudding if you ask me."

"Please, don't," I said, cringing. "Please, don't make a scene."

He sat up like he was suddenly filled with a new surge of energy.

"Why not? Does causing trouble make you uncomfortable, huh? Are you that self-effacing that all you want to do is run around and help people, save the world, save lives here and there, but lo and behold you should demand anything for yourself or cause any ruckus in life?"

"Excuse me?" I said, beginning to feel a little offended.

"What is so wrong with demanding the best or standing up for yourself?" he asked, getting agitated and gesticulating. "In my opinion, people let restaurants get away with way too much. No one should eat bad food or drink horrible white wine. You need to grab life by the horns, Eva Rae. Don't fear people getting upset or causing a scene. Demand the best. Stop letting life toss you around."

I wrinkled my forehead. "No one is tossing me anywhere. I am perfectly capable of taking…"

"Then tell me this. When's the last time you sent back an under-cooked steak or one that was cooked too much? When did you last tell someone that they didn't do their work good enough? When did you last ask to speak to the manager, huh? When did you last make a lot of trouble for nothing? When did you last even complain about something?"

I stared at the man, getting agitated. Who the heck did he think he was? Just when I was beginning to think I actually liked him and felt sorry for him, he pulled something like this. Insulting me on so many levels, I could hardly speak.

"You've never done that, am I right?" he answered his own question. "You've never complained about any food or drinks in a restaurant. You're too…nice for that. Too busy making sure everyone is happy. Just like you let that guy move in with you even though you didn't want him to, just because you don't like to make people angry with you. You can't stand making people sad. But the thing is, Eva Rae, in life, you're bound to hurt people at some point. No one can go through life without hurting someone. Not even you. And once you finally realize that letting him move in with you was a mistake, that's when you'll hurt him even worse than if you had just told him it was too early from the beginning."

I stared at the man in front of me, wanting desperately to punch him in the face. He grinned and emptied his glass while I could swear that smoke was emerging from both my ears. It felt like it, at least.

I rose to my feet and grabbed my purse.

"You don't know anything about me," I said, steaming. "And I take my words back. You're not a nice guy. You're a sick bastard, and I don't know which is worse. The fact that you are one, or the fact that you're proud of it."

Chapter 32

JAMAL ROBINSON TOOK a bite of the juicy burger. His momma and sister were sitting across the table from him, eating in silence. His mother suddenly burst into a huge grin.

"Canada, son? I can't believe we're really here. How did you keep it a secret, huh?" she asked.

The colder air had felt so wonderful on their skin, but now he was happy to be inside while the snow fell on the windows. The city of Montreal's lights danced in the darkness. In the distance, he could see a cruise ship as it was docking, bathed in bright lights. They had found a burger joint that was called something French by the harbor in the old town. People around them were mostly American or European. Their cab driver, M&M, as he called himself (not like the rapper, but the candy), had been beyond cool, and Jamal couldn't stop himself. He had to record him and live stream it to his YouTube channel. He believed it would be okay as long as he didn't use Twitch like that FBI woman had told him. M&M had been quite spectacular on the video, telling Jamal's viewers all about the town.

"I want to go to that market we passed on our way here," his sister Asia said. "Tomorrow. I want to get myself a hoodie or maybe a cap. And a snow globe. I love snow globes."

"We can do that," Jamal said happily, trying to let go of the gnawing anxiousness he was feeling inside his stomach. He was thrilled to be able to give his family this treat, but he wasn't very happy that it was under these circumstances. He knew he was far from home, yet he couldn't help feeling nervous.

"How's your burger, Jamal. You like it?" His momma asked, chewing on a french fry. No one had been prouder than Momma Robinson when Jamal had taken the World Championship home six months ago. She had always scolded him for being on his computer too much, but as he brought home the check for three million dollars along with so many sponsors that she never had to work a day in her life again, there would be no more complaining. His momma had bad knees from working as a cleaning lady for years and years. It had always been Jamal's dream to support her, so she never had to clean up white people's dirt again. And now he had.

"It's good," he said and took another bite. "Juicy."

"I can't wait to see the town," Asia said. "It's supposed to be gorgeous."

Jamal had rented them a small apartment downtown for two weeks. After that, it should be safe to go back home again. At least he hoped it would. He couldn't really stay away forever. Plus, he had to keep giving his viewers updates and new material, or they'd unsubscribe, and he'd lose his sponsors. He was used to making live stream videos nonstop all day, of everything he did and especially of his gaming, of course. The past twenty-four hours, he had been unusually quiet, except for the small driving video from the taxi, and the viewers would begin to wonder.

Jamal drank his Coke and looked at his family when out of the corner of his eye, he noticed that the waitress came to the table next to them, and a second later, the people sitting there got up and left. Normally, it wouldn't be a cause for concern if he hadn't seen her continuing to the next table and the exact same thing happening. The couple sitting there got up and left, leaving their food and their bill unpaid. When he looked around, he soon realized they were all alone in the restaurant.

Every customer had left, and he couldn't see any of the waitresses either.

Chapter 33

"DANG IT, JAMAL!"

I tapped on my iPhone, trying to call him but kept getting his voicemail. I stared at the computer screen in front of me, where Jamal was driving around Montreal with a taxi driver who was telling stories about his town.

"Why would you do this? Why would you make a video revealing your whereabouts? When we specifically told you to keep a low profile!"

I was yelling at him on the screen since I couldn't get ahold of him on the phone. My heart was racing in my chest, and I was shivering. It felt so devastating because there was absolutely nothing I could do.

There was a loud knock on my door, and Liam's voice yelled from the other side. "Eva Rae? Open up!"

I opened the door and let him inside. "Are you okay?" he asked while walking in, wearing nothing but a bathrobe over his boxers.

I showed him the screen and turned on the video. "This is from today. From Montreal. Jamal just revealed his whereabouts to the entire world."

"Oh, dear," Liam said and looked at the video, then up at me.

"I subscribed to his videos to keep an eye on him," I said. "When I saw the notification that he was live-streaming, I just about had a heart attack. How could he be this stupid? Can you explain this to me?"

"He's fourteen," Liam said and sat on my bed. "He doesn't think."

I looked at Liam. "Were you sleeping? It's eight-thirty?"

"Yeah, well, I like to go to bed early. I usually get up at four-thirty to get a good start. Then I go to the gym before I eat my oatmeal and then head to the studios for the taping of my show. I also have nine restaurants that I need to make sure are running properly. They're located around the world, so I often make a lot of calls in the early morning hours to check in on them."

"Wow," I stopped him, feeling exhausted just from hearing this. "I don't think we could ever be friends. All that is just a little too intense for me."

Liam chuckled. "It is for most people. And I am not here to be your friend anyway. I don't have friends; I have no time for them in my schedule. I am here to catch whoever killed Tim and make sure they pay."

"Okay. It was just an expression, but I'm glad we got that cleared up," I said with a deep sigh. I stared at Jamal on my computer, feeling all kinds of worry in my heart. Why wasn't the kid picking up his phone?

"Can we call someone?" Liam asked. "The local police? Can we warn them, maybe? Tell them what might happen?"

"They're probably not going to believe us."

I grabbed my phone in my hand, then searched on the computer and found the number for the City of Montreal Police Department.

"But I guess it's worth a try. Here goes nothing."

Liam placed a soothing hand on top of mine and looked into my eyes. It startled me and puzzled me at the same time. I couldn't figure this guy out. He kept pushing me away, then being extremely nice to me. The strange part was that it sort of made him oddly attractive to me, even though I fought it with every fiber of my being. Was it possible to hate someone yet desperately want them to kiss you at the same time?

Chapter 34

"WHAT'S GOING ON, Jamal? Why are you suddenly so pale?"

Jamal looked at his momma, fighting the panic attack that was about to erupt inside of him. His hands were shaking terribly as he leaned forward and whispered.

"Momma, I need you to remain calm now, okay?"

"Calm? What do you mean calm?" she asked loudly, doing the exact opposite.

Jamal stared at the big window leading to the street. They were sitting upstairs, but he could still see the blinking lights outside and had spotted at least three men in uniform setting up outside. The street had been closed off. There had to be at least a dozen police cars. Some of the cops were hiding behind their vehicles with their rifles pointed at the door.

Were they here for him?

"What's happening, Jamal?" Asia said, her voice quivering slightly. She was a smart girl and had figured out that something was going on. "Where did everybody go?"

"They went outside," he said. "And in a few minutes, the police are probably going to come in here…"

"The police?" his mother squealed.

"Yes, Momma. Now, you listen carefully, both of you. They're coming here because someone…"

Jamal didn't get to finish his sentence before the door was kicked open, and they heard the sound of heavy boots on the stairs. Jamal couldn't breathe. His chest felt so tight it was like it was impossible to get any air into his lungs. He took small short breaths that felt like they got stuck in his throat and made him feel dizzy.

"What's going on, Jamal?" his momma wailed when they came storming and yelling up the stairs in their black uniforms, Kevlar vests, helmets, and assault rifles pointed at the three of them.

"Stay calm," Jamal said. "And do as they tell you to."

"Calm?" his momma yelled as the SWAT team came closer, yelling at them. They knelt and kept their guns pointed at them. They were still yelling, and Jamal knew it was in French, but he didn't understand the words. It became clear to one of the officers, and he switched to English.

"Hands up. Keep them up!"

"What in the…?" His momma looked at them, then at her son. "Did you do something? Are they here for you? Did you get yourself in trouble, son? I knew this vacation was too good to be true. It always is."

"Just do as they tell you, Mom," he said and shot both of his hands in the air. His sister did the same, but his mother was reluctant.

"Put your hands up," the officer yelled again, "and then get up slowly and come over here. Slowly."

"I ain't doing no such thing," Jamal's mother suddenly started. "I am on vacation. And now you people come in here yelling and pointing those things at us like we're some darn terrorists or some-thin'. Now, if my son did something, then at least tell us what it is. We have a right to know why you are arresting him."

"Come over here," the officer repeated. "I'm not playing around. Come over here now."

Jamal did as he was told. He walked slowly toward the officers, keeping his trembling hands up in the air. He was barely able to walk because of the waves of fear rushing through his body, yet he managed to take the few steps it took to get to them. One of them approached him.

"Are you carrying any weapons?" he asked. "Answer me!"

Jamal shook his head. "N-no."

Another officer started to pat him down, then shook his head when he didn't find anything. Jamal could hear a chopper circling the air outside.

"Can I get an explanation back here?" his mother complained.

She still hadn't gotten up from her seat, and Jamal knew that once she got into that mood, it was hard to get her to calm down again. But he really desperately needed her to. He needed her to for once be gentle as a lamb.

Just this once, just for today.

"Why are you treating my son like this, huh? He ain't done nothing to you people. Is it just because he's black? I'll tell ya what we call this where we're from. We call it racism. This is racist."

Her words made the officers turn their attention and their guns on her.

"Ma'am, would you please come over here too?" the officer said, still pointing his gun in her direction. Asia was crying now, and Jamal wanted to comfort her. She was standing with her hands in the air, her small body shaking with fear. The officer told her to come closer. She whimpered but stood frozen in fear. It was like she couldn't move even if she wanted to.

"Please," Jamal said. "She's scared."

Jamal's mother rose to her feet. "Leave her alone. She didn't do nothin'. We're just here on vacation; that's all. You have no right to do this to us."

Jamal turned to look at her, but as he did, he felt a hard blow in the neck as the officer hit him with his rifle. The blow caused him to fall forward to his knees while he fought to stay conscious. Everything inside of him whirred, and there was a ringing in his ears. He couldn't hear what was going on outside of his body and suddenly felt a forceful push in the back as two men were on top of him, pressing his face into the ground, a knee in his back. He looked at his mother and sister, then saw his mother take off toward him, her massive body bolting forward, her mouth torn in a distorted scream. In the distance, he could hear muffled voices yelling, and he realized he was slowly getting his hearing back. As the shot was fired and the bullet whistled through the air, then ripped through his mother's chest, and she fell to the ground with a loud thud, he heard everything. He could hear every little brutal detail, and he knew instantly that he would be hearing it for many more years to come when waking up in sweaty nightmares.

Chapter 35

I STARED at Matt across the kitchen counter in my house. I had come back from New Orleans as soon as I learned what had happened to Jamal and his family. There was nothing more I could do, and I needed to be with the people I loved. As soon as I came in through the door, I had thrown myself in Matt's arms and told him everything, while crying. He poured me a glass of Chardonnay while he had a beer.

"I know I should have told you the story a long time ago, but, well…at first, I wasn't sure I was right, and then I was scared that you wouldn't believe me or that you would think I was crazy or something."

He scoffed and ran a hand through his thick hair. His soft eyes lingered on me, and I felt guilty for having admitted to finding Liam attractive. I had the best man in the world right there, and there was no one else that made me happy the way he did.

"Sometimes, I feel like you don't know me very well, Eva Rae, even though we've known each other since pre-school. Of course, I believe you. I've heard about swatting in the gaming community before, as a means of punishment for killing someone in a game or just to play a prank on someone. But this? This is insane. You mean to tell me there is someone deliberately killing people by swatting them?"

"I believe he has killed twelve people so far, yes. But there could be many more. The thing is, he's not limited by where he lives. He can call any police station in any county in any state in the country, well apparently also out of the country as we just have seen. He can simply tell them that there is a hostage situation, a bomb, or whatever he comes up with. He could be doing it right now as we speak. There's nothing holding him back. All he needs is a phone and an address. The police have to act on it; they have to send in their strongest team for a situation like that. They're nervous and scared because the killer has told them he'll shoot them if they come, or that he'll blow everything to pieces like he told them in Montreal. They don't know who is holding the bomb or who poses a danger, so they'll shoot first and ask later. And it can end fatally for anyone present, even a poor mother running to help her son, trying to protect him from what she believes is police brutality."

"She died?" Matt asked.

I nodded, biting my lip. I was giving my nails a break for once since they were almost completely gnawed down to the roots.

"In the ambulance on their way to the hospital. Jamal is inconsolable. So is his sister. Their aunt has come to Montreal to be with them. She'll take them in, but those kids…man…they're destroyed, Matt. Completely broken."

"What does the Montreal Police Department say?" Matt asked and sipped his beer.

"They've given the children a public excuse, but how is that going to help them? The prime minister has even held a press conference where he said publicly how awfully saddened he is by this horrific incident and that they'll prosecute the officer who shot. They've released the transcripts from the call, and I have to say, I can't blame them for reacting the way they did, for being terrified. You know how it is when coming into a situation like this. The caller clearly states that he has a bomb in his bag and that he is going to blow the place up. He also states that he has killed his father and that the entire family wanted to die doing this."

Matt swallowed and put the beer down, giving me a look. "There's a couple of things I don't understand here. You told me that most of the calls come in at 8:56 p.m. This one didn't."

"No, it came at seven-forty. My guess is the killer needed to do it at that time," I said. "That getting to Jamal weighed heavier. Maybe he wanted it to happen in a public place."

"Why? He could have sent them to the apartment they rented instead. In the middle of the night."

I nodded. It was true. Was the guy changing up the game? But why? Usually, serial killers would only divert from their MO if they were afraid of being caught, but this guy didn't know we were onto him. Did he?

"My second question is, how did this guy know where to find Jamal Robinson? Hadn't you just told him to leave and not tell anyone where he went?"

"He made a live video during the taxi drive from the airport," I said. "I watched it. I had told him to keep under the radar, but he must have felt he needed to give his viewers something, or he might lose them."

"So, he made the video just shortly before the swatting happened?" he asked.

"Yes."

"Seems awfully close, doesn't it?"

"What do you mean? He could have seen it, just like I did, then made the call."

Matt nodded pensively while taking another sip.

"You don't think so?" I asked.

"No, no. Of course, it's a possibility. Guys like him are always on or near the computer, but I just don't understand how he knew exactly where to find them. If he made a video in the taxi, then did he also say where they were going out to eat? Did he mention that in the video?"

I shook my head. Matt had a point.

"Did you know where he was?" Matt asked.

I wrinkled my forehead. "I guess there are other ways to find out...."

"Did you? Did he tell you?"

"He did. He texted me from the airport and told me that they had landed and that he was looking for a good burger joint. He also said that the guy helping them with their luggage had given them the name of a place; it was something French…where are you going with this?"

He shook his head again. "Nowhere. Just thinking out loud… could he have texted anyone else?"

I shrugged. "I don't know. I told him not to. But he might have. I also told him not to make any videos, and he still did that. His agent might have known. Maybe a friend, a girlfriend, who knows?"

"And you'll probably never find out, but it is odd that he was found," Matt said, sipping his beer. "And I do think that this killer knows you're onto him. He must know you talked to Jamal. That's why he's changing his tactics. Either to try and lose you or maybe because he wants to play games."

"And me getting to Jamal before he did has angered him," I said. "Up until now, he's believed himself to be invincible, to be able to commit the perfect murder. I've disrupted that."

"And you know what that means."

"I have put a target on my own back."

Matt sighed deeply.

"Exactly."

Chapter 36

"WITH US THIS morning on a Skype call from her hospital bed is Amal Bukhari. In case you don't know who Amal Bukhari is, she's one of the world's most popular YouTubers and online gamers. She was recently shot on an airplane when the police thought she was carrying a bomb. Ever since, she has been hospitalized and gone through surgery after surgery to get back to life. Good morning to you, Amal. How are you feeling today?"

Amal smiled at her camera. The hostess on *Good Morning America* had briefed her shortly before they went live, and the connection had been terrible, but now it seemed to be better.

"Good morning. I'm okay," she said. "But I am quite outraged."

"And why is that?"

"Because it has happened again. Two days ago, Jamal Robinson, or Buddha as we call him in the gaming world, lost his mother in a restaurant in Montreal."

"It's been all over the news," the host said. "I think most people have heard about it, but in case you haven't, let me quickly explain that the police in Montreal went to the restaurant after receiving a bomb threat for the restaurant, and they shot and killed Jamal's mother, who was forty-eight. A terrible tragedy that has sent shockwaves through all of us, especially in the world of social media and the gaming community, naturally."

"It makes me so angry because it was exactly the same thing that happened to me," Amal said. "They shoot first and ask questions later. The police brutality we are experiencing in this day and age is worse than anything in history. We are going in the wrong direction. We are going backward."

"And you believe it is racism?"

"Look at my brown face," Amal said. "The SWAT team did and immediately believed I had to be a terrorist. Would they have reacted the same way had I been white? Would they have shot Jamal's mom if she had been a white mom trying to help her son? Would they have knocked the kid to the ground if he hadn't been black? I don't think so. We all know this is happening all over the country and even out of the country too. Why not say it the way it is? They look at our skin color and decide our lives aren't as important as someone who is white."

"The police call what happened to you 'an unfortunate accident.' How do you react to that?"

Amal scoffed. "They try to kill me and then they call it an accident? I don't buy it. There is something wrong deep inside our system and within our police force. And that is why I want the officer who shot me to pay for what he did. I am bound to a bed right now and will never live a normal life again."

"They tell me he was fired afterward; isn't that enough?"

She shook her head. "No! If you try to kill someone, you need to go to jail. I want this guy to serve time."

"So, you're filing a civil lawsuit," the anchor said.

"Yes, and last night I just received word that the case will go to trial. Meanwhile, I am arranging a demonstration in Washington, D.C., and I urge everyone to come out and join me. It's time we stop this from happening. We can't just watch while our sisters and brothers and our children are being shot down in the streets. This must end now. We demand action right now. We can no longer rely on our justice system. We will take matters into our own hands if necessary."

"Thank you, Amal Bukhari, for joining us," the hostess said and looked directly into the camera, addressing the viewers, while adding:

"The protest will take place on January fifteenth. Anyone who wants to know more can follow Amal on social media where she will be updating about the event."

Chapter 37

THEN:

FanTAUstic345: I need your help.

DeVilSQuaD666: Sure. What's up?

FanTAUstic345: Having some trouble with someone.

DeVilSQuaD666: With who?

FanTAUstic345: Someone who's getting on my nerves. Slayer-Alpha32.

DeVilSQuaD666: What'd he do?

FanTAUstic345: He owes me money. Refuses to pay up. I asked him about it, and then he killed me in the game. Took everything I had.

DeVilSQuaD666: I hate those types. You shouldn't let him get away with it. You want to strike back?

FanTAUstic345: What do you mean?

DeVilSQuaD666: I know how.

FanTAUstic345: Really?

DeVilSQuaD666: Sure. Tell me who he is, and I'll make sure he's punished properly.

FanTAUstic345: You sure?

DeVilSQuaD666: If you pay me.

FanTAUstic345: How much?

DeVilSQuaD666: 1000 bucks will do.

FanTAUstic345: That's a lot of money.

DeVilSQuaD666: You want it done or not? You won't have to lift a finger. No one will know it was you.

FanTAUstic345: I don't want to do anything illegal.

DeVilSQuaD666: Don't worry. You're just teaching this guy a small lesson. Nothing bad.

FanTAUstic345: Okay. If you say so.

Chapter 38

I WATCHED the interview with Amal Bukhari on *Good Morning America* on my computer. The kids had taken off for school, and I was holding my warm coffee between my hands. Matt was rummaging around the kitchen, getting himself some breakfast, while my mom was filling the dishwasher. The kids had been arguing all morning, and I had ended up yelling even louder to get them to shut up. Now I felt awful and wished I could go back and just hold them tightly in my arms instead or at least speak like a normal person and not yell. The atmosphere had been horrid when sending them off, one kid more furious with me than the other.

Elijah had stayed out of it and not said a word. The kid was smart, no doubt about it. There was something different with him and Matt since I got back. Much to my surprise, Elijah was actually speaking to him. Not many words, but a few here and there, and sometimes even an entire sentence. I was pleased to see that their relationship was improving. I had noticed that Matt no longer treated him like he was fragile, and he was actually telling him what to do, like this morning he had told him to put his cereal bowl in the dishwasher after he was done eating. I had watched in awe as the kid actually did as he was told and put the bowl in the dishwasher. My kids didn't even do that.

"What are you watching?" Matt asked as he came into the living room, holding a bowl of Cheerios in his hand that he ate, standing up, slurping the milk. It was like watching a child eat breakfast.

"Amal Bukhari. She's arranging some sort of protest demonstration soon."

"Protest? Against what?"

"Police brutality."

"She was the one that was shot on the airplane, right?"

I nodded and sipped my coffee. "She thinks it was because of her skin color. That they reacted erratically because she's of Pakistani descent."

Matt shook his head. "An awful story. I feel for the officer who accidentally shot her. Not only was he fired, but he's also being charged with attempted murder. That is serious stuff. The guy's life is ruined."

"So is hers," I said. "She's had a ton of surgeries. Had all kinds of organs removed and patched up. Her body will never function properly."

"I guess there are no winners in these types of cases. The guy was just trying to do his job. The way I see it, it could happen to any of us. I'm not even sure you have to be racist to shoot someone in a situation like that."

I nodded and drank more coffee. Even though I had met my share of racist colleagues in blue, it didn't really have to have anything to do with that. Situations like these could so easily escalate and end badly.

"But he hasn't tried to kill her again, has he?" Matt asked and finished his breakfast by drinking the rest of the milk from the bowl. A few drops escaped and ran down his chin, which he wiped with the back of his hand.

"What do you mean?"

"You're saying that this was the Swatter, right? The guy who called in the bomb threat that led to her being shot? That it was the same guy as in the other cases."

"I have reason to believe it was, yes, why?"

"She didn't die. Do you think he'll try again?"

"That's a very good question," I asked. "If he does come for her, then he might also come for Jamal. But I'm not sure that's his motive if you know what I mean. I'm not sure that killing the person that he swats is the actual purpose. I think he chooses them carefully because of their popularity or because their death will obtain media coverage. He doesn't have an outstanding issue with the person or any other specific motive for killing them. At least none that I have found."

"So, killing Jamal's mother or simply hurting Amal Bukhari will be enough for him?" Matt asked. "Because it gets the coverage he wants?"

"That's my theory, yes. He has some sort of higher purpose that I have yet to figure out. But once I do, he won't be able to hide from me anymore."

Chapter 39

EVERY INCH of the four walls of my bedroom was covered with everything I could possibly find online about the Swatter's victims. And that was a lot. Some of them were big celebrities in the gaming world and had millions of followers, while others were smaller gamers, but all used Twitch for their live streams. And then there was Jamal's mother. Twelve people so far had been killed by the hand of this guy. All looked like accidents from the outside, unfortunate incidents.

Boy, this guy was good.

I'd been Googling for hours on end all day, and now I was staring at the collage on my walls and the many yellow post-it notes plastered on top of it. I had tried to find a connection between the victims, anything beyond the fact that they played Call of Duty and live-streamed on Twitch. I was hoping that there would be something else...that there was something I had missed. Anything that could direct me to this guy's motive for doing these things, for killing these people.

Did it have something to do with the game?

Matt had left for work, and my mom had gone to Orlando for the day, so I had the house to myself, which was good for thinking. I didn't even notice when Alex came home from school in the afternoon until he flew through the door to my room, a big smile on his face.

"Hi there, buddy. How was your day? Come here and give me a hug," I said.

He made a face like it was the worst thing in the world. "Mo-om!"

Then he ran back out. I stared in his direction. Was that it then? No more hugs from my little man? Had he already grown out of snuggling?

I wasn't going to let him go that easy.

"I'm hungry!" he yelled from his room.

I went to the kitchen and pulled out the bread to make a couple of peanut butter sandwiches when my phone rang. It was my dad.

"Hi there. What's up?"

I had asked my father to help me with the case since he knew everything about computers and gaming. At least a lot more than I did. He worked in cybersecurity and could gain access to almost anywhere online. I enjoyed working with him, and I sensed he did too. Working together on this made us closer, and I liked that. We had been apart for thirty-six years until he suddenly popped into my life a few months earlier. That was when I learned that I also had a younger half-brother, Adam.

I had asked my dad to play Call of Duty for me for a few days so I could take time off to dig deeper into my research. I needed him to keep an eye out for FaZeYourFeaRs.

"Did he show up?" I asked while smearing peanut butter on the bread and holding the phone between my shoulder and neck.

"He did," my dad said. He sounded strange. I put the knife down and grabbed the phone in my hand.

"What's wrong?"

"He's...everywhere."

"What do you mean? I don't understand?"

"He's teaming up with many different players. He's been doing this for the past twenty-four hours, and I'm just trying to keep track of him, but every time I find him, he's teamed up with someone else."

"He's changing the game," I mumbled. "He knows we can't warn all of them."

"I've been trying to keep track of each and every one of them and finding their real-life names and addresses, but there are so many now."

I sat on a stool, my pulse quickening. What was this guy up to now?

"He's telling us he knows we warned Jamal. So he'll just change it up, so we can't do that anymore. He wants us to watch from the sidelines," I said. "He's cornered us."

"Sounds almost like it's *Game Over* for us."

I exhaled and pinched the bridge of my nose. "Yeah, well, we'll just have to up our game too. Send me the list of names you have so far, will you? Defeat is not a word in my vocabulary, as he'll soon learn."

Chapter 40

SHE WAS BURNED OUT. She knew it, and so did everyone who knew her. Susan 'SSweatpea' Johnson stared at her computer screen and her headphones lying next to it.

"You don't have to do it, Susan," her husband Rob said, coming up behind her. He put a hand on her big stomach and smiled cautiously.

"It stresses you out, and I don't want that. Not in your condition."

"But I'll lose all my sponsors. We'll be poor."

He shrugged. "So what? With the money you've earned already, we can make it pretty far. The house is paid off, and we'll come up with something. I still have my job."

"You're an elementary school math teacher, Rob. You make no money."

"We'll figure it out, Susan. I don't want you gaming sixteen hours a day and stressing yourself out. You have to face the fact that it is over, honey. And you can't do it once the baby arrives anyway. You'll be busy taking care of our little girl. She'll need to eat often and have her diaper changed. There's no extra time when you take care of a baby."

Susan sighed, exhausted, knowing Rob was right. She had known for quite some time now. She had no idea that being pregnant would be this tough. She had thought she could at least continue until the baby arrived. But she felt so tired and so emotional that there was no way she could keep up in the world of professional gaming anymore.

Susan was one of the veterans in the gaming community. Before becoming a professional video gamer in 2009, she had been an ordinary high school student, working at the local post office in the summers. Her parents were poor, and they never had much while she was growing up. She always had to wear her brother's old clothes, which made her look like a boy since her mother insisted on keeping her hair short too, cutting it herself to avoid getting lice or anything else that might *cost them a fortune.*

Money was tight when she was growing up, and her parents didn't understand this new world that Susan had entered when she just started. So, when Susan told them there was money to be earned when gaming, they told her she was insane and that she needed to keep her job at the post office. Susan hid it from them in the beginning, but when she entered a tournament one spring, she won five thousand dollars. It was a heck of a lot more than she could earn at the post office over an entire summer. And as she told them this, she had her parent's full attention. They spent the five thousand on a new gaming computer and whatever else she needed. Two years later, she signed a three-year contract with tournament operator MLG-Major League Gaming, earning two hundred and fifty thousand dollars.

Today, playing esports had become highly competitive. The prizes were bigger too. The last tournament Susan had entered, the winner took home fifteen million dollars, whereas it was only one million ten years ago. The competition from the sixteen-year-olds was fierce too. Today, Susan was sponsored by Red Bull, Nike, and Honda, who paid her millions every year. She had seventeen million subscribers to her channels, and she was still quite good at what she did. She just didn't enjoy it anymore.

But was she ready to retire…to turn her back on this world and all its money? To no longer be adored by fans all over the world?

"What is it they say about gamers?" she said and leaned on her husband's shoulder. "Get big, burn out, retire young."

He chuckled and caressed her stomach. "I know you were a big star, sweetie, and you always will be in my eyes and the eyes of our little princess, but it's time to call it quits while you still can. You can't sit through tournaments that take ten to fifteen hours anymore. The life of a pro-gamer requires discipline and perseverance like no other job. There's no room for failure; your fans won't forgive you if you're not up to the game, and you only make real money if you're the very best. It requires intense focus and demands quick reactions, much like athletic sports, which young minds and bodies are most capable of sustaining. It's not suited for an almost thirty-year-old woman who's having a baby. You always knew it was an *all-in, all-out* kind of affair."

Knowing he was right and that the decision was made, Susan nodded and kissed his cheek, feeling sad yet relieved.

"I'll just do this one last tournament this Friday, and then I'll retire, okay?"

Chapter 41

NATHAN LOOKED over his shoulder as he rushed out of school, down the stairs, and toward the bus stop. He liked to be the first one there and the first one to get on the bus. Plus, the day hadn't been very good at school. He had been bullied at lunch again by Travis and Dexter. It was a long story that ended with his lunch on the ground of the cafeteria and him starving the rest of the day.

Nathan also had another reason for being in a hurry. Today was the day his grandmother would come over after school, and she had promised to bring him a new baseball glove, the one he had wanted for so long. Nathan didn't know why he was getting it now since it wasn't his birthday, and he hadn't gotten straight As or anything, but he assumed his grandmother was just trying to be nice.

The bus arrived, and they all got on. A kid pushed him, and he almost fell on the way up the stairs, while someone else gave him an elbow in the side and almost made him yell out in pain. But Nathan managed to get into his seat on the bus and placed his backpack by his feet. With butterflies in his stomach, he waited patiently for the bus to finally take off.

He sat alone, as usual, on the bus, but he didn't mind. He'd rather sit alone than be assigned to sit with someone who clearly didn't want to sit next to him like in school. He hated those looks he always got from his classmates when they were forced to sit next to him.

"Come on; come on," he mumbled impatiently while his legs bounced up and down. The bus stopped, and two kids left. There was only one more stop until he was getting off. Nathan had been dreaming about getting this glove for two years, at least. He was going to play with it all afternoon, and he would most definitely sleep with it tonight.

Maybe his dad could throw a few balls?

His dad had been out of work for a few weeks now and didn't have much else to do, as far as Nathan knew. He could definitely do it. If only he could be in a better mood than he had been in the past couple of days.

The bus approached his stop, and Nathan rose to his feet, backpack in hand. He walked out of the bus, three other kids coming out with him. He put his backpack on his back, then began the walk toward his house, waving at the bus driver on the way as he always did. No one liked Ms. Pat much, but he did. She was always nice to him and only yelled at all the other kids.

"See you tomorrow," he yelled as the bus took off and disappeared. Meanwhile, Nathan sped up when a car drove up on his side and a window was rolled down. An African American woman looked out at him, then stopped the car next to him. Puzzled at this, Nathan stopped walking and stared at her.

"Hey, kid," she said. "You Nathan Downey?"

The boy nodded. "Y-yes."

The woman opened the door of the car and got out. With her came two girls, whom Nathan recognized from his school. They were a few years older than him. The way they looked at him frightened him. Nathan backed up.

"I...I..."

The mother was the first one to act. She reached over and grabbed him in her strong arms and held him down. Then she yelled at her two daughters, and they came running, and soon punches were thrown at him from all sides. Nathan tried to scream and get loose, but the mother held him down, using her weight to press him into the pavement while the girls punched him again and again, harder and harder each time. A kid who was walking by pulled out her phone and began filming it. That made the mother let go of Nathan, and he stumbled to his feet, blood running from his nose and ear. As he tried to rise to his feet, one of the girls took another swing at him, punching him so hard he fell headfirst into the lamppost next to him.

Chapter 42

"ARGH!"

I threw my stapler across the room in anger. It knocked against the wall and fell to the floor. Matt came rushing into my room, looking confused.

"What are you doing in here?"

"I can't figure it out, Matt," I said, feeling tears well up in my eyes. I had been at it all afternoon and gotten nowhere. I had been looking through all of the gamers that FaZeYourFeaRs had teamed up with in the past twenty-four hours, but the list felt endless. And they were all so alike; there was no way of telling who his next victim would be. I had tried to cross-reference them and find similarities with his earlier victims, but all of them seemed to have the same differences and similarities. There was nothing that stood out to me, and time was passing. For every hour that went by, we were getting closer to this killer striking again.

It was unbearable.

Matt grabbed me in his arms and held me close. "It's okay, Eva Rae. You're doing what you can."

"But it's not enough, Matt. It's not good enough. Look at what happened to poor Jamal's mother, Mrs. Robinson. Look at what happened to Amal Bukhari. I knew they were his next victims, but it didn't matter."

Matt sighed and held me close. "You can't do any more than what you do, Eva Rae. You're wearing yourself out on this case. You can't be so hard on yourself. How about you come downstairs and watch some TV or we could play cards? Or what about you and I go out for dinner tonight, huh? Your mother will be home and can watch the kids for a few hours. Let me take you out for once. Just you and me."

"It's sweet, Matt, but I can't. I would never be able to relax anyway."

Matt gave me a disappointed look and let go of me.

"You're sad," I said.

"Yeah, well, can you blame me? We never do anything together, just the two of us anymore. Meanwhile, you're constantly running around somewhere hanging out with that Liam guy, eating dinners with him, and having drinks. Why can't you do that with me? Why is he more important?"

I gave him a look. "You're kidding me, right? Tell me you're kidding right now because I really hope you are."

"No. I'm very serious. I can't believe you won't go out to dinner with me, but you can race across the country to meet up with him… sleeping in hotels and eating expensive dinners."

I shook my head. "This isn't happening. Tell me it isn't happening."

"Well, it is. I'm tired of having to beg you to hang out with me, Eva Rae. I moved in so we could spend more time together, but so far, you haven't given me anything."

"So, what? You moved in for my sake?" I asked.

"No. I moved in for us. But so far, you're not in it at all."

"Well, excuse me if I'm trying to save lives here, Matt. Silly me; I thought you might think that was important, being a detective and all."

"That was low. You know, I take you very seriously. And I am the only one who is. But the fact is, you're always trying to save someone, Eva Rae. Even though you know just as well as I do that you can't save everyone."

"Well, I will still try," I said. "I can't just sit still when I know someone is about to be killed. I thought you'd understand this."

"You're running," he said.

"I'm what?"

"All this. It's a cover for the fact that you can't stand being here. You're running. You're running away from me constantly and from the grief."

"What are we talking about now, Matt?"

"You haven't cried. Not even once since Chad died."

I exhaled and rubbed my forehead. "Not that again."

"I'm serious, Eva Rae. You haven't shed a single tear since he was shot. At the funeral, you were like an ice sculpture."

"Wow, what a picture. You're a true poet, Matt."

"What's going on with you? Why are you constantly running away from me?" he asked.

"I'm not," I said, avoiding looking at him. "I'm just...busy. People are dying here, Matt.

I can't just let this guy get away with it. No one sees it."

"No, it's more than that, Eva Rae. Is it that guy?"

"Liam?"

"Yes, is something going on with you two? Is that it?"

"Matt, please. No. His son was killed, and he wants to find the person who did it; that's all. I don't even like him. He's a prick. But he is good to have on hand when I want to get to those celebrity gamers. When they hear he wants to see them, they want to meet. I can't get to them by myself."

"That means it's me then," he said. "If there's nothing going on, then that means you're running from me, not to Liam."

He stared at me, and our eyes met briefly when I saw something change in his.

"You blame me for Chad's death, don't you? I've asked you this before, but you didn't give me an answer. I want one now."

I rose to my feet. "No...Matt, I..."

He shook his head, backing up. "No. I think I'm right. He took a bullet for me, and every time you look at me, you're reminded of that. That's why you can't stand being with me or even in this house. That's why you're burying yourself in all this instead of being with the ones who love you. You feel guilty about it, about feeling this way, but you can't help yourself."

My shoulders slumped. I stared at Matt, speechless. There were so many things I wanted to say in this moment, so many words I could have said to calm him down, to reassure him that it wasn't the way things were. But they never came because they wouldn't be true.

Matt sucked in air, then nodded. "Yeah…that's what I thought. I'm being punished for something I had no say in, but I guess that's just life, right? It's just that unfair."

Matt walked to the door and opened it. I took a step toward him, wanting to stop him, but then I paused for a second too long, and he was gone.

As I sat on my bed, feeling heavy at heart, I heard him go to the boys' room and get Elijah. I could hear them rummaging around for a few minutes, then jumped when I heard the front door slam shut. To my surprise, I didn't cry when I heard Matt's car start up and drive away. I didn't shed a tear. But I did feel like someone had just ripped out a big chunk of my heart.

Chapter 43

"WE NEED TO TALK."

Chris Branson, Amal's agent, closed the door behind him and walked to the window next to her hospital bed. Amal tried to sit up, but couldn't. She had gone through yet another surgery the day before and felt awful. Her brother, Samir, was sitting in a chair by her bed, scrolling on his phone.

"What's up?" she asked, strained with pain.

Her agent rubbed his forehead. "I take it you haven't heard what happened yesterday?"

"Well, duh. I was kind of busy all day yesterday."

"Oh, yes, the surgery," Chris said. "I forgot for a minute."

"I sure didn't," she said with an exhale. "But what is it? What happened?"

Chris shook his head and looked briefly out the window, then back at her. "It's awful. Officer Downey's kid was attacked by some mom and her kids. They beat him up."

Amal grimaced. "How bad is it?"

"Bad. Real bad. He's still in the ICU. Hit his head against a lamppost and cracked his skull open. They don't know if he'll ever wake up."

"Oh, dear Lord. That is terrible."

"I know, but there's more."

Amal looked at him. "I don't like the sound of that."

"It was all recorded by some other kids and has gone viral. The mother and the girls have been arrested, but the reporters got to them first. There was an on-camera interview with her where she says that it was all for you."

Amal's eyes grew wide. "For me?"

Chris nodded. "Because of what happened to you. To punish Officer Downey for shooting you."

Amal placed a hand on her chest. "That's awful."

Chris shook his head and looked out at the view again. "They say it's because of what you said on TV, on *Good Morning America*."

"What?"

"You said something about taking matters into your own hands. You encouraged people to vigilantism."

"I did no such thing," Amal said, appalled. "I told them to come out for a protest. I never told anyone to beat up some kid. What on earth is happening?"

"I need you to be careful what you say from now on," Branson said. "You've got to think about it more than once before you say stuff like that. You make all these videos from your hospital bed, and millions of people see them and sympathize with you because of what happened to you."

Amal stared at him, surprised at this. "You're telling me to censor myself?"

Samir looked up from his phone. His eyes met Amal's, and he shook his head. "You can't do that."

"I'm not saying you should censor yourself. But you've got to realize what kind of power you hold right now," Branson said. "And be cautious. That's all. Maybe you should even hold back on your language toward the police, and if I'm being perfectly honest, I'd advise you to cancel the protest march. You're in no condition to follow through with it, and I'm afraid it's gonna end badly."

Amal couldn't believe it. Wasn't her agent supposed to be

supportive of her? She shook her head, even though the gesture sent shockwaves of pain through her body. She lifted her finger at him.

"It's not my fault there are idiots out there who take what I say the wrong way. I am sorry, but I'm not going to stop what I've started. This is probably the most important thing I have ever done in my life. This is a movement involving millions of people, and if you can't back me up in this, then you're not the right agent for me."

Chris Branson looked at her, then lifted his eyebrows. "Wow. I guess I'm not the right agent then. But before I leave, I want to warn you. If you follow through with this, it's gonna end in a blood-bath, and you'll be the one who has to live with the guilt. I hope you're prepared to do that."

"Oh, I'm more than prepared. Now, if you'll please leave, I have a video to make. My viewers are worried and want to know if my surgery went well yesterday."

Chapter 44

"WHERE ARE MATT AND ELIJAH?"

Olivia came into the kitchen as I was eating my cereal the next morning. I had put extra sugar on it, thinking it might cheer me up, but it didn't really help.

"They left," Christine said, glaring at me. "Mom kicked them out."

"I did no such thing," I said, putting my spoon down in the milk so hard that milk splattered on the breakfast counter.

"They left? What do you mean they left?" Olivia squealed. "Are they not coming back?"

"We don't know," Christine said. "Mom had some fight with Matt last night, and then he and Elijah left the house carrying their suitcases."

"You're kidding me, right? I go on one sleepover at a friend's house, and when I come back, you've ruined everything." Olivia grabbed a box of Cinnamon Toast Crunch forcefully. "I don't know how you do it. You just keep pushing him out of your life. How many times do you think he's going to take you back?"

"Why do you both assume that it was my fault?" I asked, surprised at them.

"Because it usually is your fault, Mom," Christine said and got up from her stool. She went to the sink and poured out the leftovers, then placed her bowl in the dishwasher.

"Since when did you start cleaning up after yourself?" I asked.

"Since Matt told us to do it," she said, then walked past me, giving me a disappointed glare.

"She was getting used to having Matt here," Olivia said after Christine had left. "She was starting to like him. You wanna know why? Because he was around. Yes, he worked full time, but when he was home, he was here, hanging out with us. He didn't stay in his room, avoiding having to deal with us."

"Very subtle, Olivia," I said and got up as well. I put my bowl in the dishwasher while my poor heart was aching.

"It's gonna destroy Alex; you do realize that, right?" Olivia said. "He loves Matt and was so excited to share a room with Elijah. How's he taking it so far?"

I exhaled tiredly and rubbed my forehead.

"You've got to be kidding me, Mom. You haven't told him; have you?"

"Yes, I told him," I protested. "I said they went to visit Elijah's grandmother for a few days."

"Why didn't you tell him the truth?" Olivia asked.

"Because I don't know what will happen yet," I said. "I don't know if they'll come back or not, and I don't want to break Alex's heart for no reason."

"Who's gonna break my heart?" Alex's small voice came from the door. My little guy had gotten himself dressed even though he had turned the shirt inside out. His hair was still messy from sleeping.

Olivia gave me a look. "Now, you have the chance to tell him, Mom."

Alex approached the counter and crawled up on a stool. "Tell me what?"

"Tell you that we're out of Cocoa Krispies," I said and grabbed the box of Cinnamon Toast Crunch. "So you'll have to have these instead. I hope it's okay."

Alex made a funny face. "Of course, it's okay. I love those."

I poured him some, my heart beating fast in my chest. Olivia left, sending me a disapproving glare. I knew she was right. If Matt and Elijah weren't coming back, I'd have to tell the kid at some point. But that meant I had to admit it to myself first, and I didn't want to do that. To be honest, I didn't want to deal with any of it. I didn't know what I wanted except to find the Swatter and take him down for good.

Chapter 45

I WATCHED the video of Officer Downey's kid being beaten up with great horror. I followed up by listening to an interview with the crazy mother who believed she was entitled to take action against a kid because of what his father had done.

It absolutely terrified me.

The poor kid.

I couldn't believe a mother could be so irresponsible and help her daughters attack another child by holding the kid down. What kind of a mother did something like that?

Luckily, they had all been arrested now, but it was too late for Nathan Downey. He was fighting for his life in the ICU, and his life would never be the same again, even if he did make it.

Neither would his father's.

"It's like the domino effect," I said to my dad when I spoke to him later. "Like what happened to Amal Bukhari is causing ripples across the water, and it keeps affecting people. It's like it won't stop. The video of the attack is all over the internet, and so is the interview with the mom where she told why she did it. Because of what Amal Bukhari had said on TV. To end police brutality."

"Fight fire with fire," my dad said. "Unfortunately, it's often what happens."

"There are no winners in this," I said. "That's what Matt said."

"Well, he's right about that."

I paused when thinking about Matt. "Do you think I'm running?"

"What do you mean?"

"Matt seems to think that's why I'm throwing myself at this case, why I'm devoting all my time to finding this killer because I don't want to deal with Chad's death."

My dad went quiet on the other end. I realized it was probably asking too much of him. We hadn't known each other very long.

"He might have a point," he said. "Dealing with grief is tough, and we all do it in our own way. For you, it might be digging into work and burying yourself with it for a little while."

"So, you don't think there's anything wrong with me doing it?" I asked.

"That's not for me to say," he said. "You'll have to listen to your own heart, sweetie. Only you know what is best for you."

"That was very diplomatically put," I said with a chuckle.

"Well, I like both you and Matt. I just hope you can figure things out."

I sighed and sipped my coffee. "Yeah, me too. I also wish I could find the Swatter and stop him before he kills again. I've been up and working on it for most of the night, but none of the names you gave me stand out. I've Googled each and every one of them and matched their profiles with the earlier victims to see if there is a deeper pattern to reveal which of the twelve names you gave me will be next. But nothing has come out of it. Absolutely nothing."

"We'll keep working on it," he said. "It's all we can do."

"I just hope we can figure it out in time. I won't be able to live with myself if more people are killed or even hurt by this guy. It's gotta stop. He simply has got to be stopped."

Chapter 46

SUSAN FOUGHT her way through the fog and finally managed to open her eyes. She blinked a few times while reality came back to her. Her head was pounding, and everything was in a hazy light. It took a few seconds for her to remember where she was and what had happened. The last thing she remembered was going to the bathroom for the tenth time this morning, thinking that it felt like the baby was having a dance party on her bladder.

The baby. Is the baby okay?

Susan remembered coming out of the bathroom and then the taste of the nasty fingers covering her mouth. She remembered biting those fingers and someone screaming behind her. Then she remembered trying to run away, getting loose, and then…then the sound of the person behind her swinging something through the air and it hitting her in the back of her head. After that, she remembered nothing else.

Someone had been in her house. Someone had tried to kill her. Was this someone still here?

Susan felt the baby kick and sighed with relief. She was okay. Everything seemed okay. There was no unexplained pain and no bleeding. The baby was fine.

That was more than you could say for Susan's head. It was aching painfully, and she closed her eyes for a few seconds to try and make it go away. When she opened them again, there was someone standing, hovering, and bending down above her. Seeing this, she tried to move but realized she couldn't. Her hands were tied behind her back, and something that tasted awful had been stuffed inside her mouth. The eyes looking down at her were unknown to her, the face covered by a ski mask.

"Oh, good. You're awake," said the person behind the mask. The voice wasn't one she knew or recognized either.

What do you want from me?

She wanted to scream the words, but she couldn't. They remained muffled sounds behind the ill-tasting gag. Susan felt like she was about to choke and breathed raggedly through her nose while panic threatened to devour her.

Take my computer. Take my credit cards, take anything, just leave my baby and me to live. Please, don't hurt my baby.

Tears ran down her cheeks as she stared into those cold eyes above her. There was something about them so terrifying it made every fiber of her body want to scream. Instead, Susan cried. She cried because she was scared and because she wanted to wake up from this horrid nightmare and because she wanted her life back; she wanted to feel happy again like she had this very morning when kissing Rob goodbye and waving to him, promising him that she wouldn't spend all day on the computer, that she'd go for a walk and smell the flowers or do something that felt good.

She hadn't done any of that. She had been playing all day, wanting to do her best in this last tournament that was approaching, wanting to keep up with the younger generation that was surpassing her in all levels these days, refusing to admit that it was possibly over, that she was ready to retire.

Please, don't hurt me or the child. Please. I'll retire, God. If you spare us, I'll retire today and never play again for other than fun.

The masked person walked to the front door and peeked out the window next to it. Susan didn't understand what was so important out there until she heard the familiar sound of a car door slamming and footsteps approaching the front door, followed by a gentle whistling. While her eyes grew strained in terror, Susan saw the masked person get ready behind the door, lifting his gun.

Susan's eyes grew big and wide, and soon she screamed desperately behind the gag.

Not Rob! Please. Not Rob!

Chapter 47

MY MOM MADE us some vegan dinner, and I ate fast without complaining since I was just so glad she wanted to cook for us, so I didn't have to. As soon as I was done, I rushed back to my computer in my bedroom, continuing my research.

Later that evening, I put Alex to bed, read from his favorite book about the firetrucks, and sang a couple of songs for him—or more like twelve since he kept asking for more before I could return to my work.

I stared at the wall in front of me, where I had put pictures of all the victims, trying to connect them, comparing things they had in common. I had been at it all day and still not found anything useful. It bothered me greatly that I couldn't figure out this killer. What was his deal? I didn't believe anyone killed just for the fun of it. There was always a deeper meaning, always a deeper motive, even if he killed people with whom he had no immediate connection. It was all about finding that deeper purpose of his killings that would bring me to him. But I still couldn't see it clearly enough.

I closed the lid on my computer when Christine came in and sat on my bed with a deep sigh.

"What's going on, sweetie?" I asked, knowing my thirteen-year-old daughter wouldn't come to my room unless there was drama in her friend group or if there was something she wanted from me.

She cleared her throat. "I was just wondering…"

"Yes?"

"Why don't we ever go to church?"

I stared at her, quite surprised. We had gone to church back in Washington, D.C. when the kids were a lot younger and we had more time, but once I got busy with my work, it had slowly faded out of our routine. Chad had never wanted to go much, so I started to feel like I was forcing him, and I didn't want to have to fight about it once I was finally home on a Sunday.

"I don't know," I said. "I guess we just haven't been in the routine of going for the past few years. We haven't even looked for a church here. Why do you ask? Do you want to go to church?"

She shrugged and looked away shyly like she was embarrassed to ask this of me. "Kind of."

I nodded and sat next to her on the bed. I took her hands in mine, then looked into her eyes, making sure she knew it was okay.

"Because of your dad?"

She swallowed, then nodded. "I just keep thinking…wondering… Do you think he's in Heaven?"

"Of course, he is," I said with the most reassuring voice I could muster at this moment. I was fighting not to tear up like always when the conversation fell on Chad. "He risked his life to save someone else. If that doesn't qualify for going up there, then nothing will. God's totally into that stuff."

Christine's face lit up. "Like Jesus. He sacrificed his own life, too, right?"

A tear shaped in the corner of my eye. I nodded while moving a lock of hair from my daughter's face. It amazed me how, at times, she seemed almost like an adult, and then at others, she was still just a young child who needed her mother's comfort.

"Yes, just like Jesus."

"I like that thought," she said with half a smile. "Do you think he'll meet Pebbles up there?"

Pebbles was a cat we had for about two months before it ran out in front of a car. I had never liked that cat much since I was more of a dog person, but the kids had begged and begged, and I had finally given in, probably mostly due to the terrible feeling of guilt I carried everywhere back then. They could probably have asked me for anything at that time, and I would have said yes; that's how bad I felt for never being there for them. The cat had ended up scratching our couch to pieces, my favorite couch, and it peed in one of my best shoes, so it is safe to say it wasn't exactly popular with me.

"I'm not sure he made it in, to be honest," I said with a sly smile.

Christine laughed. "He was kind of annoying; wasn't he? Remember how he always scratched us when we tried to pet him? I'm not sure he even liked humans very much. At least not us. Dad was the only one who could handle him. Pebbles was always nice to him for some reason. Do you remember that, Mom?"

I nodded, caressing her hair, then pulling her head close so I could kiss the top of it. The talk about Chad made my stomach churn, and I felt the tears well up in my eyes. I didn't want them to do that. I didn't want to feel them or the grief nagging inside me. I just wanted it to go away. Just like I wanted my children never to feel this way again. I wished so terribly that I could go back in time and stop what had happened to their father.

But then Matt would have died, and I hated that outcome just as much. So many times, I had gone through that event, and so many times, I had thought that if only Matt had never gone there, then it wouldn't have happened. But then again, Matt had saved my life and my grandmother's as well, and naturally, I was thankful for that. I just wished that it hadn't ended the way it did.

If only…

"So, will you go to church with me this Sunday?" Christine asked. "And say hi to Dad?"

I stared at my daughter's adorable face. She still had a little baby fat around her cheeks that she would lose within the next year or so, but it made her look so incredibly cute, and I felt like kissing her small cheeks the way I used to when she was younger.

I nodded. "Sure. Let's all go this Sunday."

Christine smiled widely, then got up and pecked me on the cheek. "Yay."

She left, almost skipping out the door and closed it behind her. I sat on the bed for a few seconds as a thought popped into my mind. It was one of those thoughts that wouldn't let you go again until you finally realized its importance.

Then I gasped and stared up at the wall in front of me, wondering why I hadn't seen this before now.

Chapter 48

"DRONE CAMERA CAUGHT eyes on two people inside the house."

Deputy Gailor, or *GayLord* as he was lovingly called among peers, approached Sheriff Howard. He looked at him nervously. He hadn't been in uniform long, only a few months, and this was his first real situation. The sheriff was standing behind his car, gun directed at the house.

The call had come in just before nine o'clock: an active shooting situation, a domestic dispute. A man threatened to shoot his wife and their unborn child. Howard had seen his share of husbands killing their wives in anger and even the children too. Just a few weeks ago, they had recovered the bodies of three children that the father had admitted to killing with a baseball bat. The wife, he had stabbed to death, he said, and she had been thrown in the river. There was also a guy six months ago who drove around with his wife's dead body in the car for weeks before he was caught when he crashed the car, and the arriving police smelled a foul odor.

It wasn't uncommon, and Howard hated it.

"One man and a woman," Gailor continued. "The light coming from the living room made it easy for the drone to take a picture."

He showed the picture that the drone had taken to Howard. It was hard to see what they were doing, but there was a woman on the floor kneeling, holding her hands above her head while a man hovered above her, holding something in his hand. There was no doubt about it in Howard's mind. It was a gun.

"So, we've got a hostage situation on our hands," he said. "We need to get the SWAT team."

"I'm on it," Gailor said and walked away.

Howard felt his pulse quicken when thinking about the poor woman in there. Howard had lost his own sister to an abusive husband who ended up beating her with a hammer in a fit of rage. There was nothing that angered him more than when men misused their physical superiority and took it out on poor defenseless women and children. He had seen so many of them in his time as sheriff in Indian River County. Those poor women even made excuses for their men's bad behavior.

It was disgusting.

"I am not losing one today. Not on my watch," the sheriff mumbled to himself and pointed the gun at the door in case the man decided to come out. Last time Howard had been through a hostage situation, it had ended in a nine-hour standoff. In the end, the guy had gotten himself killed, and the child he was holding hostage had been saved and returned to her mother. But Howard had also had a deputy get hurt, and he wasn't seeing that again today either. Deputy Towers never returned to active duty and was now retired and on a disability check at the age of only thirty-two.

"SWAT team is en route," Gailor said as he returned. "Two minutes out."

Howard felt his Kevlar vest and nodded. His deputies had surrounded the house and were covering all exits. Howard felt sweat prickle on his forehead and wiped it off with the back of his hand while wondering if they had minutes to spare...if the woman inside had that long. He wasn't losing her and her unborn child.

Not today.

Chapter 49

"THEY DO all have one thing in common," I said, almost yelling it into the phone.

Liam paused on the other end.

"I'm waiting," he said, "for what it is."

"They're all outspoken atheists."

He went quiet for a few seconds, then said: "Atheists, you say? You think it's a religious thing?"

"I don't know. It kind of surprised me too. But it's the only thing I've been able to find that they all have in common. Well, all except for Peter James, victim zero. I haven't been able to find out anything about his religious beliefs, but the rest of them, all of them have clearly stated that they are atheists on their online social profile or even publicly in interviews, like Amal Bukhari. She has been very outspoken about denouncing her family's Islamic religion and told the world how her parents had turned their backs on her because of it and because of what she does for a living. And you have been very clear about this in the past too, right?"

Liam exhaled into the phone. I could almost sense his deep feeling of guilt and how he blamed himself for his son's death through the phone. He already did, after I warned him and he didn't take it seriously. Now, I had added another dimension to it, another thing he could blame himself for.

"I'm sorry," I said. "I didn't mean to…"

"No, it's okay. I asked you to keep me updated," Liam said. "I'm a big boy, as you might know. I can take it."

"Anyway, I'm not sure that's the connection, but when something is this clear, then I have to go after it. It was something my daughter said; she asked me why we didn't go to church, and that led me to realize this."

"Clever."

"But the fact remains that if this is part of his pattern, then I can find the next victim in the list my dad gave to me. And I think I have."

"That's the good news, then," he said.

"Only one of the players on the list is an outspoken atheist, which I could see in her profile. Her gamer name is *SSweatpea*, and it was pretty easy to find her real name…"

"Susan Johnson," Liam interrupted me.

"Yes, that's her."

"She's one of the biggest names in gaming, or at least she used to be. I met her once at some charity event in California. Tim used to watch her videos all the time when growing up. You sure it's her?"

"Sure sounds like someone our killer would pick, right?"

"You're the expert," Liam said.

"Now, I just need to figure out how to find her," I said. "I thought that maybe you could help me with that?"

I stared at the TV screen in front of me. I had turned on the local 24-hour News Channel but muted it while I was on the phone. My mom was asleep on the couch next to me, and the big kids were in their rooms getting ready for bed, while Alex was sound asleep. At that moment, as I was talking to Liam, the picture shifted, and a banner appeared, reading: BREAKING NEWS.

Then the anchor returned with a serious face while the text underneath her said:

POLICE IN FELLSMERE DEALING WITH HOSTAGE SITUATION.

The blood ran cold in my veins.

"Hold on a sec," I said and turned the sound up so I could hear better.

"What's going on?" Liam asked.

I stared at the screen, listening to the anchor telling the details. They didn't know much yet, she said, but it was a developing story, and they would return to it later. They did, however, tell me exactly enough.

"You're not going to believe this, but I think I found her," I said.

Chapter 50

"ELIJAH, it's nine-thirty, and I told you to go to sleep a long time ago. What are you doing up?"

Matt stared at his son, eyebrows lifted. Elijah had come downstairs while Matt was watching TV.

The boy stopped in his tracks. That was when Matt realized the boy looked like he had been crying.

"Are you okay, buddy?"

Elijah barely dared to look at him. He stared at his feet as a tear fell from the tip of his nose onto the floor below. That made Matt jump to his feet.

"What's wrong? Elijah, look at me."

Finally, he lifted his glance and stared at Matt, eyes filling.

"Did you have a bad dream or something?"

Matt's heart raced in his chest. Elijah had never shown any emotion like this before. It was overwhelming.

Elijah nodded as his lips cringed downward and tears spilled down his cheeks. Matt stared at him, not knowing what to do. Following his intuition, Matt simply grabbed him in his arms and hugged him, holding him tight. Elijah didn't protest. Instead, he wrapped his small arms around Matt and put his head on his shoulder.

Matt could barely breathe.

"Mommy," Elijah said between sobs.

Matt's heart dropped. "You dreamt about your mother?"

Elijah nodded and sniffled.

"I bet you miss her, huh?"

Elijah nodded again.

Matt placed a hand on his back and held him as close as possible as his own eyes filled up as well. His love for the boy had been growing so rapidly lately, and he had to admit he had been longing for this kind of closeness with him.

"I think I know how you feel, at least a little bit," Matt said. "See, I lost my dad when I was a teenager."

Elijah lifted his head. "Really?"

Matt nodded while memories of his father rushed through him. "I used to dream about him all the time. Back then, my mom said that it was a way for my dad to tell me he was fine. She believes that the dead come to visit us in dreams, so we'll know that they're in a better place and so we can continue our lives. See, all they want is for us to be happy. Did you know that?"

"No," Elijah said, shaking his head.

"They don't want you to go around being sad all the time. Remembering them is okay, it's good actually, and we can talk about your mother as often as you want to, but we need to move on. It's not doing them any good if we stop living our own lives, you see?"

Elijah nodded with another sniffle. It was amazing to Matt how this boy suddenly seemed so fragile. Everything had been a fight with him from the beginning, and Matt had believed he'd have to be tough and hard on him, and he did have to create boundaries, but he had to remember that all he really was, was sad. And he just needed a little guidance, that was all—a little love and help to get through his grief. It wasn't as complicated as Matt often made it out to be.

"How about some hot chocolate, huh? Would you like that?" Matt asked. "That usually helped me when I was sad. My mom would make it for me and then put a marshmallow in it. Do you like marshmallows, Elijah?"

His eyes grew wide, and he nodded. Matt put him down on the ground, grabbed his hand in his, and they walked into the kitchen. They talked about Elijah's mother and even laughed while drinking the hot chocolate before Matt finally put the boy back to bed and left his room with a deep sigh. In the hallway, he met his mom, who had been in her room all night, reading. She smiled and kissed his cheek.

"That was some serious adulting right there, Matt," she whispered, then disappeared into the bathroom.

Feeling prouder than ever, Matt went downstairs to clean up the kitchen when there was a loud and rapid knock on the door. He went to open it.

"Eva Rae?"

Matt closed the door behind him and came out toward her on the porch. His heart dropped at the sight of her. It was pouring down rain, and she had been soaked just from running from her car to his porch. The rain was drumming on the metal roof above them.

"What's going on?" he asked when she didn't speak. It was like she had to find the courage.

She took a deep breath. She was in obvious distress and seeing this made his pulse quicken. For a second, he worried that something had happened to one of the children.

Her eyes met his as she spoke:

"I need your help with something. It's important, Matt."

Chapter 51

THE BLUE LIGHTS from Matt's police cruiser lit up the palm trees next to us on the road as we took the exit leading to Fellsmere. Matt was literally flooring the accelerator, siren blaring. It had taken a few minutes to convince him to help me out and that I needed him. Driving there in his cruiser was the only way I would stand a chance to make it there in time. Matt had at first tried to call the sheriff's office in Indian River County, but they couldn't put him through to Sheriff Howard, they said. There was no other way than to get there, and hopefully in time.

"Are we ever going to talk about us?" Matt asked as he reached the end of the ramp, leaving I95. "About what happened?"

I cleared my throat and swallowed. "Not now, Matt. We're kind of in the middle of something here."

He ran a red light, making sure traffic was holding back for him, then floored it again. The cruiser jolted forward aggressively. Matt grumbled angrily at a car that didn't move out of his way fast enough.

"Okay. I guess we aren't talking about it then," he said.

"You're the one who left," I said. "Just like that. Like you did when we were on Amelia Island too."

"You didn't exactly give me a reason to stay."

"I thought we weren't talking about it," I said.

"Well, now we are."

"What do you want from me, Matt?" I asked when he took a sharp turn, and I was thrown against the door.

"I want you to be there. I want to feel like I'm important to you," he said. "I mean, I move in, and you hardly notice. I spend most of the time with your children and not you. I feel like you don't want me there at all."

I looked at my watch, my heart pounding in my throat. I really just wanted to get there fast and not deal with all this right now. I knew Matt was hurting, but people's lives were on the line here. A pregnant woman and her husband.

Matt scoffed at my silence. "You're not even trying to deny it."

"What do you want me to say?" I asked and threw out my arms.

"Tell me it isn't true. Tell me that you want to take our relationship to the next level. I want you to stop running and be here with me. Let us be a couple."

"I'm not running, Matt. I've told you this a million times. I am trying to save someone's life. I am trying to catch a killer that no one else seems to understand is out there, killing. That's all it is, Matt."

He shook his head in disbelief. "You're just too much; do you know that?"

"Well, if I'm that much, then why were you so eager to move in with me, huh?" I asked. "Why did we have to rush into it like this?"

"Is that how you feel? That we rushed into it? Because I thought it was about time and a natural move by now."

I stared at him as he approached the address, bumping down a dirt road till we reached a small two-story house. There were a lot of things I wanted to say in this instant, but I didn't because it would have destroyed us. It would have broken his heart. Instead, I opened the door as he parked the car behind the police blockade, and we spotted the many police cruisers surrounding the house in the driveway. Instead, I got out without a word, suppressing all my emotions like I was getting so good at.

Chapter 52

MATT RAN up to the sheriff, holding out his badge to the deputies that tried to stop him, and I followed close behind him. The sheriff was standing behind his cruiser, his gun aimed at the front porch. I could see the SWAT team's wagon had arrived. Heart in my throat, I wondered if they had made their move yet. Everything seemed quiet, and I assumed they hadn't.

"Sheriff, Detective Matt Miller," he said, running up behind him, waving his badge. "I need you to stand down. We have information that your situation is a swatting call and not a real hostage situation."

Sheriff Howard didn't move. "No can do, I'm afraid, Detective."

"Please, sir," I said. "Just tell your men to stand down, and we'll explain everything afterward."

"This is Eva Rae Thomas," Matt said.

"The rogue FBI profiler? Yeah, I heard about you. What are you doing here?" Sheriff Howard said without looking at us. His focus remained on the front door of the house.

"I'm working on a case," I said. "Please, tell your men to…"

"As I told Detective Miller, there is no way we can do that," he said. "We have drone footage from inside the house, showing the man holding a gun to his pregnant wife's head. Now, if you'll please get out of here before either of you get caught in the line of fire."

Matt and I shared a look. I couldn't believe what I was hearing.

"You say you have footage of this?" I asked.

Finally, the sheriff looked at me. "Yes. We sent in the drone close to the window as we arrived, and it captured it all on video."

Matt glared at me. I shook my head. "But...it can't be."

"Would you please stand back, ma'am?" Sheriff Howard said.

But I didn't move. I stood like I was frozen, a million thoughts rushing through my head. I couldn't understand how this was possible if this was a swatting call. Had I chosen the wrong person? Had I been wrong about the connection between them?

Matt grabbed me by the arm and pulled me away.

"I don't...understand," I said.

"You had me drive here for...this? You had me barge in and use my name to try and stop something that seems to be a legit hostage situation?"

I shook my head. "But it's not. It can't be."

Matt threw out his arms. "They have the footage to prove you wrong. How do you explain that?"

I couldn't. If my theory of the Swatter was right, he sat somewhere else in the country, far away, and called these events in, then let the police do the rest. If the man really had a gun placed against his wife's head, then maybe...it was real? Maybe her husband had lost it and was trying to kill his family?

But how could it be?

What if he...

I stared first at Matt, then at the house with a small gasp.

"What?" Matt asked. "I don't like that look in your eyes, Eva Rae."

I spotted the SWAT team as they crawled closer to the house, popping up like roaches. The operation had begun.

"Eva Rae?"

I stared at Matt.

"Eva Rae?"

"He's here," I said. "He's in the house. He knew he had to make it look legit this time. He knows I'm onto him, so he had to make sure I looked like a fool, that no one would believe me. He's here, Matt. He made sure they got that footage somehow. I need to…"

Matt shook his head. "Oh, no, you don't. You don't need to do anything, Eva Rae."

He reached out to grab ahold of me, but it was too late. I had already taken off and was running toward the house.

Chapter 53

"STOP!"

The voices yelling behind me were all drowned out by the sound of the blood rushing through my veins, pulsating in my ears. I stormed toward the house and onto the porch, knowing very well that they might shoot me, but it was my only chance, the way I saw it. I couldn't live with myself if Susan Johnson and her unborn child were killed or if her husband was without me at least doing what I could, even if it meant being shot on the way.

I stumbled on the first step, but bounced off the fall with my hands and shot across the wooden porch. I passed a couple of SWAT officers on the way. One of them reached out to try and catch me, but I was faster than him. I had always been the fastest runner in my team at Quantico, but that was a long time and several extra pounds ago. It was good to know that I still had it in me.

"STOP, or we'll shoot!"

They were still yelling behind me, but I didn't listen. I blocked it all out, and as the shot fell, I jolted forward while I could hear Matt screaming behind me. The shot missed, and I thumped against the front door and leaped into the house, slamming the door shut behind me, gasping for air.

Nostrils flaring, my heart threatening to burst, I fell to my knees on the tile inside, then looked up and spotted Susan Johnson and her husband.

She was kneeling on the floor, bending forward, crying, while he was standing behind her, holding a gun pointed at the back of her head.

Just like in the video.

But there was something else, something no drone camera could have caught.

He was crying too, sobbing loudly and shaking heavily in fear. I reached for the gun in my ankle holster and pulled it out, then pointed it at him.

"Put the gun down!" I said, getting up on my feet. "Sir. Mr. Johnson. I need you to put the gun down now."

Come on. Come on. Just do as I say before they swat the house!

"Sir?" I said and approached him cautiously. "I need you to put the gun down. Or you'll get shot. They're coming in any second now. Please."

He was shaking heavily. "I…I c-can't."

"You can't? Why not?"

"H-he'll see me."

"Who? Who will see you?" I asked, suddenly focusing on my surroundings, pointing the gun toward the open doors behind them. "Is someone here?"

He nodded nervously. "He's watching us."

I turned around and walked behind them, then walked into the kitchen, but found no one.

"No," the man yelled as I came back. "He's watching us from there."

He nodded toward an open laptop placed on the chair next to them.

"Please," Susan Johnson said. "He told us to stay in this position."

I stared at the small camera on the computer, then grabbed the lid, but they stopped me.

"Don't close it!"

"Why not?" I asked, hand still on the lid.

"If we move or close the lid so he can't see us, he'll kill him."

Chapter 54

MATT COULDN'T BREATHE. He had seen Eva Rae jolt for the house, then heard the shot being fired, and that was when his heart stopped. Now, he felt like his chest was so tight that no air was being let in. As far as he could tell, Eva Rae hadn't been hit by the bullet, as she had continued into the house and slammed the door shut. He was pretty sure she was okay, but for how long?

Panic had spread where he was standing, and the sheriff had no idea what to do next. He had told the SWAT team to stand down, then looked at Matt and asked him what the heck Eva Rae thought she was doing.

"Is she trying to get herself killed?"

"I think she's trying to save the situation," Matt had replied. "Somehow."

"Save it? Save it?" Sheriff Howard had shrieked. "I'm gonna have to have her arrested for this."

"She believes it's a set-up," he said. "Give her a minute. Just a minute."

Sheriff Howard had looked into Matt's eyes deep and long, then told him one minute and one minute only.

Now those sixty seconds had passed, and he was addressing him again, eyes determined.

"Time's up. We need to go in."

"Please," Matt said, but he knew it was no use. For all they knew, Eva Rae had become a hostage herself.

Matt felt sick to his stomach as he heard the sheriff give the order over the radio. He had just said the words when someone yelled.

"There's movement by the door. Someone's coming out!"

"Stand down, everyone," Sheriff Howard said. "SWAT team, stand down. We have movement by the front door. Hold your positions."

All guns were pointed at the door, and Matt's eyes were glued to it as it opened slowly. His heart was pounding in his throat as he watched the woman he loved so deeply walk out, arms held high above her head.

"Don't shoot," she yelled. "I am unarmed."

"Step down from the porch slowly," Sheriff Howard yelled. "Move slowly toward us, no sudden movements."

Eva Rae did as she was told. Matt could tell she was shaking as she walked forward, knowing that one small movement could prove to be fatal, one arm falling below her waistline could look like she was going for a weapon. It could be so easily mistaken in a tense situation like this.

As Eva Rae took the final step from the porch and ended up in the driveway, Sheriff Howard yelled:

"Now, get down to your knees, hands behind your head."

Eva Rae paused for a second, then did as she was told, keeping those hands up behind her head. Soon, she was surrounded by SWAT officers pointing guns at her, searching her, then taking her away from the scene.

As she was pushed forward against a car and cuffed, she yelled. Her voice was quivering, and it occurred to Matt that she was terrified.

"I need to talk to Sheriff Howard. Please. It's important. There's something you need to know. If you want to save the lives of those people in there, then please listen to what I have to say."

Chapter 55

"FIRST OF ALL, it's not a real gun. It's a replica," I said.

The sheriff had come closer and told his deputies to stand back. My hands were cuffed behind my back; I posed no threat anymore.

"The gun in Mr. Johnson's hand," I continued, still breathing raggedly in fear and agitation. "When I was in there, I got a good close look at it, and it's not real. I guarantee you. I know my way around guns. It's not real."

Sheriff Howard gave me a stern look. "Why would he hold a replica against his wife's head?"

"To make it look real," I said. "They've been set up. They were told to stay in that position no matter what happened."

"By whom?" he asked, still skeptical.

"By the same guy who called it in."

"But the call came from the house—the man calling identified himself as Rob Johnson. He said he was going to kill his wife and unborn child."

I nodded. "I know. I know. But it wasn't him who made the call. Someone who wants to hurt them did this. He told them to sit like that, placed the replica in Mr. Johnson's hands, and said that if they moved, he would know, he would see it. He has been watching them from his computer, he placed her laptop so it could record everything, and my guess is that it has been live streaming to Twitch all this time, so others could watch along. It's what this guy does; he wants the world to watch it."

"But why did they stay after he left?" Matt asked. "He couldn't get to them once the police were here."

I sighed. "Because she has a younger brother. He threatened to kill him if they didn't do exactly as they were told. He's thirteen years old."

Sheriff Howard lifted his hat and rubbed the hair underneath it. "So, let me get this straight, I need to get the basics straightened out first. The guy is holding a replica to her head, right? He's not trying to kill her? There is no danger?"

I shook my head. "No need for the SWAT team or even weapons. They're terrified in there. They don't dare to move. Not even when I was in there, but no one wants anyone to be killed."

Matt and Sheriff Howard shared a look. "And you can vouch for her, Detective? You know her well enough to stand behind what she's saying? No matter how crazy it all sounds?"

Matt nodded. "Yes, sir. She's been tracking this serial swatter for quite some time. She knows his ways. She might not always play by the book, but she is very good at what she does."

Sheriff Howard nodded and signaled for his deputy to release me.

"All right, then. I'll buy into it…at least for now. But you've got to help me out here. What do I do next? Do I arrest Rob Johnson for holding a replica to his wife's head? Or what? The way I see it, if you're right about all this, then we have a thirteen-year-old boy that we need to save. Because if this guy, whoever he is, was watching, then he must have seen you and know that it's all been exposed."

I exhaled, relieved, as my hands were once again free, then looked up at both of them.

"You're right about that, Sheriff. And I think I might have an idea, but you're probably not gonna like it."

Chapter 56

SKYLER SIPPED his can of CULT with one hand while the other still tapped on the mouse. He reached for a handful of chips and put them in his mouth and chewed. Austin, who was sitting next to him at the Gamers Respawn Gaming Café, stared intently at the screen in front of him and didn't even notice that Skyler was looking at him. Austin was his best friend, and they had known each other since third grade when they sat next to one another in Mrs. Fischer's class.

"Oh, man!" Austin exclaimed and threw the mouse down. He took off his headset in frustration and drank from his Mountain Dew. Finally, he looked at Skyler and made an annoyed face.

"I hate that guy."

"Was it the same dude?" Skyler asked. "The one who killed you last week too?"

"Yeah, he's so annoying. I spent three hours getting to where I was. Now, I lost everything."

Back when they just met, Austin had barely ever talked to Skyler. Not until he found out that Skyler's much older sister was a famous esports gamer and YouTuber. Austin dreamt of becoming like her, and so once he found out she was Skyler's sister, they had become friends. Skyler wasn't stupid. He knew that was the reason why Austin hung out with him, not because he thought he was cool or even liked him much. Austin was one of the popular boys in school, one of those that hung out with the popular girls at lunch and on the weekends. He would post pictures of himself with them on Snapchat as they hung out by the pool at Patricia's or Malia's house. Skyler didn't care much about those no-brained cheerleading girls or hanging out at their pool, but he did care about Austin. A lot. He liked hanging out with him and felt such deep jealousy when he saw snaps of him with them.

So that was why he had promised him to help him become a famous gamer and YouTuber. Somehow, Skyler had managed to make him believe that he knew how his sister had become who she was today and that he could help him out. But the fact was that Austin wasn't a very good gamer and teaching him anything had proved harder than Skyler had thought.

"Go at it again," Skyler said.

Austin sighed. "I don't feel like it."

The thought that Austin would want to go home now made Skyler panic. He didn't want this to end, them spending time together like when they were younger before the girls came into the picture. "Try something else. We can play Call of Duty Black Ops III if you like."

"Nah," Austin said and ate chips from Skyler's bag. "It's boring."

Skyler looked at his watch. It was almost midnight. The gaming lounge didn't close till two in the morning, and Skyler had hoped they'd stay till then. His dad had told him he could stay and that he'd pick him up when they closed. It was his parents' biggest wish for Skyler to follow in his sister's footsteps and become an esports gamer, but he just didn't have it in him. He liked to play, but only for fun. He didn't like the pressure of having to win or even perform well. And he wasn't very good at it either.

"So, what do you want to play?" Skyler asked nervously. "Fortnite?"

Austin looked at his phone with a deep sigh. Skyler ate some more chips while trying to suppress the feeling of sadness that overwhelmed him from time to time, especially when he was lonely.

Austin looked at him and shrugged. He received a text and smiled when he read it. Skyler's heart dropped. He knew that smile. That meant one of those girls had texted him again. Once they did, Skyler knew that the fight for Austin's attention was lost.

Austin texted the person back, then took a selfie and sent it. Skyler rolled his eyes, annoyed, then put his headset back on and continued his game.

Chapter 57

"ATTENTION, all units. We have a possible 10-32 at The Riverside Shopping Center. I repeat we have a 10-32. Any units in two minutes or less?"

Deputy Adams stared at Sheriff Rogers, who was sitting next to him in the cruiser. He had only been with St. Lucie County Sheriff's Department for what felt like ten seconds, and was out on his first patrol, driving with the sheriff when the call came in. It had been a slow Friday night so far. They had stopped a guy who had run a stop sign and given him a ticket, and then they had gone to the burrito place to eat dinner. Adams had given up on anything interesting happening before his shift ended at midnight. But then this call came, and he could barely believe it. 10-32, that was man with gun. Did they seriously have a man with a gun on his first night on patrol?

Sheriff Rogers grabbed the radio. "217 received. En route."

"217, additional information. No shots fired yet. Call came from one of suspect's friends who said that he had brought a gun to the gamer's lounge called Gamer's Respawn Gaming Café. He is planning on attacking at midnight. Gunman's name is Skyler Griffin. I repeat Skyler Griffin. Shooter is black, wears white hoodie."

Deputy Adams looked at his watch. "Midnight? That's fifteen minutes from now."

Sheriff Rogers nodded. They were only two minutes out from the shopping center. He rushed the cruiser into the road.

"Let's get him before he pulls out that gun."

Rogers grabbed the radio again. "217 received. Advise SWAT."

"217, will do."

Rogers put the radio back, then took a sharp turn and turned on the wailing siren. Adams sat back in his seat, then felt for his gun in the holster, secretly hoping he'd get to pull it out. He had been training for this for so long. This was the type of stuff that made him want to join the police in the first place.

Was he ready for it?

As he saw the lights flickering in the distance and heard the other patrols joining in, he nodded to himself. Yes, he felt ready. Scared as heck, but ready. This kid wasn't shooting anyone tonight; Adams was going to make sure of that. He would be proud to be the one to have prevented the next big mass shooting.

Chapter 58

SKYLER SIGHED and looked at Austin, who continued to text and take snaps and send them. What was it about those girls that made them so important that Austin forgot everyone else around him? Skyler didn't get it. He didn't understand why Austin was always on his phone, either. Skyler always left his in his backpack and never took it out if he didn't need to use it. But then again, Skyler didn't have any friends on Snapchat, and he didn't use any social media, so there was no need to be looking continually at his phone. No one would be texting him either, except for his family.

"You want some candy?" Skyler asked and showed him the twenty-dollar-bill his dad had given him when driving him to the lounge. He nodded toward the vending machine by the end wall.

"Sure," Austin said with a shrug.

Skyler rose to his feet. He didn't even notice that his phone was lighting up in the front compartment of his backpack or that he had received more than thirty calls and texts. Instead, he walked to the vending machine and pressed the numbers to get a packet of Skittles and two Hershey bars, one for him and one for Austin. He knew how much Austin liked chocolate.

He looked back toward him when the phone by the counter rang, and the guy managing the store picked it up.

"Hello?"

Skyler opened the bag of Skittles and poured out a handful that he put in his mouth and chewed. The guy behind the counter looked paler than usual. He had a ton of piercings and a long beard that he was now fiddling with as he listened. Then his eyes grew wide.

"Really? What the…?"

The guy grew quiet as the other person spoke before he said:

"Yes, yes, of course. Right away, ma'am."

He hung up the phone and seemed to be gathering himself for a few seconds before he looked at all the kids in the lounge.

"Uh, guys. Listen up. I need to get you all out of here. As in right now. I just spoke to someone who said there was a bomb inside the store."

The guy's eyes grew even wider as he spoke the words like the realization was just now sinking in. Skyler was still chewing his Skittles, wondering if it was some sort of joke or if he had actually heard him right.

"I mean it," the guy said. He grabbed his phone and a hoodie, then looked at all the kids who were staring at him, eyes wide. "There's a bomb in here. Get out!"

And just then, panic set in. The few kids that had actually heard him because they weren't wearing a headset threw everything they had in their hands and stormed for the doors. Seeing this, the other kids took off their headsets and stared at the guy who kept yelling at them to get the heck out of his store before the bomb exploded.

Skyler had only one focus, and that was Austin. Austin was in the middle of playing Counterstrike and hadn't heard a thing. Skyler ran to him and pulled his headset off.

"There's a bomb. We have to get out of here now."

Austin grabbed his phone and backpack, and they ran outside, joining the others. In the distance, they heard sirens. Skyler stared at the building in front of him, then felt Austin's hand in his. With a slight gasp, he looked at him, and their eyes met. Austin seemed scared.

"Do you think we're far enough away?" he asked, his voice shivering. "If it explodes?"

"Maybe not," Skyler said. "Let's move to the other side of the street."

They walked across the road just as the police cars rolled up. Skyler's heart raced in his chest; he had never seen so many police cruisers at the same time. Being black and having been told scary stories of innocent people of color being killed by police, his legs began to shake beneath him. His parents had instructed him carefully on how to react when stopped by the police, but it still scared him like crazy.

Don't run. Whatever you do, don't run. And do everything they tell you. Make sure you tell them you are unarmed. Don't give them a reason to believe you're a threat.

Skyler watched as about ten police cruisers drove up in front of the store. At the same time, another big grey police cruiser drove up behind him and opened its side door. A set of strong hands reached out for him, grabbed him around the shoulders, and swiftly pulled him inside. Next, the cruiser took off, tires screeching on the asphalt.

Chapter 59

"PLEASE, DON'T," Skyler cried desperately. "I didn't do anything."

"It's okay, Skyler. No one is accusing you of anything," Matt said, using his soft voice to calm the boy. He was holding him tightly in the passenger seat until he relaxed, and he could let go of him. It took a few seconds for him to realize he wasn't in trouble. Skyler finally eased up, and he sat up straight, while Matt continued talking to him, assuring him that we weren't out to hurt him.

"We're here to help you, Skyler. We're not the enemy. We're going to take you to your sister's place now."

Meanwhile, I floored the cruiser, and we took off, leaving the shopping mall behind us. I could see the blinking lights of Matt's CBPD police cruiser in the rearview mirror for a long time, and I didn't feel safe until we reached I95, taking off toward Fellsmere, where Skyler's sister and her husband were waiting for us with Sheriff Howard.

When we finally got there, Skyler spotted his sister. He seemed dumbfounded yet relieved. I parked the cruiser in the parking lot by the sheriff's office, and Matt and the boy got out first.

"Skyler!" Susan Johnson exclaimed, then ran for him. She grabbed him in her arms and hugged him tightly, closing her eyes.

When I stepped out of the car, Sheriff Howard came up to me, a sly smile on his lips. "It worked. I wasn't sure it would. And I certainly didn't like any of it; you were right about that part. Still, I gotta hand it to you. Clever thinking."

"Yeah, well, since the boy didn't answer his phone, there really was no other way to get to him quickly enough when he was more than an hour's drive away in a different county, which was run by a different sheriff. I knew we couldn't make it there in time to stop them after they received the call."

"St. Lucie County was out of my jurisdiction, and before I could explain the situation to my colleagues and convince them of this strange story, it would have been too late."

"Nothing clears a building faster than a bomb threat," I said with a chuckle. "Even if it was a controversial move."

"The boy could have been seriously hurt or even killed," Sheriff Howard added. "Racial bias in law enforcement is, unfortunately, very real. And if they believe he has a gun, then…well, we've seen it happen too many times if you ask me. The climate of fear and the expectation of violence accelerates the serious risk of overreaction and excessive use of force."

I smiled. "You're a good man, Sheriff Howard."

"I still don't like it much, but it seems you might have saved the day," he said. "So much could have gone terribly wrong tonight, but instead, no one was hurt, and that pleases me."

I shook hands with the sheriff before I walked back to Matt's cruiser. Before I got in, I turned around and threw one more glance at Susan and her brother, who were still hugging.

My eyes met hers, and I felt a pinch deep in my stomach. We had won this round. It was a good feeling. I had broken the Swatter's code and found part of his pattern. It was bound eventually to lead me to him if only I kept digging. At some point, I would get to him. I knew I would.

I just hoped it would be before he made his next move.

THREE WEEKS LATER

Chapter 60

"I'M GOING NUTS HERE."

I stared at Liam, who was standing in my doorway. I hadn't spoken to him in a little more than three weeks when we had talked about Susan Johnson on the phone. I had sent him a text to update him on what happened to her and wrote that we had our first victory, right before bedtime on the day we saved her. He had answered that he was extremely relieved. But that was the last communication we had. It had been a busy three weeks. Christmas had come and gone, and so had New Year's Eve. Matt and I had celebrated both apart from one another, which felt odd, but we hadn't really spoken much since that night. It felt like we were both avoiding the issue right now. Meanwhile, I had been digging deeper into my research and trying to recreate the Swatter's pattern when Liam rang my doorbell.

"Liam? What the heck are you doing here?"

He pushed his way past me and came inside, rubbing his already greasy hair excessively.

"I can't sleep. I can't eat. I keep thinking that today he's gonna do it again. Every morning, I go through the news, combing through it to see if anything matches his behavior—if anyone has been killed by the police overnight. It's driving me crazy."

I slammed the door shut behind me. I was still in my jammies, I suddenly realized, and crossed my arms in front of my chest. School was back in session after winter break, so the kids were all gone, and I hadn't planned on seeing a single soul all day.

"Welcome to my world," I said. "Coffee?"

"Please."

I walked to the kitchen and poured coffee into two cups, then handed him one. He stared into it like he wasn't sure it wouldn't kill him.

"It's not been digested by Indonesian monkeys or cats or what-ever the best coffee in the world is supposed to be. It's just plain old black coffee. Nothing fancy. But it will wake you up and keep you going for a few hours till you need the next one."

He smiled. "I've had coffee before."

"Really? Doesn't really seem like it. There's milk in the fridge if you use that and sugar in that bowl over there. If you need Almond milk, I'm sure my mom has some in there as well."

"I prefer it black," he said and sipped it. He tried to look like he was enjoying it, but his eyes told a different story. I didn't care. I poured myself a bowl of Cheerios and put milk on it, then began to eat.

Liam stared at me, his eyes still frantic, yet so incredibly sad. "I need to catch him. I need to see justice for Tim. I can't stand the fact that this guy is still out there, and the police aren't even looking for him."

"I am," I said, chewing with my mouth open. A drop of milk flew toward him and landed on his shirt. The shirt looked expensive, so I dried the droplet off with a napkin as fast as I could. Liam stared at my hand touching his chest, then at me.

His stare seemed to look straight through me, undressing me, and suddenly, I could barely breathe. I hated myself for it, but I found him so insanely attractive, it pained me. Why did I feel this way? He was pretty much the most unattractive man I had ever met. And he wasn't even a great person. He wasn't even nice, and he didn't have a winning personality.

Our eyes were locked for a long time until I finally gathered myself. I cleared my throat, then moved away and continued to eat my Cheerios.

"I want to be more involved," he said. "I need to do more."

I turned around and wiped milk away from my lips with my hand. "Involved?"

"With the investigation or whatever you call it. I need to do something. I can't stand the fact that this guy who is responsible for the death of my boy is still out there. I can't focus on my work. I keep walking into his room, expecting him to be in there sitting by his computer, rolling his eyes at me, or even saying something nasty because he hates me. He used to hate me, Eva Rae. But at least he was there. At least he was still alive. I need to get rid of this guilt I'm harboring inside. I need to pass it on to someone else before it eats me up."

I swallowed another bite, then put the bowl down. Liam looked like he would break into pieces. I grabbed him by the shoulder and helped him to sit down. I took the coffee cup from between his hands and placed it on the kitchen table. He looked up at me.

"I'm falling apart, aren't I?"

I exhaled and took his hands in mine. "No one would blame you if you did."

Chapter 61

DeVilSQuaD666: Yo answer me this.

SlayerAlpha32: What do you want?

DeVilSQuaD666: Did the cops show up at your house last night? Yes or no.

SlayerAlpha32: No

DeVilSQuaD666: I don't believe you

SlayerAlpha32: So? See if I care.

DeVilSQuaD666: I know for a fact that you're lying.

SlayerAlpha32: Oh? How?

DeVilSQuaD666: Come on. You can't hide it. Be honest. Did anyone show up at your house last night?

SlayerAlpha32: Nope.

DeVilSQuaD666: Be honest with me. I know they were there. Admit your defeat. Did they flashbang you or not?

SlayerAlpha32: You're literally retarded.

DeVilSQuaD666: I know they were there. Why won't you admit it? I know there was a call.

SlayerAlpha32: And how do you know that?

DeVilSQuaD666: I just do. Don't ask me how.

SlayerAlpha32: Did the call say that someone shot his dad?

DeVilSQuaD666: Yes

SlayerAlpha32: Yeah, I heard about that. Police did show up.

DeVilSQuaD666: I knew it!

SlayerAlpha32: They showed up at my old address.

DeVilSQuaD666: What?

SlayerAlpha32: We don't live there anymore Bahahaha. You wasted your time, and now you're pissed.

DeVilSQuaD666: I don't get it.

SlayerAlpha32: You got trolled. You thought you were coming for me, but you sent them to the wrong house, you idiot.

DeVilSQuaD666: I don't believe you.

SlayerAlpha32: Really? Watch the news.

DeVilSQuaD666: What do you mean?

SlayerAlpha32: Your prank days are over. The police will be coming for you soon. It's over, bro.

DeVilSQuaD666: You're bluffing.

SlayerAlpha32: Am I tho?

DeVilSQuaD666: I think you are

SlayerAlpha32: As I said. Watch the news.

DeVilSQuaD666: Why?

SlayerAlpha32: You'll see why. But I wouldn't want to be in your shoes right now. Just sayin'.

Chapter 62

"AMAL, are you absolutely sure you want to go through with this?"

Samir held Amal's hand in his. He had that concerned look in his eyes that she had grown to despise. It was nice of him to worry; it was more than you could say for her parents, who hadn't even called or sent a card while she was in the hospital fighting for her life. She wasn't surprised at that, though. They had turned their backs on her when she decided to become a gamer and not succumb to the family's ways. They had their pride, and even if she were on her deathbed, they wouldn't speak to her. She knew that much. It was the price she had to pay for her freedom. But at least she had Samir. Samir was kind and gentle, and her younger brother would go through fire for her. She knew he would.

"I'm sure," she said and winced in pain as he helped her sit up so she could eat. He sat on her bed and started to feed her since she was still in too much pain to be able to lift the spoon on her own.

"The protest is in three days, Amal," he continued while she fought to swallow the soup. She had been eating mostly through a tube while she'd been recuperating, but they wanted her to start slowly to eat on her own. It was going to take some time. "Are you sure your body is up for that kind of stress?"

She nodded. "Yes, Samir. I'm sure. This is an important matter. Not just for me or you, but for everyone of color. We have been suppressed long enough. We've been killed in the streets; our brothers and sons have been shot dead just because of fear, just because of prejudice. So far, three million people have replied that they are coming on my Facebook event page. That shows how important this is, and how much people need this, need me."

"I could take care of it," he said. "You could tell me what to say, and I'd read it to them to encourage them. Or you could make a video. Their march can go on. It doesn't need you in front."

Amal scoffed and touched his cheek gently. "My sweet brother. I know you're only trying to protect me, but I think that you also know deep down inside that I need to do this, even if it means me losing my life doing it. They shot me, Samir. The police were so frightened of me, a young woman armed with nothing but a camera. I've become a symbol of the fight. They are writing to me from all over. All the big organizations see me as an important front figure, and you need to let me be just that."

Samir nodded, slumping his shoulders. "I'm just so scared that something might happen to you. There are a lot of agitated people out there. As I was coming in this morning, I had to walk through a crowd of protestors who were shouting white supremacist slogans at me. They were wearing swastikas on their arms, for crying out loud. They see you as a threat. They're demanding justice for the officer's son, who was attacked. It's like it never ends. Won't this march just make matters worse? What if they try to kill you? Or what if you die because of the stress and exhaustion on your fragile and broken body? The doctors say it's too much for you. I don't want to lose you, Amal. When I thought you had died on that plane when they called...I...I can't go through that again."

Amal reached her hand up and placed it on Samir's arm. Eating had left her in pain, and she didn't want any more soup.

"If I die, at least I would have died for something. I think there's a reason I survived being shot on that plane. I have a purpose, and that makes it worth it. That makes it remotely bearable. Look at me. My body is completely destroyed. I'll never get to live a normal life again. I'm missing several of my internal organs. There's no chance I'll live very long, even if I ever make it out of this hospital. This march makes it worth it. This gives me a reason to live, to keep fighting. Doing this march makes going through the pain worth it. I truly believe going through with this march can change the world. Let me have it; will you? Let me do this."

Samir stifled a few tears, then nodded and kissed Amal's hand. "Okay. But now you must rest. You're gonna need all your strength. Just the traveling alone will be devastating to your body."

Chapter 63

THE SWATTER WAS EERILY quiet in those days, and it was about to drive me crazy. I was terrified that he was planning something big. Liam went back to Philadelphia for a few days, but then came back and was now staying at the Hilton in Cocoa Beach, trying to stay close to me and the investigation. He was doing his share to help me out, combing through news stories about police activity, domestic disturbance calls, and so on. Meanwhile, my dad was keeping an eye out for the gamer named FaZeYourFeaRs, trying to track him down while keeping an eye out for him in *Call of Duty*. But he hadn't shown up in a very long time, and that had me worried. Not that I wanted him to because it would mean he had found his next victim, but I was concerned that he might change his pattern, that he'd start playing another game with his future victims, or that he would play with tens of different players like last time and I'd miss out, not being able to find the right one in time. His silence confirmed my suspicion that he knew I was onto him. His defeat in Fellsmere had to be nagging him, and it was forcing him to change his ways. I just wished I could figure out his next move.

It all came down to why he was doing it. I still hadn't figured that part out, and that gave him a head start. I didn't know him well enough to be able to find him. I knew bits and pieces, like the fact that all his victims were declared atheists, which had to play a big part in why he chose them. Also, the fact that most of them were people of color played a part. The chance of it going wrong was bigger, obviously, because of the fear and racial bias, but there was more to it than that, in my opinion. I knew that he was a gamer himself, so I had him picked for being young, less than thirty at least, but probably even younger.

Was he white? A supremacist?

I had written the word on a yellow post-it note and placed it in the middle of my collage on the wall. I had asked my dad to seek out those forums online where white supremacists met and had him snoop around to see if anyone knew anything about this guy. But it was a jungle.

What did he get out of doing what he did to these people? What was the purpose? To induce fear? Did he have quarrels with them? Did he do it to punish them? Was it just for the adrenaline rush, not knowing if this person would make it through this alive? Did he watch it from his computer while getting a kick out of it? Was it a power rush? The idea that he could sit somewhere far away and destroy someone's life in a matter of seconds with only a simple phone call? Was that why?

But he was there, Eva Rae. He was at Susan Johnson's house. He can't be that far away. He could be really close.

I stared at the map on the end wall of my bedroom. I had drawn a big red X on each of the towns where he had struck. The first one, Peter James, was in New Orleans, Louisiana, while the second was all the way in Indiana. There was one in Kentucky, two in Pennsylvania, one in California, Iowa, Alabama, New Jersey, South Dakota, and even one in Portland, Oregon. The latest attempt was in Florida. Jamal's mother had been killed in Canada of all places. This guy could strike anywhere.

It frustrated me more than anything. I wanted to catch this guy, especially for Liam's sake. He was a mess, and I had to admit that I, too, felt guilty because of what had happened to his son. I had known he was the next victim, yet I let Liam go that day when I confronted him about it. I could have done more. I could have run after him. I could have grabbed his arm and stopped him. I could have insisted more.

The door to my bedroom opened, and Alex came in wearing his police uniform and the fake badge that Matt had given him to wear on Halloween. He always put on this outfit as soon as he came home from school. Alex wanted to be in law enforcement, just like Matt more than anything in this world.

"Hi, sweetie," I said and smiled.

Alex came closer. He looked angry and crossed his arms in front of his chest. I reached out to take him in my arms, but he stepped back so I couldn't reach him. He spoke with great determination:

"When are Matt and Elijah coming home?"

I exhaled and felt a pinch in my heart. "Oh, buddy."

"They're not coming home, are they?"

"They're staying at his mom's house for a little while," I said. "She misses them, so they'll be there for a little while before they come back here."

Alex shook his head. "Nope. That's not what I heard."

I looked at him, surprised. "What did you hear?"

"Olivia told me that they moved out." Alex's voice grew shrill. "Is it true, Mommy? Did they move away from us?"

I closed my eyes briefly, then looked at him and nodded. "For now, yes. But I don't know if they're coming back, honey. That's the truth. It all went a little too fast and well… we both needed time to think."

"That's not what I heard either," Alex said.

"Oh, really?"

"Yup. I heard you drove Matt out. That you didn't want him here, but I wanna know why. Why, Mommy? He's really nice, and so is Elijah. Why don't you want them here with us?"

I stared at my son, unable to say anything. I searched for something clever—for something to soothe the pain that I could detect in his eyes. But I couldn't find it…simply because I didn't know why. I loved Matt; I truly did. I had always loved him; I had loved him my entire life.

But was I in love with him? Did I want to live with him?

I wasn't sure.

My silence made Alex even angrier. His small nostrils were flaring, and I saw tears shaping in his eyes. I hadn't seen that since his dad's funeral.

"You're just a meanie," he yelled.

"Alex, I…"

But the boy wouldn't hear anymore. He turned around and stormed out of my bedroom, tears rolling down his cheeks, yelling:

"I hate you!"

The sound of his harsh words hit me hard. I felt awful. I couldn't blame him for being angry, though. He was so fond of Matt and, of course, he needed a male role model in his life, especially when living in a house of only females. With his father gone, he had hoped Matt could be that figure in his life, one that he could look up to, that he could mirror.

I had hoped so too. I just wasn't sure it was enough.

Chapter 64

"HE SHOWED UP LAST NIGHT."

I had barely opened my eyes. I looked at my watch. It was seven-thirty. We had overslept. Again.

"I'm sorry if I woke you up," my dad said on the other end. I blinked to try and get back to reality. I had been up most of the night, following what I believed was another swatting case, but had turned out not to be. I hadn't fallen asleep until five o'clock.

"No. No, it's good that you did. I have to get the kids to school."

I jumped to my feet and found my jean shorts, still while clutching the phone between my jaw and shoulder. "What happened?"

"FaZeYourFeaRs entered the game last night. He played for about two hours with two different players."

I fastened my pants and grabbed the phone in my hand. "Only two?"

"Yes. I have them both here and will find their names and addresses as soon as possible."

"That's perfect," I said.

I hung up and ran into Olivia's room, then woke her up before I continued into Christine's and finally Alex's room. He had fallen asleep still wearing his police uniform that Matt had given him. The hat had slid off and was lying on the carpet below.

"Get out of there. I can't be late for history class," Olivia yelled and hammered on the door to the bathroom where Christine had just gone in. "I have a test!"

"I have a test, too," Christine yelled back.

"So what? You're in seventh grade. It's not important!" Olivia yelled back.

I kissed Alex and woke him up slowly. He opened his eyes and looked into mine. It was obvious he had forgotten how angry he was at me in the instant he shot them open. They gleamed at the sight of me, and he pulled me into a deep hug. But then he remembered, and his eyes grew angry again.

"We're late," I whispered and kissed his cheek. He turned his head away from me. "I'll drive you to school today."

I left and ran downstairs, then pulled out cereal boxes and poured cereal into bowls, then threw together a couple of lunch boxes, giving them all peanut butter sandwiches, which I knew Olivia would be angry at me for, but I'd have to take that one with her later. Now it was all about getting them out of the house in time.

I was halfway through the third sandwich when I realized my mother wasn't there. She was usually up before any of us in the mornings. Often, she'd have prepared smoothies for the kids to make sure they got off to a healthy start.

That's odd.

I walked to her room downstairs and knocked on the door.

"Mom?"

I opened the door, then walked inside. Seeing what I saw, I wished I never had. In the bed was my mom, but she wasn't the only one. Next to her was a man I had never seen before in my life.

And they were both completely naked.

Chapter 65

I SCREAMED. From the top of my lungs, I simply screamed out, waking them both up with a start.

"Mom? What's going on?"

All three kids came running up behind me, and before I could stop them, they had seen what I saw. Olivia started laughing.

"Grandma?"

"What's going on?" Alex said, unable to see much. "What's happening?"

Olivia couldn't stop laughing. My mother and the man both tried to cover themselves. I was about to explode.

"Mom?"

"I...I...," she said, but I realized I couldn't listen to it. I turned to face my kids.

"You three, get back in the kitchen, asap."

"But what is it?" Alex kept going on while I tried to get him away from the door. "What's so funny?"

"Grandma's got a *man* in there," Christine said mockingly, then added an *uuuuhhh*.

Alex looked at me, confused, as I closed the door so they could get dressed. I couldn't erase what I had seen from my mind, but I was desperately trying.

"Grandma had a sleepover. Nothing strange about that," I said and pulled him away. We walked back to the kitchen, and he sat down at the breakfast counter, where I had placed a bowl of Cheerios for him.

"But why are you so mad about it then?" Alex asked. "Isn't she allowed to have sleepovers?"

It was a good question. My mother was a grown woman, and of course, she was allowed to have a life, even when living with us. I just had never thought that she would get one, at least not so fast.

"Who is he?" Olivia asked before gulping down a glass of orange juice. I stared at the clock on the oven and realized school had already started for Alex, and there was no way we'd make it in time for the girls' school either.

"I've never seen him before," Christine said. "Have you, Mom?"

"I didn't even see him at all," Alex whined. "It's so unfair."

The door to my mom's bedroom opened, and she came rushing out, fixing her hair as she went. I just stared at her, unable to say anything.

"Eva Rae...I...I'm so sorry. He wasn't still supposed to be here. I had told him to leave and not spend the night, but well...we got going and then..."

"No need to go into further detail," I said, raising my hand to stop her.

She gave me a look. It was an odd situation to be in, me having the upper hand, her being the messed-up one. I had to admit, I kind of liked it. Okay, that's an understatement. I enjoyed it a lot.

"It's never gonna happen again," she said. "I'll ask him to take the back door and then..."

"Come on, Mom," I said. "You can't do that to him, the poor guy. Have him come out here and eat breakfast with us."

"Yeah, we'd like to meet him, Grandma," Olivia said, giggling.

"We sure would," Alex said, trying to sound like he had any clue what was going on. It was really cute, and I had a hard time fighting the urge to laugh.

"You would?" Grandma asked, fiddling with her hair. I had to admit I wished I could have frozen this moment and kept it for years to come, just seeing her face; it was priceless.

"Of course, we would," I said, biting my lip so I wouldn't crack and laugh out loud. "I'm sure he's…a very nice guy."

My mom smiled. "He really is."

"Good for you, Grandma," Christine said and smiled.

My mom gave us an insecure smile, then turned around and went back to her room. She had barely made it down the hallway before the kids and I all broke down laughing, even Alex, who had no idea why.

Chapter 66

AS SOON AS the kids were sent off to school, I returned to my bedroom and computer, leaving the two love birds alone in the kitchen. I couldn't get away from there fast enough. My mom's boyfriend, Irvin, seemed nice and all, but the situation over breakfast was awkward and unpleasant. Not that he wasn't kind; he seemed like a sweet enough guy, but I couldn't stop picturing him naked and as he reached over to grab a piece of toast from the breadbasket. I flinched, thinking about those fingers touching my mother.

It was icky. Just icky.

I rushed back to my room, leaving them to do whatever they needed to do, and hopefully, without me having to witness any of it again. My dad soon sent me the names of the two gamers as he found their real names, and I began my research. The first one was a twenty-three-year-old guy named Darnell Jackson who lived in Anaheim in California. The second was a young girl, only seventeen, named Carly Collins, living in Springfield, Illinois. Both were gamers and YouTubers, even though the girl didn't have more than three thousand subscribers to her YouTube channel and a few hundred on Twitch. She wasn't a big fish. The boy, Darnell, had more than a million subscribers on YouTube and twenty thousand on Twitch. Neither of the two was in the real big leagues, but I definitely leaned toward the boy. As if he had read my thoughts, my dad sent me a text:

BOY SEEMS LIKE THE BETTER FIT.

I nodded, thinking he was right. Darnell seemed like the Swatter's type. He wanted it to be spectacular, to make sure a lot of people watched when the victims were swatted. The boy was definitely more prolific—a better catch. If the Swatter really had a reason to do this, a greater cause if you will, then Darnell would be his choice. He was also black, and the girl white. Not that the Swatter's victims had all been people of color, but he seemed to prefer them.

I texted back:

I AGREE.

The question was what to do next. The Swatter had been playing with both of them the night before, and we knew from experience that somewhere between twenty-four hours to forty-eight hours later, they would be swatted. Somehow, I'd have to get ahold of both of them and just pray they'd listen. I just wished I could go to both of them and give them the message face to face. Getting a phone call from a crazy lady from Florida wasn't exactly easy to take seriously.

Still, I had to try. My dad had found addresses and phone numbers for both of them, so I picked up my phone and dialed the first number. I was pleased that it had been so easy to get to them. Neither of them was very famous, not like Amal Bukhari, Jamal, or Liam's son, so they were more accessible, which I found to be a little odd. It wasn't how the Swatter usually rolled. These kids seemed almost like they were too small to become his victims. But then again, maybe he was just trying to make it easier on himself. To make sure nothing went wrong this time.

The phone rang once, it rang twice, and then a third time.

Voice mail.

I listened to Darnell's voice as he told me to leave a message while wondering what to say. I couldn't really tell him the truth since he'd only think I was crazy. I had to persuade him to call me back as soon as possible.

So I came up with a lie. I told him I was from Microsoft and that we had a deal we wanted to make with him. I also told him to call back asap, then hung up. I then called the other number and got ahold of a woman, whom I assumed had to be Carly's mother.

"Yes?"

What the heck do I say?

"I'm looking for Carly Collins?"

"And who might I say it is?"

"My name is Eva Rae Thomas. I'm with Microsoft," I continued in the same lie. "We've watched her videos on Twitch and want to invite her to an esport tournament. It's invitation-only, and we need an answer right away, or her spot goes to someone else."

Boy, you can lie about gaming.

"Carly isn't home right now, but I'll let her know you called."

"It's very important," I said, beginning to feel desperate. "I need her to call me back as soon as possible. Could you maybe tell me where to reach her? I'm guessing she has her own phone?"

"Yes, she does, but we don't give that number out to strangers calling our house," her mother said.

"Of course not. Gotta be careful with those youngsters. But is there any chance she might call me back say before eight o'clock tonight? It's extremely urgent that I get ahold of her before then."

The mother went silent. "I'm not sure. She's going to be out of town all weekend, but I'll try."

"Thank you."

We hung up. I groaned, annoyed, and put the phone down. I tried Darnell's phone again, but got the same voicemail once more and hung up with a growl. I couldn't really afford to rush out to California today and spend the night, once again. This case was getting expensive, even though Liam had been nice and paid for me several times. While I was working on this, I hadn't exactly been working on writing my next book as I was supposed to, and I had to get an extension on my deadline.

Meanwhile, my latest book telling the story of my father had a good run, but it wasn't exactly a bestseller, and the money was getting low even though my mom pitched in. I should probably have been out looking for a job instead of trying to save all these people, but how could I? I had once sworn to protect and serve, and I couldn't just not try and stop this guy. I wished I knew how to make my former colleagues at the FBI listen. Isabella Horne, my former supervisor at the FBI, had tried, but she had also told me that it wasn't enough to start an investigation. They needed more. Opening an investigation was expensive, and they too had been told to cut back on unnecessary spending.

I couldn't blame her, really. I knew how the bureau worked. She had her bosses to answer to and couldn't just open up investigations here and there because an old colleague of hers *had a hunch*.

I stared at the computer screen at the two profiles on Twitch and YouTube, where I had found these gamers. I started an old video that Darnell had put out a couple of days ago, then watched him play Fortnite for a few minutes while feeling an odd sensation in the pit of my stomach.

Something was wrong here; I just couldn't put my finger on what it was. It didn't feel right.

I grabbed my phone and called my dad.

"It's the girl," I said. "I think he's chosen the girl and not the boy."

"Why? Darnell seems like more his type if you don't mind me saying so."

"I know, and that's what I don't like about it."

"Why not?"

"He's his type, yet he isn't really big enough or interesting enough. The girl seems completely wrong for him, and that's why I think it's her."

"I'm not sure I follow you."

"It's too obvious. Darnell is too obvious."

"Still not following."

"He knows we're onto him," I said with worry. "We have to assume that by now. We stopped him in Fellsmere, both of his attempts. He even saw me there; he must have seen me on that camera on the computer. He knows I'm onto him, chasing him. So, he'll want me to screw up because I won the last round. He wants me to pick the obvious one and miss his real target. That's why I think it's her and not him. Because she's the most unlikely of the two."

My dad sighed. "I have to admit, I think it's getting a little too complicated, but you're the expert. So, what do we do next? Did you get ahold of her? Does she know?"

Now, it was my turn to sigh. "I'm afraid not. I spoke to her mother and told her it was important that Carly called me back before eight o'clock tonight. But I'm not certain that she'll take it seriously enough. I fear she won't call back, and then where does that leave us? We can't go to Illinois and make it in time or afford to fly across the country all the time. We don't even know where she is. Her mom said she'd be out of town all weekend, but didn't say where. She wouldn't give me her cell phone number, either."

"Well, can't really blame her, can we? You wouldn't give Olivia's number to just anyone who called, right?"

"Sure wouldn't," I said. "Do you think you can find her cell number somehow?"

"I can try, but it might take a while."

I stared at the screen when I got a notification from YouTube that Carly had just uploaded a new video. I had subscribed to her channel a few hours ago, hoping she'd do just that.

"Wait a minute," I said and clicked on the video. Carly's young face tuned onto my screen. I turned the volume up and watched. Then I smiled.

"I know where she is. And it's not that far away."

Chapter 67

I RAN A RED LIGHT, and Liam screamed, clinging to his seat. His knuckles were turning white from the strain.

"What?" I asked, accelerating down 520, hitting the beachline toward Orlando. "Why are you screaming?"

"You ran a red light. That car to our right almost hit us."

"But it didn't," I said, passing a truck and hitting close to one hundred miles per hour.

Liam went pale as I zigzagged between the cars. I ignored him.

"You're not exactly a very good driver," he said with a snort.

"What are you talking about? I'm an excellent driver."

"Watch out for that car," he screamed and covered his eyes as I drove up behind a red Toyota and hit the brakes right before I knocked into it. I shifted lanes and passed it on the inside. Liam finally dared to look again.

"Are we there yet?" he asked, sounding like my kids.

"Still about twenty minutes," I said and tried to push my minivan harder. I had bought a new one with the insurance money I got from the old one that I lost on Amelia Island when driving through flooding due to Hurricane Damien. This minivan was five years old and had all sorts of things wrong with it, but it took me from A to B, and that was all I needed. Right now, I was definitely pushing it to its limits.

I had seen Carly as she filmed herself in a hotel in downtown Orlando. In the video, she said she was spending the evening at Disney World and that she was staying till the fireworks went off. There was no doubt in my mind that the Swatter would try and hit her while she was there. It had him written all over it. It would be spectacular, and it would be the center of media attention, no matter if she were hurt or not. Evacuating Disney World would count as a huge feather in the cap for him. It didn't matter that she was a small fish. The story would be big enough in itself. The headlines pretty much wrote themselves.

I had chosen to bring Liam because I thought that if I approached Carly on my own, she might not want to listen, but by bringing a celebrity like him, I assumed my chance of success would be a lot higher. I was glad he was with me, even though he was whining like a baby in the seat next to me.

"Watch out!"

I zigzagged between the cars, and Liam barely breathed. I didn't have time to care; he'd just have to get through it. I was getting to the girl, no matter what.

"Will we be there soon?" Liam asked again, his voice shrill.

"A couple minutes more," I said as we arrived at the exit and I turned onto the ramp, but not slowing down much. "Hold on."

Liam did. He held onto anything he could for dear life. The minivan skidded sideways up the ramp, but I managed to get it back on track, tires screeching and whining loudly. Liam let out another scream, and I floored the accelerator again as soon as it was back on track, pushing him back in his seat as we approached the entrance to Disney World's Magic Kingdom and could see the huge Mickey and Minnie figures on the horizon. The traffic slowed, and so did I. Liam finally breathed again, and as the car came to a more manageable speed, he regained some color back in his cheeks.

Chapter 68

WE HAD ALMOST REACHED the entrance to the big parking lot when I heard the sound of sirens. I looked in the rearview mirror and could see the red and blue lights blinking in the darkness behind me.

"What the...?"

Soon one police car turned to two, then three, four and five, coming up behind me, sirens blaring, blinking lights on.

"What's going on?" Liam asked and turned around to see better. I could hear the anxiety in his voice. I couldn't blame him. His last rendezvous with law enforcement hadn't exactly ended well.

"I don't know," I said, trying to sound as calm as possible. "Maybe something happened inside the Magic Kingdom. I just hope it isn't Carly they're here for."

I looked at my watch. It was seven-thirty. It was too early if the Swatter was keeping to his MO, but I had a nagging feeling that he wasn't. He had a way of changing things up every time I thought I knew his pattern that I didn't care for much.

"I...I don't think they're here for Carly," Liam said as two police cars drove up behind us and another two came up in front of us, blocking our way, forcing me to stop. I hit the brakes, and the car came to a sudden halt.

I stared at the blinking lights in front of me and behind me, heart throbbing in my throat.

What was happening?

Police officers emerged from their cars. But they weren't approaching us the way they usually would at a traffic stop, coming up to my window and asking for license and registration. No, this was different. They were hiding behind the doors, pointing their guns at us.

This freaked me out completely.

Liam was breathing heavily next to me, barely keeping it together. I reached out my hand and placed it on his shoulder.

"It's gonna be okay, Liam. Just keep your hands up at all times. No matter what you do, don't lower them, not even if you feel like you can't possibly hold them up anymore. You have to, okay?"

Liam breathed raggedly. "O-okay."

I lifted my hands, trying to show them to the officers outside. Liam followed, his hands shaking terribly. This was one moment I wished I had brought Matt instead. I had no badge anymore…no way of proving that I was one of them.

A voice sounded through the darkness. "Step out of the vehicle. Hands in the air. Step out of the vehicle, slowly!"

I shared a glance with Liam, then nodded while letting air out between my teeth. I was fighting to keep it together.

"Okay. We have to get out of here. Just make sure your arms are above your head at all times, okay? We haven't done anything wrong except for the speeding, but I don't think that's what this is about. Are you ready?"

Liam's eyes were filled with fear. He swallowed, then nodded. I gave him half a smile, trying to seem reassuring, then we both grabbed the door handle on each side and stepped out of the car.

Chapter 69

"WE ARE BOTH UNARMED."

I held my arms above my head, making sure they could see my hands and see that I held nothing in them. Guns were still pointed at us from all sides, and the sight was terrifying, to put it mildly. I knew they'd never show up with this many officers or be this tense if it wasn't because they believed we posed a significant threat. And that made it even scarier.

Not one wrong move, Eva Rae.

"Keep your hands raised," someone yelled from behind the police cruisers. "Walk slowly away from the vehicle."

We did as we were told, keeping our hands up and visible, not even lowering them one bit when my arms began to hurt.

"Drop to your knees," the voice then yelled, sounding angry and commanding. "Keep the hands where we can see them."

I did as I was told and sunk to my knees, planting them hard into the asphalt. I didn't dare turn my head and look at Liam since I couldn't make any unexpected movements. I just prayed that he was doing the same.

"Keep your hands where I can see them!" the voice yelled again.

My arms were shaking, but I kept them up there.

"Don't shoot!" Liam yelled. "Please!"

I could hear how scared he was, but I also knew that hearing this often made the police even more uneasy. They knew that nervous people were more likely to be desperate enough to pull out a gun.

"Stay down!" the voice yelled.

I closed my eyes and bent my head down, heart racing in my chest. I just prayed that they would see Liam Berkeley for the guy he was, or at least the famous chef, instead of just a big black guy that seemed threatening to them.

"Don't move!"

Keep still, Eva Rae. Just remain completely still no matter what. It'll be over in a few seconds. They'll come out from behind the cars, then come up behind you and cuff you. They'll do the same to Liam, and once they've checked that you're unarmed, they'll take you to the station. Then you can get this sorted out. You know the drill, Eva Rae. It doesn't have to end badly.

I took in a couple of deep breaths to make sure to remain calm, telling myself over and over again that it was going to be all right, that we were both going to be fine.

"Stay down! STAY DOWN!"

I heard footsteps and sensed movement, then opened my eyes as the officers approached us. They were holding out their guns and yelling at us from all sides. So much confusion, so much chaos erupted around me; I felt panic rush through my body. I lifted my glance just in time to see the fear in the officer's eyes who was standing right in front of me, gun pointed directly at me.

That was when the first shot was fired.

The sound was so loud that I instinctively lowered my hands to cover my ears, then started to scream. As the next four shots resounded, I could only think of my kids and the fact that I never got to say goodbye to them.

Chapter 70

POP-POP-POP-POP-POP!

The sound was deafening and devastating at once. I screamed and fell forward, crying for my life. The shots fell, and the bullets whistled above my head, but much to my surprise, I wasn't hurt.

The firing stopped as abruptly as it had begun, and a sudden silence fell upon us, an eerie stillness that made everything inside of me scream. It lasted for less than a second. Disoriented, I opened my eyes as the yelling began, and I finally looked up.

Liam!

He was on the asphalt a few feet away, on his knees still, his arms behind his neck, looking back at me. Seeing this made my heart jump. I couldn't breathe. My lungs hurt, my head throbbed, and adrenaline rushed through my veins as I realized what had actually happened.

Around us on the asphalt lay five police officers...each one with a bullet wound. The one lying closest to me had taken a bullet to the forehead; another had taken one to the chest. None of them were moving.

Oh, dear God!

The realization forced me to cry out in pain. Meanwhile, chaos erupted around me. Boots, feet, voices yelling, arms grabbing me, pushing, shoving, holding me down, pressing my cheek into the asphalt, and then someone cuffing my hands.

In the distance somewhere, I could see Liam receiving the same treatment, and somehow, I managed to gain eye contact with him while they were lifting me in the air, pulling me up. We held each other's gaze until they began dragging me toward the police cruiser. As they opened the door, I heard Liam yell behind me and the officers yell something back.

I was so scared. Scared because I didn't understand what was going on, frightened for Liam because I knew they were now so scared they might harm him, thinking he was somehow responsible for what happened to their colleagues.

Do everything they say, Liam. Don't resist the arrest. Let them take you in. Otherwise, you'll give them a reason to harm you.

I ducked my head and landed in the back seat right before the door was slammed shut. Hands cuffed in the back, I moved myself to the window and looked out of it. It was the scene of a real nightmare. Five officers were down, lying utterly lifeless on the ground. The remaining officers were searching the area for the shooter, guns drawn, panic and fear painted on their faces.

I heard yelling, then turned my face and saw Liam receive a hard punch to his jaw, then a kick from another officer. Then they dragged him across the asphalt toward another cruiser, yelling curse words at him.

As my cruiser took off, I closed my eyes, slumped my head, and cried while watching the ambulances as they arrived, sirens blaring, thinking about Matt and what he had said a few weeks ago:

There are no winners in this.

Chapter 71

THEY BELIEVED we were behind the attack. Of course, they did. Why wouldn't they? To them, it looked like we had lured them into a trap. They interrogated me about it all night long and most of the next day, asking me over and over again who the shooter was and where he was now.

"We will find him, so you better tell us now," the detective interrogating me said.

"I told you; I don't know anything about it," I answered over and over again, tired and feeling sick to my stomach. "We were going to Disney World because we thought a young girl was about to be killed. We wanted to warn her."

"So you keep saying. But you might like to know that your little friend is saying something else," the second detective said. I couldn't remember their names at this point, and I didn't care either. I just wanted to go home to my family. I just wanted to know that Liam was all right.

"Liam? I hardly think so," I said. "Listen, guys, I know how this works, okay? You tell me he said something different and then you hope that I'll break down and tell the truth. Don't think I haven't been there, on the other side, that is. You seem to forget I used to be FBI."

They looked at me. They, too, were getting tired.

"Here's what we believe happened," the first one, who had had very blue eyes and a receding hairline that he obviously wasn't ready to admit, said. "At exactly seven twenty, we received a call that there was a car on its way to Disney World and inside were a man and a woman who were carrying a bomb that they were planning to blow up inside of Disney World, blowing up little children and their parents while they were at the Happiest Place on Earth. Naturally, we take action and try to stop you before you get that far, taking all the precautions we have to. Only too late do the responding officers realize that it is a trap, that there's a sniper among the trees waiting for them. Five of our colleagues are shot. Four dead. One is still in ICU and most likely will not make it."

I swallowed. "I…I am so sorry. As a colleague myself, I…"

Detective Blue Eyes rose abruptly to his feet. "No. Don't give me that. You're not one of us. Not anymore."

He was staring at me, his nostrils flaring, eyes angry. The look in them terrified me deeply.

"We're asking if maybe you and Liam Berkeley planned this to get back at the police for what happened to his son," the other detective said in a calmer voice. "Maybe you and he are romantically involved, and that's how he persuaded you to be a part of it, betraying your own former colleagues?"

I leaned back in the chair. The chains tied to my hands jangled loudly.

"Wow," I said. "That is some theory there, Detectives. But you couldn't be further from the truth. Liam's son was murdered…"

"By the police. That is what you believe; isn't it?" Detective Blue Eyes asked, pacing back and forth.

"No…I mean, yes…but…"

I stopped myself, realizing I wasn't helping my case.

"You a part of that new movement?" Blue Eyes asked.

"What movement?"

Blue Eyes pulled out his phone and tapped on it, then turned it so I could look at the screen. I saw a picture of Amal Bukhari.

"She started it from her hospital bed. They're doing a protest march in D.C. tomorrow to protest against what they believe is growing police violence. They believe that around five million people are coming, making it one of the biggest marches in history, if not the biggest. Are you part of it?"

"I mean, I heard there was going to be a march. I wasn't planning on going if that's what you're asking."

Blue Eyes slammed his fist on the table. It made me jump, and my heart began to race.

"I was asking if you were part of it, part of the movement, or whatever you call it. What you did last night, the ambush on our colleagues, was that part of it too?"

I stared at him; a gazillion thoughts flickered through my mind at once, falling into places they didn't fit into earlier.

"That's it," I said.

"What is?" he said, sounding dumbfounded.

"The motive, the purpose, the pattern. Everything I didn't understand. I get it now. I totally get it."

Chapter 72

IT WAS pleasant being pushed in a wheelchair through the airport and not having to walk on her own, Amal thought. Being this tired, she could barely keep her eyes open. Samir, who was pushing her, had hired a security company to protect her. He had insisted on doing this even though she told him it wasn't necessary, and if she didn't agree, he wasn't going to take her at all. He knew she needed him, so she had finally accepted. As soon as they were through the airport, flocks of fans greeted her. They were holding signs and yelling her gaming name, IWondergirl.

Amal felt exhausted from the flight to D.C. While in the air, she had to fight her intense fear of something bad happening again and thought she kept seeing those fighter jets outside the windows. Nothing made her happier than to finally have arrived on solid ground.

Samir was by her side, and even though the doctors had told her that she was risking her life by going, that they wouldn't recommend she leave the hospital this soon, she was now happy that she did. Seeing all these people who had come there for her, for the cause, made her eyes well up with tears. She was truly making a difference by showing up, even if she risked her health and her life by doing so.

"Look at them, Samir," she said as he grabbed their suitcases. "They're everywhere. Even outside, look."

She pointed at the windows where so many people had gathered you couldn't see through them. So many faces stared in, and so many hands were touching the glass. They were waving at her and screaming her name, while some were shouting angry protest slogans against the police.

"They came, Samir," she said. "They really came."

"Did you doubt they would?" he asked and began pushing her forward toward the exit while the security guards made way for them through the dense crowds. Hands reached out for her, and she tried to high five as many as possible.

"We love you, Amal!" one of them yelled.

"I guess not," she said, addressed to her brother, while touching more hands, high fiving as many as she could, hoping that no one would leave there disappointed. "But I have to admit; I had to see it to believe it."

More than fifteen million people had joined the Facebook event group, and, of course, she knew that a lot of them wouldn't show up once it came down to it. Most people didn't leave jobs or school to go protest marching. But the experts estimated that about five to seven million of them would. Amal was overwhelmed by that number, but silently believed it might get even bigger. Up until now, it had all been nothing but a dream, an idea shaped in her mind as she was in the hospital. But now, as she was seeing all the people for the first time, she had to admit she was quite astounded by the numbers and by how deep an effect she could have from her sickbed.

It wasn't only the fans and supporters that had shown up; it was also the media. Cameras were flashing in her face while microphones were reached out toward her and questions yelled at her:

"Are you happy to be out of the hospital bed, Amal?"

"How do you like Washington, D.C.?"

"Will you be well enough to go on stage tomorrow?"

Amal didn't have the strength to answer, so instead, she just waved, and Samir responded for her. *Yes, she was happy to be out of the bed finally. Yes, she loved Washington, D.C., and especially all the people who had shown up to greet her, and yes, she was going to be on the stage tomorrow, speaking to her fans and supporters.*

"Amal will do this despite her limitations and her hardship. Because that's how strongly she believes in this cause. It's time to end police violence in this country," he added, then said *thank you* and pushed her toward the van that they had ordered to pick them up.

Amal was rolled into the back while her fans screamed loudly behind her, some trying to force their way through the security guards to touch her. One managed to push his way through, and suddenly, he was up the ramp. His eyes were wild, and he opened his shirt while he ran, so she could see his tattoo that spelled her name on his chest.

Amal gasped as he grabbed her by the arm, pushing Samir to the side. Amal looked up, frightened, while two security guards grabbed him from behind and pulled him away.

"Amal, I love you!" he yelled as he was being dragged away and the door closed behind her. Amal stared at the man with the mad eyes while he was being pulled away, her heart knocking against her ribcage.

"It's okay now," said the one guard that was with them inside of the car.

Samir gave him an angry look, panting in agitation.

"It's okay now? What if that guy had a gun? What if he had come here to kill my sister? There are just as many who hate her as there are who love her. And some of them want to see her dead. We know this from all the hateful comments she has gotten over the past days with real threats to her life. It's your job to protect her, and you just failed at that. You better up your game by this time tomorrow when she'll be on display in front of millions of people."

Chapter 73

I USED my one call to call the only person I knew who could help me out of this mess...Isabella Horne, current FBI director, and my former boss and friend. She had helped me out in Miami when I was in deep trouble down there once, and I knew she wouldn't let me rot in jail.

A few hours later, I was released. Isabella was waiting on the other side of the door as I was let out. She was wearing that look on her face that told me she was not just angry; she was disappointed.

"I'm sorry," I said, approaching her.

"Save it," she said. "I can't believe I had to come all the way down here. Lucky for you, I was already in Orlando with a couple of my boys because of the shooting last night. But I must say it doesn't look good for you. How the heck did you end up in this situation?"

I sighed and tried to turn on my phone that had just been handed back to me along with my jewelry and other personal objects that had been with me at the time of my arrest. Luckily, I hadn't been armed. I had considered bringing my gun but knew it would probably only get me in trouble...bringing a gun to Disney World.

"It's a long story, and I really need a shower. Listen, do you know if Liam will be released too?"

She shook her head. "He won't. Not now, at least. I was able to convince them that you wouldn't run away, that you had the children to think about and aren't a threat. I think I might have convinced them that you didn't know what was happening, so now they only think Liam was behind it and that you were merely an innocent bystander. You still have some credit from Miami and catching that killer on Amelia Island, at least with those sitting in higher places like me. But don't consider yourself safe yet. Every freakin' agent around here is working on this case, and if they find even the smallest indication that you knew what was going to happen, they'll lock you up. Do you hear me? And don't come crying to me again. I'm tired of having to bail you out."

"But Liam stays in?" I asked.

She nodded. "So far, no bail has been set. I don't know if there will be. If he is considered a domestic terrorist, then who knows what will happen? I'll keep an eye on it, though."

"So, you believe us?" I asked.

She gave me a stern look. "You have never given me a reason not to. At least, not so far. But stay out of trouble, do you hear me? Stay away from anyone who might be the least bit anti-police or pro the *Blue Lives Murder* movement."

I paused in my tracks. Isabella noticed and stopped too. She shook her head. "Oh, no, you don't. You're not going up there, do you hear me? You'll get arrested, and then no one will believe me. I should have left you in that jail, at least till the march was over. Eva Rae, promise me you won't go to D.C. and be in that demonstration. Promise me?"

I shook my head. "I can't. I have to go."

She pointed her finger at me like an angry teacher. "No, Eva Rae. You're not."

"But don't you see? I have to stop it from happening. Please, listen to me, Isabella. You can help me with this. I told you about the swatting. I know you believed me or at least part of you did, right?"

She sighed heavily. "I think you might be onto something. I've been wondering about the number of fake calls and how a lot of them have turned deadly. But you don't have enough for me to open an investigation, Eva Rae. We've been through that."

"I know, Isabella. But this is important. You have to listen to me. It's a war he wants. It's been a part of the plan all along. The victims he chooses, the shooting last night. It was all part of it."

Isabella stared at me, then shook her head, walking backward. "You know what? I can't take any more of this from you. I have work to do, loads of it, and I only came because we were once good friends. I have to get going. I can't deal with this right now. This is the last time I bail you out, do you hear me? Go home and be with your kids. If you go up there, I can't help you anymore. You'll risk losing everything, including your children. I can't do any more for you. You're on your own."

Chapter 74

ISABELLA WAS RIGHT ABOUT one thing. I was truly on my own. Liam was still in police custody, and Matt said he didn't want to talk to me when I called him on the way back, then hung up. The only one I could still rely on was my dad, who had helped me all along. But even he couldn't help me out with this.

I went home, took a long shower, then returned to my computer and did a couple of searches, finding some info I needed. As I dug deeper into it, more pieces were beginning to fall into place, creating a picture that frankly had me terrified.

My mom was in the house when I came back and wanted to know why I had spent the night in jail and why there were reporters all over town asking questions about Liam Berkeley.

A couple of them had even called me while I drove home, asking stupid questions about him, but I had hung up or let voice mail do the answering for me. His face was everywhere, on all the TV channels and my Facebook newsfeed. A lot of people were applauding him for his actions, being a part of the Blue Lives Murder movement, while others were writing that he had gone too far. Journalists were writing nasty stories about how he had grown angry at the police for what happened to Tim, his son, and then planned an ambush, killing four officers as revenge. None of them seemed to think he was innocent or even cared about the real truth to this story.

At one point during the day, a reporter even came to my door and knocked, but my mom shooed him away, literally. I could hear her shoo at him from my room and couldn't help laughing. No hungry reporter was any match for my mom. It made me happy to know this because if things went wrong for me in D.C., she'd have to be the one to take care of the kids.

I needed her to be a bulldog.

My kids came home while I was packing for my trip. Alex came running up the stairs, yelling, storming into my bedroom.

"Mom!"

I sighed and grabbed him in my arms, then sat with him on the bed, holding him tightly. I enjoyed the fact that he was still so small that I could actually carry him and hold him in my lap. Both my girls were too big for any of that now. I wasn't looking forward to losing that closeness with my little man as well.

You might never see him again if it goes wrong, Eva Rae.

I kissed his head, then smelled his hair. "Are you going away again?" he asked as he spotted my sports bag of clothes. My gun was placed on top of it, and I reached over to cover it up.

"Mommy has some work to do, buddy, and needs to go on a little trip for a few days. But Grandma is here, and she'll take real good care of you."

"Ugh. I hate her food; you know that. And she never reads the story the fourth time like you do, and she doesn't do the voices correctly. I'd rather have Matt take care of us. He's really good at bedtime stories and at playing cops and robbers."

My heart sank when hearing his name. He hadn't even wanted to talk to me when I called earlier. He told me he was in the middle of something important, and that we could talk later, then hung up before I could even protest.

"I know, sweetie," I said. "But I'm afraid that we'll have to try and do without Matt this time, huh?"

Alex pulled himself out of my grip, then jumped to the floor.

"You shouldn't have invited him to move in with us if you didn't plan on keeping him," he said. "It's like that dog that followed me home from school one time. You told me I shouldn't have invited it inside the house, remember? It's like that, Mommy. You should have known better."

With that, he walked to the door and left my bedroom. I sat back with a feeling of defeat as the realization sank in.

I had lost Matt, hadn't I? I had lost him for good this time.

Chapter 75

MATT STARED at the phone like he had for the past hour. He had hung up on Eva Rae when she called, but now he regretted it. He wanted to talk to her; there was no one on this planet he'd rather talk to than her right now, but he simply couldn't. He couldn't stand being dragged into more trouble or any more muddy emotions. It was simply becoming too encompassing, too much for him.

"You wanna go again?" Elijah asked.

Matt nodded and grabbed the stack of cards. They were playing UNO, their favorite game these days. Ever since Matt had put a limit on how much screen time the boy was allowed to have, he and Elijah had been spending a lot more time together, playing cards, reading, or even just talking. Elijah still didn't say much, but Matt gave him the time he needed, never pressuring him, and listened carefully and attentively whenever he did open up. Soon, he had started to learn things about the boy as he shared details about himself. Like the fact that his favorite color was purple. That he liked to watch Anime. That he hated school, but if he had to choose, math was probably his favorite subject. He also learned that Elijah didn't enjoy sports, but he loved to draw and that his big dream was to become an animator once he grew up.

Matt handed out the cards and picked them up to look at his hand. He couldn't stop thinking about Eva Rae and worrying about her, even though he really didn't want to. He was waiting for her to come to him, for her to ask him to come back, say she was sorry for how it had all gone down with him moving in.

He just feared that she never would, and right now, he couldn't even stand talking to her, let alone seeing her again. He needed a break from her and all the drama constantly surrounding her.

He didn't understand her; he had to admit. What had happened to her? It was like she didn't even care anymore. She didn't care about them anymore. Was it just because of losing Chad? Was it her grief that made her so distant?

"It's your turn," Elijah said with a sigh. "Hello? Where are you?"

Matt smiled and returned to his son. He grabbed a card. "I'm sorry. I don't know where my head is at today."

"Where it always is. With her," Elijah said with an exhale. "You're always thinking about her, you know."

"Really?"

"Yes, really."

"Oh, I'm sorry about that then," Matt said.

"Yeah, well, it's getting annoying. She's not that special, you know. There are other women out there who'd treat you a whole lot better."

Matt stared at Elijah, then down at his cards. Was the boy right? Was he just being blind?

"UNO," Elijah said.

Matt stared down at his cards, then put one down on the pile. Elijah grinned and put his last card on top of it.

"I win again."

"Argh," Matt said, laughing. He then reached over and grabbed Elijah and began to tickle him. The boy laughed loudly, and so did Matt when the doorbell rang.

"Give me a sec," he said, then rushed to the door and opened it.

"Alex?" he said, baffled.

Matt looked behind him and to the side to see if Eva Rae was with him. The boy stormed past him into the living room.

"What are you doing here…alone?"

The young boy turned to face him, his eyes determined, arms crossed in front of the chest of his police uniform.

"Matt. We need to talk."

Chapter 76

"I KNOW it's a lot to ask to have me here, but I didn't know where else to go. I can't exactly afford a hotel room since I'm not really making much money these days."

I blew on my coffee and looked up at Priscilla, whose daughter had been victim number six. I had known Priscilla for years while living in D.C., and her house hadn't changed one bit. I couldn't exactly say the same about her. Losing her daughter had burned its marks into her usually so pretty face. She had lost at least fifteen pounds and seemed so fragile I was afraid she might break. On the counter behind her stood pictures of Stacy from when she was just a child. I remembered that happy girl as she played outside in the street, learning to ride her bike, and then later, as she took care of my girls once they were born and played with them in our yard or babysat for us if we needed it. She stared back at us from those deep brown eyes like she was begging us to figure this thing out and find the person who murdered her. I had promised her mother I would, and I wasn't going back on that, especially not now with everything that was at stake.

But it meant I would have to risk everything. I was well aware of this. If I was arrested up here, during the protest, there was no way I could argue that I wasn't a part of the Blue Lives Murder movement. Isabella had convinced the investigators in Orlando that I had no knowledge of the ambush, but they could still change their minds. Cops had been shot, and they were hungry for justice. The sensible part of me knew I should have listened to her and not come to D.C., but how could I with what I knew?

"It's good to see you. You're welcome here anytime; you know that," Priscilla said, placing a hand on top of mine.

I sipped my coffee, nodding. "That's really sweet of you; thank you."

"So, what's going on?" she asked.

It was getting dark outside as the sun had set. I felt exhausted from all the traveling, but I wasn't ready to go to bed yet. I was too stirred up inside to be able to find rest. "Why are you here? I'm guessing it's not for the protest tomorrow."

I swallowed while tapping my nails on the side of my cup. "Actually, that is exactly why I'm here. See, I realized recently that I had been looking for the wrong motive. This case isn't about those that are being swatted."

A deep furrow appeared between her eyebrows. "What are you talking about?"

"One hundred and twenty-two police officers have killed themselves so far this year in the U.S.," I said. "One of them was the man who accidentally shot a young guy named Peter James in New Orleans after getting a call stating that he had just shot his dad and was about to shoot his mother and sister as well. On November twenty-second last year, dispatch received the call to nine-one-one, and Officer James Reed, leader of the SWAT team in the New Orleans Police Department, was the guy who gathered his team and surrounded the house. As the boy came to the door, they believed he went for a gun. They believed he was armed since that's what he'd said in the call, and they shot him right there on his mother's front porch. A second later, his mom comes running out, screaming, the same woman they believed he had shot. In that second, Officer Reed knew he had made a huge mistake. After the story came out, the public demanded that Reed had to be fired and prosecuted because Peter James was unarmed. And so, he was. He was acquitted in court, but he couldn't escape the hurt inside from having taken this young boy's life, so on September twenty, almost a year later, he grabbed his gun, placed it in his mouth, and pulled the trigger. His five-year-old daughter found him in the shed in the backyard. Her life is ruined too. Do you see what I'm getting at?"

Priscilla still looked at me like she didn't quite understand. Priscilla was a professor and taught math at Howard University. She was a very smart woman.

"It's like ripples in the water," I said. "As I looked through all the cases that I suspect our Swatter is behind, I see similar stories. Six of the officers who were involved in deaths during these swatting incidents have committed suicide. Eight have been fired, three have left the force voluntarily, at least two that I have found have been divorced, one is in a mental institution."

Priscilla nodded. "So, what you're saying is that they hurt too."

I nodded. "I kept wondering about the Swatter's motives. He couldn't possibly know that the people he swatted would be killed or even hurt. A lot of cases don't end badly, and that's what bothered me until I found out that they weren't his targets. It wasn't the gamers that he was attacking."

"It was the police," Priscilla said.

"Exactly. It was all about the police all along. They were the real targets. It was meant to hurt them, to make them suffer. No one will ever get over shooting an innocent boy. The gamers and your daughter Stacy were just a means to an end. This killer has a message for us all, and it's not very pleasant."

"But what does he want out of it?"

"Exactly what he is getting. He has chosen famous gamers or other celebrities like Liam Berkeley's son, just to make sure the media would write about it. Sometimes, it was even broadcasted live if they were live streaming at the time of the swatting. He doesn't just want to hurt the officers involved; he wants us to hate the police. Look at what happened to Officer Downey's son, Nathan Downey. He was beaten up on his way home from school by a mother and her children. He almost died from his head hitting a lamppost. As far as I know, he hasn't woken up yet. It's stuff like that he wants. He wants a war against the police."

Priscilla stared at me.

"You don't believe me, do you?" I asked. "Look at what is happening tomorrow. Millions of people will protest against police brutality. People are angry. Amal Bukhari, who is behind the march, was one of his victims. Look at how much hatred she has been able to stir up toward the police. I fear more people will get hurt tomorrow on both sides of this. As Matt said, there are no winners here; there's only more hurt. Meanwhile, the Swatter can sit back and enjoy his work. No one will ever know what he has done."

There was a long silence between us as I drank my coffee, staring at my old friend while she pondered this information.

"Say something," I finally said.

"I…I don't really know what to say, to be honest. It's just a little hard, you know? To see the police as victims," Priscilla said. "After what happened to my baby. I wasn't there when it happened because she was in her own condo, but they shot her, an innocent and unarmed young girl. I can't help but be so incredibly angry with them. Our kids are being shot down in the streets, Eva Rae."

I nodded. "I know. And it's awful; of course, it is. But we can't let this guy win. He's the murderer here. He's the one who made the calls, and he's doing it again and again all over the country, destroying lives all over the place. We can't let him continue, Priscilla. And we can't let hatred win."

Chapter 77

AMAL LOOKED at herself in the round handheld mirror that Samir was holding up for her. She was trying to put on a little make-up, but the eyeliner kept smearing, making her eyes look like she had been crying.

"Ugh," she said, trying to fix it.

"You look fine," Samir said, smiling. "You don't need any more."

Amal tried once again with the eyeshadow, but her hand was shaking too badly to be able to do it properly.

"Here, let me," her brother said and took it from her hand.

Amal hadn't slept much the night before. She had been in terrible pain and couldn't find rest, even though she took the pills the hospital had provided her. It was like they didn't really help anymore.

"Thank you," she said, smiling at her brother. He leaned forward, and she closed her eyes so he could get to them. She felt the brush touch her eyelid gently and swipe a couple of times to the side, then opened them to look in the mirror.

"Not bad," she said. "You're actually pretty good at this, Samir."

That made him laugh. There hadn't been much to laugh at in

the past few weeks, and especially not since they had left on the trip to D.C. She sensed in her brother that he was greatly troubled and felt terrible for putting him through such deep pain. He was worried about her doing this; there was no doubt about it. He was scared she wouldn't make it.

Amal grabbed his hand in hers and squeezed it. They were in a small camper behind the stage that had been put up for her and for the other speakers that would come out on this day. The stage was placed outside in the street with Capitol Hill in the background. So many stories of pain and suffering caused by the men in blue were going to be told from that stage today. It was going to go down in history. And she had played a significant part in it. For that, she was very satisfied.

"All right," Samir said with a sigh. "We should get you rolled out there. There's five minutes till you're on."

She swallowed and nodded. "Yes. Let's do it."

She stopped herself and winced as a wave of pain shot through her body, closing her eyes for the seconds it lasted.

"Amal? Are you all right, Amal?"

She lifted her head as the pain subsided, but it didn't go away completely. "Yes," she half-moaned, "I'm fine."

"Are you sure you're up for this? I mean, I could go out there instead if needed," Samir said. "I could tell them what you've gone through. I've been there all the way."

She chuckled and patted him on the arm. "That's sweet of you, but we talked about this before. They've come to see me. They need to see me, see what those pigs in blue did to me. It's vital for the cause, Samir. I am vital to the cause."

He nodded. "All right, all right."

Samir grabbed her chair and rolled her toward the exit, where there was a ramp. He rolled her down onto the asphalt, and as she came outside, she could suddenly hear the roar of people from the other side of the stage. It sounded so massive; she almost forgot to breathe.

"Do you hear that?" she asked.

He nodded. "I sure do."

"Doesn't it sound amazing?"

"It sure does."

The voice came from behind them, and they both turned to look. A woman walked forward into the sunlight. She was short and chubby and had her red hair pulled back in a ponytail. The security guards blocked her way instantly, and she raised her hands to show them she wasn't looking for trouble.

"Who are you?" asked Samir.

"My name is Eva Rae Thomas, and I need to talk to Amal. It's important."

"Why would she talk to you? There are millions of people out there waiting to hear her speak. How did you even get in here?"

The woman nodded with a sigh. "I know a few people around here. And you will listen to me because I have information that'll make her want to change her mind about going up there in the first place."

Samir made a face and scoffed. "Why on Earth should she listen to you? Security, we need her out of here…"

Amal stared at the woman, then remembered something. Amal reached up her hand and grabbed Samir by the arm.

"No, Samir, don't. I want to hear what she has to say."

Chapter 78

"I KNOW WHO YOU ARE," Amal said. "You were the one who sent me that email, weren't you? I remember your name, Eva Rae Thomas."

I sighed and approached her as her guards backed off and let me through. The noise from the massive crowd on the other side of the scene was overpowering. Amal stared at me, head slightly tilted, eyes narrowed.

"You knew I was going to be shot. You sent me an email telling me I was going to get shot by the police. I didn't read it till after it happened. So many times, I've thought about how stupid I was for not reading it. It wasn't like I didn't see the email. I saw it before I got on that airplane, but I just didn't read it till later because I was waiting for what I thought was an important email, one that I believed was more important than yours trying to save my life. How silly I was, huh? Maybe it could all have been avoided, had I only taken the time to read what you wrote."

I came up to her, and she reached out her hand. I placed mine in hers. She was pale and weak, but underneath it all, you could still see the beautiful woman she had once been.

"Why have you come?" she asked me.

I breathed heavily. "I needed to get to you before you got up on that stage."

"Why?"

"Because you'll be helping him out by going up there. This is what he wants. This was his plan all along, to make people hate the police."

A furrow grew between her eyes, and she gave me a suspicious look. "What are you saying? He? Who is he?"

I swallowed. "The guy who tried to kill you. The same guy who sent the police after you on the airplane. Have you ever wondered who placed that call that made the police think you were carrying a bomb?"

"Of course, I have."

"Well, I've been chasing him. You're not the first he did this to; I have a list of people, and a lot of them have ended up dead. For a long time, I thought he was trying to get back at you because of who you were, that he held a grudge of some sort, or maybe it was a revenge issue, but lately, I've come to realize that it's a lot bigger than that. This guy has a bigger agenda, and you're playing a huge role in that. If you go out there and speak against the police, encouraging the hatred, then you're just helping his mission."

"It's nothing but a peaceful protest march," she said. "I don't see…"

"Five cops were shot two days ago in an ambush. All orchestrated by this same guy who tried to kill you. These five men have families. They have children, wives, brothers, sisters. They're someone's children."

"But this is a peaceful event."

"For now," I said. "Until he ruins it. I bet he is out there right now amidst all these people, riling them up. All it takes is for him to find a few bad seeds and get them to do something stupid. The police are on edge as well; they'll overreact at the smallest thing. Maybe he's not even alone in this. It's the easiest thing in the world to make sure this all goes wrong. You're handing it to him on a silver platter. You've got several million angry people out there right now. It can so easily go wrong. Think about it. Please."

"Listen, we need to get going, Amal."

Amal's brother came up to us. Amal had told him to leave us alone so we could talk, but now he had come back.

"They're waiting for you."

"Please, Amal," I said. "Don't do it. Don't let him win."

"Of course, she's doing it," her brother said dismissively. "Do you have any idea how much effort it has taken to get her here? To arrange all this? People have come from all over to be a part of this movement."

"Think about Nathan," I said. "Nathan Downey."

Amal's eyes met mine, and they locked for a few seconds, her nostrils flaring lightly while she pondered what I had said. I had struck something inside of her by mentioning the boy's name; I could tell I had. Amal had to know what happened to him and that he was yet another innocent victim in this sick game the Swatter was playing. But was it enough?

"I'm sorry," Amal said and looked away. "I have to get up there now. They're waiting for me."

With that, her brother grabbed the wheelchair and turned her around, then pushed her up the ramp toward the stage. I stared at her as she disappeared behind the big black curtain while the crowd chanted her name on the other side.

Chapter 79

AMAL FELT a wave of adrenaline rush through her body as she was rolled onto the stage and the roar emerged from the crowd. She couldn't believe her own eyes as she stared out at the ocean of faces. Screaming fans, banners, and people as far as the eye could see. Amal took a deep breath, taking it all in.

This was truly spectacular. Seeing this, the politicians had to listen. They had to know that the people demanded a change.

It wasn't for nothing. All that happened to you wasn't in vain.

Amal lifted her hand and waved at the crowd while her brother parked the wheelchair and handed her a microphone.

"We love you, Amal!" someone yelled.

Amal smiled. A tear had escaped her eye, and she wiped it away. The crowds were still roaring, but slowly subsiding as they waited for her to speak.

"Oh, wow," she said into the microphone, half choking up. "Look at all those faces, all those people. Look at you! I can't believe you all came out for this. But I am so glad you did."

She swallowed while preparing to begin her speech, then turned her head to see that Eva Rae Thomas was standing on the side of the stage, watching her. Amal bit her cheek while thinking about what she had said right before she went up to the stage.

She had mentioned Nathan Downey, the kid who was beaten up just because he was the son of the officer who had shot Amal. He had no part in this. He had done nothing wrong. Was this what Amal wanted? An eye for an eye?

Amal looked away. She focused on her speech and the people who were waiting patiently for her to begin.

The microphone feedback howled loudly as she lifted it back up to her lips. Amal winced, then spoke as the sound disappeared:

"Protests work when groups are willing to be bold in their tactics and persistent in their approach. It serves as a powerful signal to the rest of society that something extraordinary is happening." Amal looked down briefly at the piece of paper in her hand where she had written what to say, then back up at the crowd. "Today, the media is weaker; the institutions meant to be watchdogs aren't as watchful as they're supposed to be. But marches like this mobilize people, wake Americans up to the gravity of the situation. It can push progressive politicians to action. It can confront those who do nothing with their cowardice…"

Amal paused and looked down at her notes, then cleared her throat. She couldn't find where she was at. It was like the words were jumping around on the page, like they wouldn't stand still, no matter how much she willed them to. She kept seeing Nathan Downey's face. She had watched all the news stories about him she could find, and she'd read all the articles about the little boy who was attacked on his way home from school just because of who his dad was. She had kept telling herself that what happened to him had nothing to do with all this, that is was unfortunate and terrible, yes, but she couldn't do anything about it. But now, as she sat there, she realized it was all connected just as her being shot was connected to something bigger. And if it was ever to change, it had to start somewhere.

It might as well be here.

Amal looked at Eva Rae Thomas once more, briefly, then crumpled up the paper in her hand, lifted the microphone, and looked at the crowd.

"But it can also divide us further and create a situation that will hurt more people than it benefits," she said.

Chapter 80

"I WAS SHOT," Amal said, grabbing the wheels of her chair and rolling it closer to the edge of the stage. I watched from the sidelines, holding my breath as she crumpled up her paper and went off-script. I had no idea what she was going to do.

"And I was angry about that. For a very long time, I was very angry. I had done nothing wrong. I was just a woman on a flight, and I believed I was shot because of my skin color. I'm still angry at what happened to me, sometimes furious, since my life will never be the same again. I mean, look at me...my body is completely destroyed."

As she paused, people yelled slogans against the police, chanting for *those blue pigs to die*, calling them *murderers*. Amal lifted her head and looked out at them, then spoke again, this time sounding more determined than earlier:

"But...recently, someone reminded me of the importance of forgiveness. The men that shot me had families, and Officer Downey's child was attacked. He was beaten half to death and is in a coma right now. I need you to understand that I never wanted that to happen. That is not how it's supposed to be. We're better than that. I have not come here to create division; that's not what I'm all about. I want to build bridges. I want to put down my anger and blame, and I need you to do the same. Therefore, I ask you all to welcome with me a former FBI agent with whom I have recently become friends. Please welcome Miss Eva Rae Thomas. She is with the police, and also my friend."

Amal turned to look at me, then stretched out her arm toward me, nodding. I stared at her, not knowing what to do. Not only was I terrified to be on stage, but I also had to keep a very low profile. There was no way for me now to argue that I wasn't involved with the movement. Cameras were recording all of this, some broadcasting it live, and Amal's brother was also live-streaming it to her YouTube channel. My face was going to be all over the news in a few seconds, and that was exactly what Isabella warned me against. She would no longer be able to protect me if they wanted to prosecute me for being involved in the shooting of the five officers in Orlando.

"Come on out here," Amal said, smiling.

My feet refused to move. I stared at the woman in the wheelchair, holding out her hand, urging me to come while the crowd had gone completely silent.

This is not what they came to see. This is not what they want.

I couldn't breathe, and every part of me screamed not to, yet I did it anyway. I took a step forward, then another, and soon I was walking onto the stage, out into the open where every set of eyes could see me, and every camera had me in their lens. I wanted to build bridges, too; I wanted to help.

"Eva Rae Thomas, ladies and gentlemen," Amal said and grabbed my hand in hers. She lifted them into the air. The crowd looked dumbfounded like they didn't know what to say or do. Amal saw it, then said:

"I say we all hug an officer today, huh? When we march through these streets, let's at least hug one officer each. Let's help spread the message of love instead of hatred. That should be our real mission. I'll start by hugging Eva Rae Thomas."

She pulled me into a hug, and I bent down to put my arms around her. As we hugged, the crowd broke out into a spontaneous cheer behind us that kept going for a very long time, getting louder and louder.

As she let me go and I turned away, I spotted movement on one of the rooftops nearby, and too late, I realized what was happening. I threw myself forward, trying to cover her when the shot echoed through the air.

Chapter 81

THREE BULLETS TORE their way into her chest. Her upper body went into spasms, and seconds later, she went completely still, head slumped to the side.

NO!

I shook her, crying.

"Amal, no, please."

People came running onto the stage from behind the curtain, but I hardly saw anything anymore. I kept looking in the direction where I had seen the shooter on the rooftop, but of course, he was gone. The crowd stopped clapping and cheering and had turned to screaming in shock. Police officers came running onto the stage and tried to get people away from Amal's dead body.

I stopped one of them.

"I saw someone on the rooftop over there," I said and pointed. "Over there, to our right side."

The officer looked where I was pointing. "We'll get a team up there asap and surround the neighborhood. He's not getting away."

"I sure hope not," I said, not feeling very hopeful. If this was the Swatter, then he was too smart to get caught.

I waited there for hours while the police finished up. An ambulance arrived, and they took Amal out of her chair, carrying her onto a stretcher. They closed the body bag over her head, and just like that, she was gone. Tears sprang to my eyes, and I wept as they took her away, leaving her brother behind looking confused and lost.

Meanwhile, the crowd was taking their anger to the streets. There was yelling and screaming, and suddenly, there were loud crashing noises as they smashed in store windows. Several cars were set on fire along with dumpsters that they rolled into the street. The police set in with their forces, trying to calm the crowd, but that only made things worse. As I came down from the stage and looked out at the town, it felt like a war had just begun.

Amal's brother, Samir, came up behind me. His eyes were filling, the words coming out of him as choked sobs, "They say someone said it was a cop that shot her. That's why they're angry."

"Do you believe it was a cop?" I asked.

He nodded. "Yes."

"Why would they shoot her and make a martyr of her?" I asked.

"Why not? She spoke up against them and their violence. She was a symbol of a movement against them."

I looked up at Samir. He looked so much like Amal, it was almost scary. He exhaled deeply, then grabbed his phone. "Anyway, I need to call our family."

"I am sorry for your loss," I said. "I truly am. She was a remarkable woman."

He gave me a look of brokenness, then left, phone pressed against his ear. The whole scene was one of chaos, and, to be honest, I had no idea where to go or what to do. I had given a brief statement to the first responders, but the investigators looking into Amal's death would want to get more later, so I thought I'd better try and get back to Priscilla's house somehow. I had borrowed her car and, as I walked to where I parked it, protesters were running around in the streets, yelling slogans and fighting the police. I rushed to the car, then got in as a large police vehicle drove onto the road, and about fifty of them jumped out, wearing full body armor, running toward the roaring crowd.

"This is never going to end well," I sighed as my phone vibrated in my pocket. I pulled it out. It was a text from Liam of all people.

HOTEL PHOENIX, it simply said.

Chapter 82

PHOENIX PARK HOTEL wasn't very far, but trying to drive through a town full of protesters with them rioting and the police trying to stop them wasn't exactly easy. I kept running into road-blocks or into crowds of people who were throwing rocks at windows while yelling out their anger. I repeatedly had to turn around and try to go the other way while chaos governed the streets around me. At one turn, I drove toward a huge crowd, and they started to bang on the car with sticks. I tried to go back where I had come from, but the crowd had surrounded me, and now the police were beginning to knock them down. I got out of the car, ducked down, and tried to elbow my way out of the crowd. A huge store window of a Books A Million store was shattered, and the books thrown into the street, then set on fire. I made my way out of it, then ran down a small street before pulling out my phone to look at the map.

I wasn't far from the hotel now.

I ran onto a bigger street, looking carefully for protestors or police, then crossed it and ran through Lower Senate Park while the sounds of screaming and yelling behind me pushed me to run as fast as I could.

I spotted Liam standing outside the hotel, wearing a hoodie over his head. He saw me and waved. I ran up to him.

"This is hell," I said. "We have to get out of here."

"Not much worse than running from the reporters as I have been all day since they released me this morning on bail," he said. "My lawyer fought quite the battle to get them to let me out. Thank God for expensive lawyers. It all came down to the fact that they have no evidence that links me to the guy who did the shooting. He advised me not to travel out of state while waiting for my court date, but the judge allowed it since I have to go home at some point, and it might take months. Have you read any of the crap they've written about me?"

"You can't care about that now," I said. "The Swatter has started his war. Look at this town!"

I couldn't hold my tears back anymore, and Liam saw it. He grabbed me in his arms and hugged me as the emotions of the past hours' events overpowered me.

"Hey, hey."

"It's all my fault," I said. "I've been so close all this time. I knew this was what he wanted. I shouldn't have let her go onto that stage. I should've…"

"What a load of nonsense," Liam said.

I pulled away. "Excuse me?"

"You're not going to get me to feel sorry for you if that's what you want," he continued. "It's not happening."

"I…I wasn't…"

"Yes, you were. You think that you could have stopped this? What else do we need to blame you for while we're at it? War in Afghanistan? Syria? My boy dying?"

I swallowed and looked at him, confused.

"The fact is, there was nothing you could have done. Things happen. Life happens, Eva Rae. Yes, you're chasing a killer, but you are not responsible for those he kills. He is. Didn't they teach you anything at Quantico?"

I stared at him. "You have to be the most annoying man on this planet."

"It's only annoying because you know I'm right."

I snorted, feeling my tears dry up. "So not."

"There's my girl," he said, smiling, looking into my eyes, causing me to blush. "That's the look that I wanted to see. There's the look of determination."

"Save it, will you? Stop patronizing me."

"What? What did I do wrong?"

As a flock of protestors approached us, I started to walk away, pulling his arm to have him follow me inside the hotel.

Chapter 83

THEN:

FanTAUstic345: Yo, you there?

DeVilSQuaD666: Yes.

FanTAUstic345: It went wrong. It was the wrong address. I can't believe it. Did you see the news?

DeVilSQuaD666: I saw it.

FanTAUstic345: OMG! Then you know that guy was shot? He was shot right there in his own home.

DeVilSQuaD666: Calm down.

FanTAUstic345: How can I? A guy died. You made that call to the police. You told them to go there, to his house.

DeVilSQuaD666: I know. But they'll never find out.

FanTAUstic345: How can you be so sure? They could track you down somehow. You'll go to jail.

DeVilSQuaD666: I just am. They'll never find out. I promise you. Trust me. They won't find out it was me. I've done this hundreds of times, and they've never found out it was me.

FanTAUstic345: This is different. This isn't like when you clear out a school with a bomb threat. The guy is dead. It's murder.

DeVilSQuaD666: I didn't kill anyone. I didn't. It's not my fault.

FanTAUstic345: Yes, you did. You made the call.

DeVilSQuaD666: Well, you made me. You're the one who wanted him punished, remember? You wanted to teach him a lesson.

FanTAUstic345: I didn't mean for this to happen. It was supposed to be like a prank. A joke. But it wasn't even the right guy. It was someone else. It was the wrong address. This guy was innocent. He had no idea.

DeVilSQuaD666: So?

FanTAUstic345: So, that makes us murderers.

DeVilSQuaD666: No, it doesn't. It's not our fault they thought he was armed and shot him. Maybe he was a bad guy. We don't know everything.

FanTAUstic345: But he had nothing to do with it. We swatted someone innocent, and now he's dead. I'm scared they'll come for us. I am afraid they'll somehow find out who we are and nail us for this.

DeVilSQuaD666: Take it easy. They don't know I made the call. I'm skilled. They can't track me.

FanTAUstic345: I know.

DeVilSQuaD666: But you won't talk, right? Tell me you won't.

FanTAUstic345: I won't if you don't.

DeVilSQuaD666: Good. Keep a low profile. Never talk about this again. We should delete this chat and never talk again. Just in case.

FanTAUstic345: K. Good luck.

DeVilSQuaD666: Same.

Chapter 84

LIAM BOOKED US A ROOM, and we went upstairs to hide, trying to avoid the clashes going down all over town. We could hear sirens in the distance and see flames licking at the sky as it was growing darker still.

Later, as day had become evening, and the protests had died down outside the windows, Liam ordered some food for us, and we ate together while the TV ran in the background, showing pictures of the riots. I felt awful but decided to not blame myself for not being able to stop this. Liam had been right about that. It wasn't my fault. The Swatter had started all this, and it had been his plan all along. I was done blaming myself for not being able to save everyone.

Including Chad.

He had been killed by a murderer, and there was not a darn thing I could have done differently. It had taken me a while, but I had finally realized that I had to forgive myself for what happened to him.

It wasn't my fault.

"You okay?" Liam asked, tilting his head.

I shrugged and took another bite of my burger. Liam had laughed when I ordered a burger from the hotel's room service.

"You can have anything," he said. "You could have lobster or duck, and you choose a burger and a milkshake?"

"I needed comfort food. I guess it's hard to be very happy right now," I answered, "when I feel like I'm farther than ever from finding the Swatter. He's out there somewhere; I truly believe he's in D.C., but where? I wish I knew why he was doing this, why he was killing. If I did, I'd be able to find him."

My phone vibrated in my pocket and I pulled it out. It was my dad.

"Hello?"

"You've got to check the scanner," he said, sounding agitated. "Something is happening, something big."

"What do you mean?" I asked. "Anything other than the riots?"

"Yes, this can't just be that. I've been listening for a few hours since Amal Bukhari was shot, and I spoke to you right after. But about ten minutes ago, something happened."

"What?"

"Dispatch received seventeen high-priority calls at the exact same time. Seventeen!"

I sat down on a chair, heart pounding in my chest. I looked at my watch. "Let me guess. At eight fifty-six?"

"Exactly."

"Dear Lord."

I hung up and told Liam what my dad had said, then opened my police scanner app to listen in. My dad was right. A lot seemed to be going on at once. Several bomb threats, an active shooter situation, and a hostage situation. All life-threatening situations that will have highest priority.

"What's going on?" Liam asked.

"It doesn't sound like the riots," I said. I grabbed my jacket from the chair and put it on.

"Where are you going?"

"Do you have a car?"

"Sure. I rented one at the airport. It's parked in the back."

I plotted a couple of addresses I had heard on the scanner into the GPS on my phone, then asked it for directions. I pointed at one of them.

"This one is pretty close to us."

Liam nodded and grabbed his phone and car keys. "I'll drive."

Chapter 85

AS WE DROVE DOWN 19th Street in downtown D.C., a tingling sensation shot up through my spine. It felt like a premonition of something horrible about to happen, something I couldn't do anything to prevent. It was accompanied by an unpleasant feeling of utter helplessness.

What is going on here? What is he up to now?

"Take a right here, and then we're there," I said. "The address is at the end of the street."

It wasn't hard to find once we took the turn and came around a building. There was already what looked like fifteen or maybe twenty police cruisers there, along with a SWAT team, and they had set up a perimeter. I spotted the guy in charge in an instant, then bolted out as soon as Liam stopped the car and ran up toward him. An officer stopped me as I was almost there. His name tag said Steinberg.

"Hey, this is a restricted area. You can't be here."

"Can you tell us what's going on, Officer?" I asked and stopped. The guy I needed to talk to was only a few feet away, but too far for me to be able to yell. Besides, if I did, they'd just think I was a crazy person. I needed to look into this man's eyes to make him listen to what I had to say.

It was a lot easier said than done.

"We received a call about an active shooter inside this building in one of the apartments," he said. "You better leave now. It's not safe here."

My heart started to race in my chest. I stared at the sergeant in charge as he obviously was giving directions to his men. I couldn't escape this odd feeling inside of me that wouldn't go away. Something was off.

"Do you have a headcount? Is he holding hostages?"

"I...we don't know much as of right now. But I do need you two to...say, don't I know you? You're that chef, aren't you?"

He stared at Liam, and Liam sent him a crooked smile.

"Weren't you just arrested down in...Orlando for...?"

"Listen," I said. "We need to speak to someone in charge. I think this might be a trap. Can you hear me, sir? Sir?"

The officer shook his head, still staring at Liam. "What are you doing here? You were in that car down in Orlando, when...when...I read that..."

"Listen to me," I said. "You need to listen. Don't go inside that building, please."

As I spoke, I watched from the corner of my eye as the entire SWAT team was sent in.

"No," I said. "No!"

I stepped forward, but the officer held me back by placing a hand on my chest. I looked at him, terrified.

"Please, stop them."

But it was too late. The men disappeared inside the three-story red brick building while I held my breath. It felt like an eternity but was probably just a few seconds of complete silence before the officer spoke again:

"Now, I need you two to lea..."

Boom!

Chapter 86

THE WINDOWS on the third floor of the building in front of us were blasted out, followed by big balls of fire shooting flames into the air above. Then, the second floor followed up with another explosion before the first floor did the same. Three explosions at the same time shook the entire neighborhood. Bricks were sent flying, along with glass and other debris.

Oh, dear God!

I was thrown to the ground by the force of the explosion, cracking my forehead into the pavement while waves of glass rained from the sky. Blood ran from my forehead down my cheek and nose while I struggled to figure out what had happened. The building in front of me wasn't just destroyed. It was gone.

And so were the people who had been inside it.

Somehow, during it all, I saw Liam go down as well. His legs gave away under him, and he fell face-first into the pavement right next to me while the sound blasted out my ears and kept echoing for minutes after, pounding inside my head.

Please, make it stop, please!

Liam yelled something, but I couldn't hear what it was. I tried to yell something back, but he couldn't hear me either. Black smoke and dust filled the air and the neighboring buildings in front of us were completely engulfed in flames. I stared at the scene, mouth open, gasping for air, while an inferno raged inside of me.

The worst part was that it wasn't over yet.

As I was almost on my feet again, another explosion blasted through the air. This time, it came from another part of town, and as I scrambled to my feet, another one came, and then another one followed, and I fell forward to my knees, holding my hands above my head to shield myself from the terror.

Stop. Please, stop!

I counted seventeen explosions, all at almost the same time or right after one another, coming from all over town. It was like an earthquake, one of the bad ones, where you aren't safe anywhere, where the very ground beneath you caves in, and every house crumbles around you.

As the ground shook and bricks, glass, and debris landed on the pavement in front of me, Liam reached out his hand toward me, and I grabbed it, holding it as tightly as possible like it was the very last thing connecting me to this world. A wooden electrical pole fell from the sky and smashed down scarily close to us, and I let out a scream.

Liam then covered me with his long coat and with his big body. He was hugging me tightly, protecting me, while the entire town seemed to be crashing around us. People were spilling into the streets in panic, crying out to God. I saw the officer from earlier, the one that had held me back, dragging the remains of the sergeant across the pavement, struggling, his face smeared in dirt and sod while the sergeant was barely alive, missing his right leg.

That was when I closed my eyes and covered my head completely. I didn't want to witness any more. I simply couldn't bear it.

THREE DAYS LATER

Chapter 87

IT WAS like looking at a warzone. Several big buildings downtown had been completely demolished by the seventeen explosions. Hundreds of people had died. Hundreds. They still didn't know the exact number since they weren't done searching through all the fallen buildings. But they knew that sixty-nine of them were police officers, twenty-two were firefighters, and there were four emergency responders, along with an uncertain number of civilians. So far, twenty-five had been dragged out of demolished buildings, but it was believed there would be a lot more as the work for digging them out progressed. A baby had miraculously survived two days in the rubble and was dug out by firefighters, bringing a flicker of hope to us all.

Other than that, it was bad. It was really bad.

I was in the hospital for several days, being treated for a concussion and smoke inhalation. I was one of the lucky ones, though. My injuries were far from as severe as most other people.

The Swatter had outdone himself.

Liam was another lucky one. He only spent one day in the hospital before they discharged him, and he went back to his home in Philadelphia. The airports remained closed for three days, and the roads were clogged by people traveling by car instead of air, so my mom and the kids couldn't come up to see me. And I told them they didn't have to. I'd be home as soon as I was done in D.C.

Matt did come, though. As soon as he realized I had been hurt, he drove all night and all the next day to get to D.C. He stayed by my side for all three days while I was in the hospital, and I was so happy that he did.

"Actually, it was Alex who told me to come," he told me on the last day when he had come back with coffee from the vending machine. "He came to my house after you left and we had a little chat."

"Alex did?" I asked.

"Yes, he ran away from your house, and I called your mom immediately. He ended up staying the night, sleeping in Elijah's room. I think those two are becoming really good friends. Anyway, Alex told me he wanted us to come back to the house, to your house and live there because we were needed. You needed me, he said. You were just too proud to tell me."

"Wow," I said.

"I know," Matt said. "That little kid sees more than you know."

"He sure is smart," I said.

"Anyway, I was thinking that Elijah and I should just come back to the house as soon as we get back from here. It's all been silly, really. I don't even remember what I was so mad about earlier. It's all water under the bridge."

I swallowed. I smiled, thinking I should be happy about this, but somehow, I wasn't. I had that feeling once again like someone was choking me—like I couldn't breathe. I cleared my throat and shook off the feeling.

"Yes, sure, of course."

He took my hand and kissed the top of it. For some reason, I winced, and he saw it. A shadow went over his face for a second, then disappeared. He smiled gently.

"That's a deal, then. We start all over once we get back."

"Yeah, about that. I might need to stay in D.C. a few days longer," I said.

"What?"

"Isabella, my former supervisor, has put together an anti-terror task force to catch whoever was behind the attacks. She wants me to join them as soon as I'm ready. Which I guess is tomorrow when they let me out of here."

"So…you're not coming back then?" A furrow appeared between his eyebrows, signaling disappointment, but it swiftly disappeared. It was replaced by another smile, one that seemed awkward and forced.

"Not yet. I will as soon as we catch this guy. I promise you, okay?" I lifted his hand and kissed the top of it with a smile.

Matt smiled nervously and let out a small, seemingly insignificant scoff. I knew this wasn't exactly his plan, but that was life for you, right? Plans were bound to be broken from time to time.

As were hearts.

Chapter 88

IT WAS strange to be back. My old workplace at the FBI Headquarters on Pennsylvania Avenue hadn't changed much, if at all. Isabella waited for me in her office. I knocked, then walked in.

Isabella smiled warmly.

"There she is. Returned to the land of the living. Please, have a seat."

I found a chair and sat across from her desk. She kept looking at me, shaking her head.

"Remind me never to dismiss your theories again, will you? I mean...you knew this would happen. You saw it coming, you spotted it, and you tried to tell me in Orlando, but I wouldn't listen. I feel like such a fool. I will never forgive myself for not listening to you."

"I...well, I didn't exactly know that *this* would happen," I said. "Not the explosions and all. But I had a feeling something awful was about to go down, yes."

"And you knew they would target our men in blue," she said, pointing at me with her pen. "Seventeen calls led to seventeen ambushes. All were bombs placed inside the buildings with tripwires that were set to explode as soon as they entered. The calls led them straight into the traps."

Isabella rose to her feet, then walked to the window and looked out. I could tell she was truly shaken up, and that said a lot. Isabella was solid as a rock; nothing shook her. I had never seen her like this before.

"This case has the highest priority," she said. "President's orders."

"Of course."

"We have all our terrorism experts on this, day and night."

"I saw plenty of activity when I walked through the building to get here," I said.

"No one has claimed it yet," Isabella said and turned to face me. "Which means we have no idea what we're dealing with here. ISIS? Al Qaeda? Another terror network that has managed to stay under the radar? Who are these people? It's been four days now, and you'd think they'd at least want to claim it by now."

"What do the experts say?"

Isabella sighed and pinched the bridge of her nose. "Nothing useful, that's what."

"Have they made a profile?"

Isabella nodded. She handed me a piece of paper. "This is what I wanted you to see. We think we're dealing with a terror organization, which is kind of a given at this point, but…"

"I don't think so," I interrupted her. "Sorry, but I'm guessing that's why I'm here, right? To give you my opinion?"

Isabella gave me a look, then sat down. "Please. Go on."

"I think we're looking for one guy. I call him the Swatter. He's American, born and raised here. He's also a loner. A computer-savvy gamer, which makes me think he's not very old, but I could be wrong about that since my dad is a genius with computers and he's in his mid-sixties. I believe he is most likely ex-military with his knowledge of explosives and how to place them. He might have shown signs of PTSD and could have been stationed in Afghanistan. He is most likely black, fighting for black rights, and against police brutality.

He's had some sort of collision with the police, maybe been a victim of police brutality since that is his focus. He's chosen his victims to make sure it's spectacular, and it's the same with the bombings. He wants attention. He wants people to see and understand his mission, maybe even start a revolution. He killed Amal Bukhari on that stage to get the people to riot, and then placed the calls to lead the police to his bombs. It all went down in one day. It's all very calculated, so he's also extremely intelligent. My guess is that he's also deeply religious, based on his targeting of declared atheists like Amal, who had denounced her family's Muslim faith. He also has an attachment to the exact time eight-fifty-six p.m. He's made most of his calls at that exact time, and that goes as well for all the calls to dispatch that led to the bombs four days ago. This is what I believe you're looking for, not an overseas organization, but that's just my opinion."

She stared at me. "Really? You think this entire attack was orchestrated by only one person?"

I shrugged. "Yes. That's what I believe."

"And how is that possible?"

"I don't have the details yet. But he makes me think of the Unabomber. He targeted people who were involved with modern technology, issuing a social critique opposing industrialization while advocating a nature-centered form of anarchism. We're looking for someone like that. Someone who wants to change society for what he believes is the better."

"Crazy as a bat, you mean," she said.

"The Unabomber was a mathematics professor, and if you asked him, he wasn't crazy. He never pleaded insanity for that very reason."

Isabella leaned back in her chair, mumbling under her breath. "I'll be…"

"That's my profile; you can do with it what you want," I said. "I know the so-called experts might call you insane, but…"

"No, no, no," she said. "That's not why I'm so surprised."

"It's not?"

She shook her head. "Before you got here, I just spoke to one of our technicians. They've gone through all the recordings of the calls that came to dispatch from the night of the bombings."

"And?"

She took a deep breath. "Well, there's no doubt that it was the same voice. He was using a modulator app to make it impossible to recognize, and to fool our recognition software, but they analyzed the voice, the audio patterns, the emotions, the stress to his voice, and the syntax to locate any accent to identify where he could be from, and his breathing pattern and all that. There's no doubt it was the same man who made all seventeen calls at once. We haven't been able to locate a single phone number connected with any of the seventeen calls. They believe he used a computer and some software that can hide your identity. How that is possible is beyond my understanding. I'm not very tech-savvy, as you probably know."

"He must have used recordings, then," I said. "He must have pre-recorded each and every message with the address and high-priority incident. They must have been automated calls that he timed. You can find software for that online; it's no big deal. Like they do for schools when they want to send a message to all the parents at once. That's the only way that this is possible."

Isabella nodded. "That's what Tom, the tech, said too. But it being the same voice fits well with your theory, now, doesn't it?"

I nodded, leaning back pensively in my chair.

"It sure does."

Isabella looked at me. "The question is where the heck he is now and what's his next move? That's where you come in. So far, you've been the only one who seemed able to predict his patterns. I need you to do that again, so we can catch him. And please do it fast, before anyone else dies."

Chapter 89

THEY GAVE me a small office to sit in, and I logged onto the computer and into the system. It was so strange being here again, yet it felt so familiar. The only thing that had really changed was me, I realized.

As I sat there staring at the screen and the empty wall behind it, I felt tears well up in my eyes. Everything there reminded me of the time when I was still married to Chad, when we had been a family. A quite dysfunctional one, one that only survived because we forced it to, but we had still been one.

Now, all that was gone.

And so was Chad.

He wasn't just a cheater who had run out on the children and me anymore. It wasn't just a divorce. He was dead and gone.

Oh, dear God.

And right there, it finally happened. I finally realized that Chad was definitively gone, that I could never call him for advice about the children anymore, nor could we laugh about them or be proud of them together. Realizing that he was completely gone felt so definite, and it overwhelmed me with a deep sadness. I hadn't wanted to admit it to myself, but I missed him. I missed him terribly. Realizing that did the trick. The tears that had been piling up inside of me, that I had refused to let out, came gushing out, overpowering me completely. I leaned forward and just bawled my eyes out, sobbing, my torso in spasms while finally getting it all out.

And it felt amazing.

Afterward, I felt lighter than ever. It was like this huge knot growing inside of me had finally burst and all the pressure lifted. I was still sad and realizing that I was never going to get the man I had loved, the father of my children, back, hurt like nothing else, but facing it made me feel better.

I stared at my phone, wondering if I should call Matt, then put it down. I knew he would be there for me; I knew he would talk to me and be understanding as he always was, but for some reason, I just didn't want to.

I had to handle this grief on my own.

I found a pack of Kleenex in the bag Matt had packed for me and brought to the hospital, then dried my eyes. I then found the FBI files on the bombings and opened the first one. There were almost a hundred files that I needed to read through, so I was planning on making it an all-nighter. We were running out of time. I was determined to get through everything, combing it meticulously for details—anything, no matter how little and seemingly insignificant —that had been overlooked. I was desperate for anything that could lead me to the Swatter's identity. So far, I had nothing. Not even a lead suspect.

"Who are you, you ugly bastard?" I mumbled as I opened the first file on the bombing that I had witnessed myself and began to read. It wasn't easy to read about, and I had to get my Kleenex out now and again as I read through the reports and interviews with the few that survived, among them Officer Steinberg, who I had spoken to in front of the building before it happened. There was also my testimony and Liam's. I read through them as well, just in case. A note was attached to the report, and I opened it. I wrote down a number on a post-it note and did a search.

Then I froze.

Could it really be? Could it really be this easy?

I shook my head and looked down at the screen again, making sure I had read it right. I had. There it was, right there on my screen.

The answer to who the Swatter was.

It had been right there all this time.

Chapter 90

IT HAD BEEN A LONG DAY. Officer Ben Ross drove his patrol cruiser down the main street of town. He spotted a couple of teenagers from the high school by the ice cream shop, goofing around, punching each other jokingly, then slowed the car down and looked at them through the window. Seeing this, the teenagers scattered, disappearing behind the building.

Officer Ross continued, taking a right and going around the corner, driving toward the bar areas. It was getting dark out, and soon the drunks would gather here, maybe get themselves into a fight. Some of them had been drinking since happy hour started at four. After almost five hours of drinking, they'd be toasted by now and ready to get themselves in trouble. And he'd be right there, waiting for them.

He parked his vehicle on the street in front of the parking lot of the Sports Bar, where most of them would hang out. Placing himself there would work to hinder both the drunks and people speeding on the road.

He opened his computer and started writing his report from earlier. He had been down on the beach where someone had called about a bum sleeping in a tent several nights in a row. Officer Ross had told the bum to get off the beach, but the guy had been drunk and wanted to put up a fight. He had called him all sorts of names and curse words, getting in his face, threatening him. Ben Ross was already in a bad mood as it was because of Ilene, his wife. She had told him she wanted a divorce this very morning and handed him the papers to sign. It wasn't like he didn't know that they weren't doing well; of course, he did. He just thought they'd be able to work through this, especially for the sake of Bryan, their seven-year-old son. But Ilene had met someone else, and she wanted to be *set free*, as she put it.

Whatever that meant.

Not only was she ruining his life, but she was also destroying their son's life, and that made Ben Ross angrier than anything.

"Attention all units," the radio scratched. "We have a possible 10-32 at 121 DeLeon Road; it's a private residence. Any units available?"

Ben grabbed the radio. "This is 46. I'm less than a minute out. En route."

He put the car in drive, then put the siren on. He rushed down the side street behind the Sports Bar and across the parking lot, then drove onto the small street behind the building and approached the main street of town, flooring the accelerator. A 10-32 was a man with a gun. The address was residential, so it was possibly a domestic dispute gone awry. Ben took a deep breath and felt for his gun in the holster. Two other units were coming up behind him now, and he felt more reassured. It was less than a year ago that he had made a traffic stop where the driver had pulled a gun on him from his glove compartment. Staring down that barrel into the face of death had made it hard to sleep for months afterward; heck, he still woke up bathed in sweat from time to time. Ben had ended up drawing his gun and shooting the guy inside his car. It tormented him to this day, and he often thought he could still see the guy's mad eyes, especially when he closed his eyelids to go to sleep. To this day, Ben still didn't know whether the guy would have shot him or not, or if he was just high on drugs, trying to get away from the police. But he couldn't really take any chances, could he?

"It was him or you. It's as simple as that," his chief had told him afterward when he had addressed his concerns and worries.

Ben Ross turned down DeLeon Road, four patrol cruisers following on his tail, then parked in front of the mailbox carrying the number 121, heart throbbing in his chest.

Chapter 91

IT WAS LATE, but luckily, Publix was open till ten. Matt pulled down toilet paper and then ten big bottles of Dr. Pepper that he placed underneath the cart so they wouldn't squash all the bread and meat. His mother was addicted to those things and had been since he was a child. It was all she drank. How she had lived this long and never gotten sick or even overweight was beyond him.

Matt had stayed late at the station today but promised to grocery shop for his mother on the way home. She had strained her thumb while walking the dog. The dog had seen another puppy across the street and suddenly yanked the leash so hard her finger got twisted, and now she couldn't carry anything. Matt was used to shopping for her, so it was no problem to drop by on his way home. Except he hadn't known that it would be this late. Chief Annie had him on a case of ATM-fraud. A group had placed fake skimmers on ATMs several places in town and copied people's credit cards. He had spent most of the day and evening interviewing the victims and then talking to the neighboring police departments in the towns of Satellite Beach and Cape Canaveral, who had experienced the same.

In cases like these, it wasn't very likely he'd ever catch them, which was extremely dissatisfying.

Matt paid for the food, then rolled the cart to his car and placed the bags in the back, then went to the driver's seat. He took off, driving through town. He was in his mom's car since his police cruiser had to go to the shop this morning.

As he stopped at a red light, he thought about Eva Rae. He had called her at lunch, but she hadn't picked up.

Probably busy with catching terrorists.

He wasn't jealous or anything, but he did miss her. Like crazy. He didn't like how they were always away from one another and how he constantly felt like she was drifting away from him.

He called her again while the light was still red. She picked up.

"Hi there," he said. "You busy?"

"You could say that," she said, sounding distant.

"So, I take it you're still working even though it's nine o'clock at night?"

He could hear her tapping on her computer. She sounded agitated.

"Listen, I'm really busy…"

He held the phone between his shoulder and ear as the light turned green. "Are we okay? You seem really far away. Like you're drifting away."

"Matt, seriously. I can't do this right now. I'm just about to break op…"

Matt heard the sound of sirens, then looked up in the rearview mirror. He pulled the car to the side of the road to make room for the police cruiser, and as it passed him, sirens blaring, he saw it turn down a street ahead of him. Seeing this, his blood froze.

"Eva Rae?"

She answered with anger. "What, Matt?"

Matt followed the police cruiser down DeLeon Road, and as he saw the blue blinking lights in front of Eva Rae's house, his heart stopped.

"Something is going on here; what the heck…?" he mumbled, still holding the phone between his jaw and shoulder.

Hearing his voice change, Eva Rae suddenly shifted too.

"What? What's going on, Matt? Is something wrong?"

He parked behind one of the cruisers.

"I'm afraid so, Eva Rae. Your house, it's…"

"My house is what? Matt? What's going on here? What's going on with my house? Are the kids okay?"

"There are police everywhere," he said and got out of the car. He saw four officers approach the house, wearing Kevlar vests, weapons drawn. He knew all four of them and yelled out to one.

"Officer Ross, don't…"

But it was too late. Matt saw them kick down the front door, while Eva Rae yelled at him on the other end.

"Tell me what's going on. Why are the police at my house!"

Matt ran toward them, yelling out their names, but they were already inside. His heart throbbed in his chest, threatening to explode. The phone was now in his hand, and Eva Rae was yelling in the distance while sweat sprang from his forehead as he ran through the driveway and stormed up toward the entrance. Just as he reached the doorstep, he heard yelling from inside, a child screaming, then an officer yelling:

"Hands up!"

"Sir, there's no need to…" a voice said.

"Keep your hands where we can see them!" an officer yelled.

"Get down! GET DOWN!" another officer yelled.

"STOP!"

Matt screamed at the top of his lungs and stormed inside the living room just as the panic erupted. Loud voices were yelling at one another, and then a shot was fired.

Chapter 92

I WASN'T BREATHING. I stood in my small office, yelling into the phone, but receiving no answer.

"Matt? Matt? What's going on, Matt?"

But there was nothing but yelling and screaming. And then came the shot. The terrifying sound of a gun going off.

Inside my home? Inside my house where my children were?

I screamed into the phone and fell to my knees.

"NO!"

I heard scrambling and realized the phone had fallen to the ground. Matt had dropped it, and now I could hear him whimpering in the far distance, and then he screamed again.

"No! No! No!"

"What happened?" I said, feeling more confused than ever, fearing the worst. Had any of my children been shot? Had my mom?

"Someone, tell me, please; what's going on!" I yelled into the phone, feeling desperate, crying in fear and worry. I imagined the most horrifying scenarios.

My poor children. My poor, poor kids.

"Please," I said, sobbing. "Please, just tell me what happened. Is someone hurt? Who was hurt?"

It was eerily quiet on the other end—only the sound of someone sobbing loudly. After a few minutes, I realized it was Matt. He was crying, and I could also hear a child crying. It sounded very much like Christine.

Was Christine hurt?

Please, say it isn't so.

"Hello?" I said, fumbling nervously with the collar of my shirt, pulling it till it almost ripped while tears were gushing down my cheeks.

"Hello?"

"Oh, dear God," Matt said. "Why? Why?"

I heard more sirens now and figured it had to be an ambulance approaching.

Someone in the distance mumbled, "I thought he had a gun; I really did."

He? Could it have been Alex who was hurt? *Oh, dear Lord, say it isn't so.*

"Please," I said. "Please, say it isn't so." I bent forward in anguish, crying heavily when there was scrambling on the other end, and a small weak voice spoke.

"Hello?"

I almost screamed. "Christine!?"

"Mom?" she said, her voice shrill and wailing. "Mo-om? Oh, Mom, it's terrible."

"What happened, Christine? Tell me what happened."

She was speaking through sobs, making it hard to understand. "I...I was in the living room; the police came, they thought... Grandma...she..."

"Was someone shot?"

"Yes," she said. "Grandma came out as the police burst into the house screaming and...and...yelling and then..."

"Was Grandma shot?"

"No," she said, sniffling.

"Then what happened?"

"Irvin…was here," she said.

"Irvin, Grandma's boyfriend?"

"He was here for dinner, and he came out too, and they just went berserk when they saw him, pointing their guns at him. He was holding a baseball bat in his hand because he and Alex had been outside playing ball, and they thought…they must have thought it was something else because they yelled and screamed…and…and… then he tried to calm them down, but then they asked him if he was armed, and he…he said…yes, he was carrying, but he had a license for it and to calm down, but they didn't listen, oh, Mommy, they wouldn't hear what he said. They just yelled at him after that, and then they fired a shot."

"Was Irvin hit? Was it Irvin?"

Christine whimpered again. "No. He…he moved, and they missed him, but the bullet, it hit someone else."

Oh, dear God!

"Who, Christine? Who did it hit?"

She sobbed, trying to speak, but hyperventilating too heavily. I was crying so badly now that my stomach was cramping.

"Please, Christine, tell me who it is."

"Elijah. It was Elijah."

Chapter 93

"I'M COMING HOME, Christine. As soon as I can, okay?"

I sat on the floor for a few seconds, gathering myself, tears gushing down my cheeks, unable to comprehend what had just happened. An ambulance had arrived, Christine said, and they were taking Elijah to the hospital. Matt was going with him. I asked her if Elijah was breathing or even moving, but she said that she didn't know. She couldn't get close enough to see.

"He doesn't look good," was all she could give me.

Then she handed the phone to my mother, who was completely out of it, understandably. I told her I was coming back home as soon as possible and to make sure the kids were all right until then.

"Of course," she said.

"How are Alex and Olivia?"

"Crying," she said. "I can't blame them—what a mess. And the door is completely destroyed. Irvin said he can put up a temporary one."

"Good," I said. "Thank him."

"I...I don't know how this could have happened, Eva Rae. I thought these people knew us, knew you and...and Matt?"

"They do," I said heavily. "But they have to react when a call like this comes in. My guess is that someone called in an active shooter situation and it gets highest priority, and well…they didn't know Irvin. They didn't know he wasn't the gunman. He could have been holding all of you hostage."

"But who would make such a call?" she asked.

I think I might know this one.

"Poor Matt," she continued, and I could just see her shaking her head and tightening her lips like she always did. "He was completely crushed."

My heart was aching for him as we said our goodbyes and hung up.

I checked online to look for a flight but wouldn't be able to get on one till the morning. And they were all filled up till the one at ten o'clock. I looked at my watch. It was a thirteen-hour drive. I would get there faster if I drove. I rang Isabella in the taxi on my way to Avis Car Rental and told her, sobbing, what had happened and that I was going back there.

"Of course," she said. "That is awful, Eva Rae. Send Detective Miller our deepest sympathies."

As I got into my rented car and plotted in the address to my home, I felt like everything exploded inside of me. I stared at the GPS on my phone, heart pounding in my chest, ears ringing, while thinking about everything.

It had to be him, didn't it? Of course, it was him. The Swatter had struck again. And this time, it was personal.

"All right," I said and changed the address in the GPS. I floored the accelerator, and the car jolted into the street with me hissing in anger and spitting as I spoke:

"If that's how you want to play it, then so be it."

Chapter 94

THE DRIVE WAS two and a half hours in the wrong direction, getting me farther away from my family, but I still did it. I loaded up on Red Bull and coffee, then drove the entire way there in one stretch, not stopping once, speeding excessively most of the way, cutting about twenty minutes off the drive.

I arrived after midnight, parked the car in the street, and got out. I grabbed my gun between my hands and hurried up the walkway leading to the front door. I looked inside the windows and saw him in his kitchen.

Cooking at midnight, of course.

I lifted the gun, then reached over to grab the door handle, but it was locked. I then snuck around the house, found a back door, and tried that as well.

Also locked.

I stared at it for a few seconds, then made the decision. I kicked the door down. It slammed open, and I rushed inside, holding up my gun. I had barely made it inside before a knife darted through the air, whistling past my face, stabbing me in the shoulder. I saw it too late to move out of the way. The hand holding the knife let go of the handle, and the person stepped backward. The pain in my arm made me drop the gun to the floor. Blood gushed out of the wound, and I fell forward to my knees.

A set of well-polished shoes stood next to me. They stopped by the gun, which was picked up. I lifted my head, wincing in pain from where the kitchen knife had penetrated.

Liam reached down again, grabbed the knife, then pulled it out forcefully. I screamed and held a hand to my wound, which was gushing blood. I felt lightheaded. Liam handed me a towel. I pressed it against the wound, then looked up at him, biting back the pain.

"Don't look so surprised," he said. "I was expecting you."

I closed my eyes, trying to remove the black spots dancing in front of them, obscuring my sight, then rose to my feet, straining with pain.

Liam had his back turned to me, and I stormed toward him and slammed into him headfirst.

"You bastard!"

Liam was pushed forward and fell to the tiles, sliding across them. I stood above him, grunting like a bull.

"Matt's son was shot. Elijah was shot. Because of you."

Liam lifted the gun and pointed it at me, signaling for me to back away. I didn't obey. I stared down at him, blood dripping from my wound onto his black shoes.

"What do you care? You don't love him anyway," he said and stood up. I felt like punching him, but the gun in his hand kept me from it. And perhaps the throbbing pain in my arm and shoulder.

"You don't know anything about that," I hissed. "I have loved Matt my entire life."

"Why are you running away from him then?" Liam asked. "In all the time I have known you, that's been all you've done."

I shook my head. "What's it to you?"

The look in his eyes changed. He burst forward, grabbed me around the throat, and lifted me in the air, pressing me against the wall behind me. I screamed and then fought to breathe, gurgling. Liam kept pressing harder and harder until my face felt like it was about to explode.

"Please...Liam, let...me...go."

His expression changed, and he let go of me suddenly. I slid to the floor below, coughing and fighting to catch my breath. I crawled across the floor, trying to stand up, but he kicked me hard in the stomach, and I fell, face first, unable to move.

"That was exactly what she said," he said and kicked me again. "But you didn't let her go. You and your pigs just let her die right there while she fought for her life."

Chapter 95

"HER..." I spoke between coughs, spitting up blood. "You...mean...
your wife, you mean Anna?"

Another kick fell, this time in my side. It felt like he broke every
rib in my body.

"Don't you dare say her name. People like you...pigs like you
don't even deserve to say her name."

"She was killed, right? She didn't die from pancreatic cancer like
you told everyone. She was killed. At a traffic stop?"

"So, you know, huh? How did you find out?"

I rolled to the side while holding a hand to my stomach. "There
were two notes in the reports from the blast in D.C. Two numbers
had been written on the side of the document. One was the case file
number from your arrest in Orlando. When I ran the other number
in the system, your wife's story came up. Someone in the FBI had
run your name in the system and found those two cases and put the
numbers in there. They just didn't put the pieces together the way I
did because they're not profilers. They thought we were still looking
for a terrorist organization, not just one mad lunatic. They didn't
know what I knew, that the person we were looking for is someone

who holds a grudge against the police because of what happened to him, or rather to the one person he loved the most in this world."

Liam sat down in a chair heavily, placing the gun on the table in front of him. I looked at it, then at him. I tried to move, but it hurt too much. He stared into thin air, tears shaping in his eyes.

"I did love her more than anything in this world; you're right about that."

"But she was sick?"

"She got sick. Six years ago, she suddenly lost her appetite. She was fading away from us, and then she got the diagnosis. She went through treatment, but it wouldn't kill it. It kept eating at her, and soon she was nothing but skin and…"

Liam stopped talking. I could tell he was getting emotionally distressed by talking about this. He grabbed the gun in his hand again and clenched it.

"But then she got better, much to everyone's surprise," he said, clearing up suddenly. "She got better for a little while. She was still heavily medicated, but we had hope, you know? The doctors said she was responding well to the chemo and that the second time around, it was like she was finally fighting off the cancer. She was getting better. We thought she might actually make it. Then, one day in October, five years ago, she wanted to go buy herself a new scarf. We had a charity event we were going to the coming weekend, and she wanted to look nice for that. I told her she didn't have to go if she wasn't up for it, but she said that for once, she actually felt like it. She had energy enough for small talk and all that other stuff that she used to hate. Going to this would make her feel normal again, she said. Like she didn't have cancer. So, I agreed. I asked her if I should drive her to the store, but she brushed me off, saying I was treating her like she was a child. I laughed and kissed her on the cheek before she left. I can still feel her skin against my lips when I think back on it. She tasted like fall, like rain and fallen leaves."

"But she never made it home?" I said, finally able to push myself up on my only good arm and sit up while groaning heavily in pain.

Liam shook his head. "No. She didn't. Because of people like you."

Chapter 96

"I SAW it happen on the footage from the officer's body camera," Liam said. He had taken my phone from my pocket and was playing with it in his other hand, turning it between his fingers while talking. "My lawyer had it released to me. I wanted it; I wanted to see what had happened, how she died. At first, I wished I had never seen it, but today, I'm happy that I did. It opened my eyes to what is really going on out there."

I stared at my gun in Liam's hand while blinking my eyes to focus better. My head was spinning from all the pain, and I couldn't really see straight. I needed to buy myself some time.

"So, what did happen to her?" I asked. "How did she die?"

Liam sniffled and wiped his nose with his hand. "She was stopped because she failed to signal when turning at an intersection. That's the police officer's story. In the video, you see him walk up to her car and open her door. Anna is scared at this point. You know how we hear all those stories. She'd seen those videos online. It was her biggest fear—that Tim would be one day be chased by the police and killed in the street. You don't know this, being who you are, but as a black person, this is a mother's greatest fear and one you live with every day. A simple traffic stop can become deadly.

Now, Anna was scared, naturally, so she started to scream when the officer opened her door. She yelled at him and asked him why she was being stopped. "You're coming into my own car and threatening me,' she yelled. 'Why am I being apprehended? Why are you opening my door?'"

"And all the officer yells back is, 'Get out of the car. Get out of the car.' The officer has now pulled out a stun gun that he is pointing at her while he continues to yell at her to get out of the car. Anna doesn't dare to get out, so she keeps yelling for him to explain why he has stopped her. 'I will light you up,' he says. But Anna doesn't come out of the car. She is screaming in fear, and he reaches inside, then shocks her with the stun gun. Anna screamed even louder, and then he told her again to 'Get out of the car.' She finally got out, and he used the stun gun again. Now he was mad and yelling at her, and you see her fall to her knees, screaming, while he shocks her again and again. Anna begins to scream for him to stop, telling him that she has cancer, but he doesn't listen. He keeps going, again and again, shocking her a total of seventeen times. All you can hear is her screaming, 'Let me go; let me go.' Finally, she fell to the ground, lifeless, and that's when the seriousness of the situation finally occurred to the pig. Anna was taken to the hospital in an ambulance and died that same night from heart failure."

"Because she was weak after a year of chemo and radiation treatment," I said. "Her heart couldn't take it."

"At exactly eight fifty-six that night, the doctor at the hospital declared her dead. And my world crashed. She was my everything."

"Why didn't you tell the world? Why did you keep it a secret?" I asked. "You could have filed a civil lawsuit?"

"My lawyer advised me against it. I was too weak back then, too destroyed with grief to understand how powerful it would have been if I had spoken up right away. But later, I could see the possibilities in it, as soon as the haze was gone, and I could see things more clearly."

"That was when you began swatting," I said. "Seeing how it hurt the officers and discredited them, showing the world what was happening by choosing victims that were live broadcasting while gaming and who were famous and had millions of followers who would be angered by this and maybe one day take it to the streets. That is what you wanted, right? To change the system by breaking it apart. But what I really want to know is how did you do it? When I found out that you fit the profile almost perfectly, I kept going back to that one thing that didn't fit."

Liam gave me a look. "And what was that?"

"Your age," I said. "I was so sure the Swatter was a man in his early twenties or maybe late teens, not a man in his late forties. How did you even think of swatting? How did you learn how to do it so you weren't traceable? My profile was a hacker and a gamer, and I've seen you with a computer. That, you are not."

Faster than I could react, Liam rose to his feet and rushed toward me. He slapped me across the face with the gun. I fell backward, sliding across the tiles until I hit the wall behind me with a deep moan. Blood filled my mouth. Tasting it, I panicked. I rose to my feet, stumbling behind curtains of blood in my eyes, biting back the pain. I tried to run forward, to get away from him, but my head snapped back so hard my feet flew out in front of me. Liam had grabbed me by my ponytail, yanking me toward him, and was dragging me across the floor toward a door. He opened it, slamming it against the wall behind it, and a staircase leading down appeared. He dragged me by the hair downward, my back bumping on every step, me screaming for him to stop.

He reached a door in the basement, then grabbed the handle and pulled me up, so he could look into my eyes. His words came hissing between his teeth.

"I have something to show you."

Chapter 97

THEN:

Hunter Perry, aka DeVilSQuaD666, stared at his computer screen. His fingers touched the keyboard lightly, but then he removed them. He hadn't been on that darn thing for weeks now. After his last conversation with FanTAUstic345, he hadn't dared even to log on. He was so terrified that the police might be able to trace him.

It had gone wrong. What was supposed to be a prank had gone so terribly wrong, and it was all his fault. He hadn't meant for the guy to get shot; he had just wanted to scare him a little and make a thousand dollars. But the guy had been shot, and that terrified him. Because now they were calling him a murderer.

He had watched them say it on the news when he was upstairs with his grandmother. Hunter lived with her since his own mom couldn't afford to take care of both him and his younger sister. She worked two jobs, and yet it was barely enough for one child. He had never known his father.

"Whoever made the call might be charged with murder," the reporters had said over and over again.

"Swatting is no prank," some guy in a suit had said. The text

281

below him told Hunter that he was the US Attorney for the District of Oregon. "Sending police and emergency responders rushing to anyone's home based on utterly false information as some kind of joke shows an incredible disregard for the safety of other people. In this case, it resulted in murder and should call for a prison sentence."

"Prison," Hunter now said to himself, sitting in his room. He shook his head violently and felt tears in his eyes. He was fifteen for crying out loud. How could he go to prison? It was just a joke?

Hunter felt his eyes burn from all the crying he had done the past weeks. His grandma wasn't home, so he stood up and walked upstairs to the kitchen, where he found a pack of donuts that he opened and began to eat. The house was dark and empty, and Hunter didn't like it. He didn't feel safe anywhere these days, and every day, when he went to school, he was terrified of being picked up by the police. If he saw a cruiser, he'd run. He felt like everyone knew what he had done; all eyes were staring at him no matter where he went. But worst of all, he hated that he'd probably hurt his grandma. She'd be so disappointed once she found out what had happened. It would all be revealed. Not just the swat that led to a man dying, but also all the others. The bomb threats to his school, the times he'd cleared out conferences far away, like the Comicon in Chicago, but also all the others. People online had paid him to call in bomb threats to their school so they'd get time off. Some had even paid him to swat other gamers because they killed them in the game. Hunter had never thought someone would actually get killed from it. Especially not some stranger that wasn't even the person he was trying to swat.

Hunter sighed and swallowed the rest of his donut. He felt awful. But he couldn't really tell anyone what he had done, could he? He'd end up in jail.

Hunter heard a noise coming from outside and gasped. He walked to the window and looked out into the street. A trash can had tipped over on the pavement. That was probably the loud noise.

It's okay, Hunter. You're fine. You're safe. The guy was killed in Oregon. It's so far away from California. They'll never find you. Stop worrying.

Hunter heaved a sigh of relief, then walked away from the window. He wanted to play on his computer so badly but still didn't dare. He then spotted his old PlayStation and decided he'd just revive some of the old games. He'd missed playing them anyway.

Hunter grabbed the controller in his hand and started up the PlayStation when there was a knock on his door.

He looked at the clock. It was five to nine. Who could it be at this hour?

Maybe Grandma forgot her key.

Hunter chuckled when thinking about how forgetful his grandma had been lately, then opened the door. But it wasn't his grandma who stood outside; it was a man, a big man wearing a hoodie.

"Yes?"

The man smiled. "Can I come in?"

Hunter shook his head. "No."

The man looked like he wasn't going to go away and wouldn't take no for an answer, so Hunter tried again.

"Listen, mister, I don't know who you are, and it's late so…"

He tried to close the door, but the man placed a hand in the opening and pushed it open. As he stepped into the light, Hunter suddenly recognized him. It was that guy from the cooking show, the one who yelled at everyone and was meaner than his grandma when she got angry at Hunter.

"That may be," Liam Berkeley said, "but I know what you've done."

Chapter 98

I STARED into the small dark room. Liam had opened the door and forced me to look. Five huge computer screens, a desk, and an office chair. On the chair sat a young boy, probably no more than the age of Olivia. He was gagged and tied to the armrest. His fear-struck eyes stared back at me, and he groaned behind the gag like he was trying to warn me.

"Hunter, meet Eva Rae Thomas. Eva Rae Thomas, this is Hunter Perry, also known as DeVilSQuaD666, back in the day."

Liam dragged me inside and slammed the door shut behind us. I stared at the young boy whose eyes glared back at me like he wanted to scream at me to *get the hell out now!*

"Now you'll know him as FaZeYourFeaRs," Liam continued. "Hunter here does all the work for me. He's the one who records the calls and makes sure no one can track them. He's the one who taught me everything I needed to know, including who the important people are in the world of gaming, who has the most followers, and so on. The thing is, Hunter did something bad one time, and he knows that if he doesn't do as I tell him to, I'll tell the police what he did. It was Tim who told me he even existed. He had heard about this guy who would swat people for money, or call in a bomb threat at your school for money. He told me this over dinner one night after Anna had passed away. It caught my interest, and I had Tim help me write to him. So I started chatting with him, calling myself FanTAUstic345. I followed what he did with great interest as he would often brag about it afterward in the chatrooms. I then told him I'd pay him to swat someone for me, and he did. The guy ended up being shot by the police in his own home. And the best part was that it wasn't even the right guy. It was someone completely random."

"And that fit your mission perfectly, I suspect," I said, wincing in pain. He was holding my ponytail so tight it felt like a screaming headache.

"It gave me the idea," Liam said, "of how I could tell the world about the injustice being performed constantly by our very own law enforcement. This was my way of breaking them down. Keep swatting till they messed up, and boy did they mess up. Again and again, it was beautiful. I kept at it, knowing that if this continued, the anger toward the police would get me the result I wanted, what we all needed. A revolution."

"Are you really so crazy that you would sacrifice your own son for this cause?" I asked as he finally let go of my hair and I could fall to my knees.

Liam smiled. "Tim wasn't really my son. He was Anna's when we met. I adopted him, but never cared much for him, and the feeling was mutual. He hated my guts."

"You called it in on him to prove a point. You sacrificed him. He was dispensable to you. Did he really mean so little? The son of the woman you loved?"

"I didn't know he'd get killed. I didn't know what would happen. That was the beauty of it. They might as well have killed me on that night. But yes, his death became a means to an end. Swatting myself and losing my step-son sure made headlines. It also served as a way to keep the focus away from me. I had a feeling I was being watched —that someone was onto me, and the day you came to me, I knew I was right. It was also the time I learned that Hunter here had been going behind my back."

"You didn't know he was playing *Call of Duty* with the victims?" I asked. I looked at the boy. "Because he was trying to warn them. That was why."

"Yeah, well, he tried to chat with them in the game and tell them they were in danger since he knew I would never see it in there. But you told me this when I came to you, and I put a stop to that. Instead, I used it to get you to where I wanted you. But he endangered the entire mission."

"And so did I," I said. "That was why you kept close to me. You kept showing up at my house, wanting to be close to the investigation. I should have seen it then. You were only there to make sure I wasn't getting too close to the truth. And you arranged all the bombs before Orlando happened. But who shot at the police if you were in my car?"

"It's not hard to find help when you're fighting injustice," Liam said. "I have a network of people online who have joined the revolution. They helped me shoot in Orlando, and they helped me start the revolt in D.C. After what happened to Amal Bukhari on the airplane, it wasn't hard to recruit people."

"Did you shoot her?" I asked. "Amal Bukhari? Was it you on that rooftop?"

"Yes," Liam said. "I wanted to do that one by myself. It was so important, like the shot that killed Archduke Franz Ferdinand of Austria in Sarajevo in 1914, that started the First World War. I wanted it to have the same significance. I wanted the world to look back at the shot as the beginning of the revolution."

"And since you served two tours in Afghanistan, I read this in your files last night, you knew about explosives and were a trained sniper," I said.

Liam smiled. "I can do more than just cook, you know."

Chapter 99

LIAM GRABBED an office chair and rolled it toward me. Then he grabbed me by the collar and pulled me up from the ground. Blood and spit were dripping from my broken lip onto the floor. I slid into the seat, and he tied my hands to the armrests using black strips.

He then walked to the desk and found a piece of paper that he handed to me.

"Here, read this. I need you to know it well before we record it."

"What is this?" I asked, looking at what was written. The letters were dancing, and I couldn't focus properly on the words.

"I wrote this before it all began, and I want you to read it while I record it," he said. "Go ahead."

"Liam," I said, staring at the text. I blinked and blinked, but it made no sense. "I...I...can't..."

"READ IT!" he screamed directly into my ear. It sent a spike of pain through my head and down my back. The scream was followed by a punch directly on my nose. My head was yanked backward, and I felt dizzy, fighting not to pass out. As my head bopped back up, Liam gave me a look.

"Read it."

I stared at the paper. More blood dripped from my nose down

onto it. I cleared my throat and tried to say the words, sounding them out, almost like a Kindergartener before cracking the reading code.

"I…It's t-time…t-to…"

Liam pulled the paper from my hand. *"It's time to create…"* he said, reading it. He continued:

"…a substantial change within the American police force."

He looked at me like it was the easiest thing in the world, which it was to him, but not to me. Not in my condition.

He handed me back the paper. "Read it again."

I looked down. The words seemed clearer now. Liam grabbed his phone and began recording me. I glanced briefly at Hunter. He was crying behind the gag. I wanted to tell him I was going to get us both out of there, but I was no longer convinced myself. Liam slapped me again, and it burned my cheek and eye.

"Read it."

I blinked a few times again, then started all over.

"I-It's time to c-create a substantial change within the American police force. The big problem is that people don't believe a revolution is possible…" I paused to catch my breath, biting back the pain, then continued. *"And it is not going to happen precisely because they do not believe it is possible. To a large extent, I think the Black Lives Matter movement has achieved many great things, but I don't think they're going far enough. They need to go further if anything is to change. I think what has to be done is not try to persuade the majority of people that we are right. I believe we must try to increase tension in society to the point where things start to break down and finally collapse. To create a reality where people get angry and scared enough that they're going to rise against the injustice being done to them. The question is, how do you increase those tensions? How do you reach that level of anger in a population?"*

I looked up at Liam, who tapped on his phone, then smiled. "There you go. Now the whole world will think you are the one who started it all, that you are the Swatter. I've left a written confession on your Facebook and Instagram profiles along with this audio file that I just recorded and will upload…now. There we go. Now, it won't be long before the police will look for you, and when they do, they'll track your phone that I'll leave right here on the desk. Once they get here…guess what?"

"What?" I asked, spitting out blood.

He leaned forward, putting his face very close to mine.

"Kaboom," he said. "All gone. You, Hunter, all the police officers who come in here looking for you. All are gone. They'll think I died here too. Blown to pieces like the rest of you."

Chapter 100

I STARED UP AT HIM, nostrils flaring. I felt so stupid for not seeing this earlier, for trusting this guy. Matt had been suspicious of him from the beginning. I should have known better than just to brush him off as being jealous. I should have at least figured it out when he found Jamal at the restaurant. I was the only one the boy had told where he was, and Liam was with me when I received the text. He could easily have read it while I was doing something else or when I briefly left the room.

"Tell me one last thing."

"Yes?" he said.

"Why the atheists? Why did you prefer them? You're not religious yourself."

"I'm not, but Anna was a devout Muslim. She always said that atheists had no honor. To her, religion is the foundation upon which family, community, morality, and identity are built. I chose them to honor her. It's as simple as that."

Liam shrugged. He leaned forward and came close to me, placing his hands on the armrests of the chair. He stared down at me, breathing heavily.

"It's too bad you're one of them, you know. I was quite attracted to you. It was the first time I'd felt drawn to a woman since Anna. And I know you probably won't admit it now, but I had a feeling you were quite attracted to me as well, am I right?"

He was right about the part that I would never admit it; that was for sure. I didn't say anything. I just stared at him; every part of my body throbbing in pain. His eyes locked with mine, and he bent forward further, leaning in for a kiss.

Big mistake.

I moved fast. I lifted both my legs in a V shape. Seeing this, Liam tried to pull away, but I was too fast. My strong legs wrapped around his neck and held him tight, holding him in a Triangle Choke. I then squeezed as hard as I could, holding him tight, making it impossible for him to move. Liam's face turned strained; a vein popped out in his forehead. He sputtered and coughed and grabbed my legs while trying to pull them apart, but with no such luck. I kept him in this position till his eyes rolled back and he lost consciousness. Then I let him slide to the floor and, panting for air, I pushed my chair to the desk where my phone was. Pushing it with the tip of my nose, I managed to get it close enough to my hand so I could grab it with the tips of my fingers. I tapped it a couple of times and managed to make a call.

"Eva Rae?"

"Isabella…I…"

I didn't make it further before someone grabbed my leg and pulled me forcefully. I screamed as I jolted across the room, looking down at Liam, who was pulling on my leg.

"Eva Rae?" I heard Isabella yell.

Liam was on his feet, moving fast, and slammed a fist into my face. My head flew backward, and I heard a loud ringing in my ears. Liam grunted loudly and panted for breath while I fought to remain conscious. A sea of stars tried to lure me in, and it was hard not to give in. I blinked my eyes to see through it, then spotted Liam grabbing the gun. He walked to me and placed it on my forehead. I kicked him in the stomach, hard, and he flew backward, landing against the wall. Grunting angrily, he slid to the floor, but was up on his feet fast, storming toward me, finger moving on the trigger. I closed my eyes, waiting for it all to end here.

Chapter 101

MY EYES WERE STILL CLOSED when the door slammed open. Liam's finger was still on the trigger, but the shock of the sound made him ease up. As the SWAT team burst into the room, they fired one shot, one that hit Liam in the shoulder, causing him to drop the gun. Boots and men in heavy body armor surrounded him. There was a lot of yelling, and Liam screamed in pain.

Meanwhile, I finally let go and dozed off into the unknown, letting the stars guide my way. I didn't feel the hands on my body as they freed me and carried me off on a stretcher. I think I heard Isabella's voice in the distance as I was rushed off to the hospital, but that's all I remember.

Until the next day, late in the afternoon, when I woke up in a hospital bed. I blinked and reached for something to drink, feeling overwhelmed with thirst.

A hand made sure to guide mine to a glass and helped as I pulled it to my mouth and drank. Slowly as the liquid did its work in me, I woke up completely, only to see Matt's gentle eyes looking down at me.

"Matt? Are you here?"

"Isabella called me right after they had taken you to the hospital. I took the first flight here early in the morning."

I grabbed his arm and pulled it forcefully.

"Elijah," I said. "What about Elijah?"

Matt's expression changed. Tears welled up in his eyes, and my heart began to break.

Oh, no, please, no.

"It was all an unfortunate accident…" he said, "I know it wasn't the guy's fault, but…"

"What happened to Elijah, Matt?"

He lifted his glance and looked me in the eyes. I couldn't stand seeing him tormented like this.

"He was shot in the right arm. They had to amputate it from the elbow down. Something about too many fractures and shattered bones. They said it…they tried, but they couldn't save it."

"But…he's going to be all right?"

Matt nodded. "Except for the arm, yes."

Tears welled up in my eyes, and I started to cry, now with joy. "You have no idea how glad I am to hear that. You have no idea, Matt."

Matt reached out and hugged me, holding me very tight. He was crying too now and sniffling.

"I was so scared, Eva Rae. Within less than twelve hours, I almost lost both of the people I love the most."

I swallowed and looked at him, then chuckled. "You still love me?"

"Of course, you silly," he said, wiping his nose with his hand. "Why wouldn't I?"

"I haven't exactly treated you well," I said. "I haven't appreciated you enough. I know I could have been better; I shouldn't have been…I just felt so bad about Chad and what happened to him— about losing the only man who'd understand if I bragged about my kids, you know? I felt so guilty, and then I blamed it all on you, I guess. It was just easier, you know? And you were so right. I have been running. But it's over now…I mean, I think I'm finally done running now."

"Easy there, Eva Rae. I'm not blaming you. Not anymore. It was just as much my fault. I moved too fast," he said. "I was so scared of losing you that I wanted to move faster than you were ready for. Elijah and I will move back in with my mom until you're truly ready for us. It's what's best for all of us."

"So, we're good?" I asked.

He smiled and kissed me. As our lips parted, he whispered: "We're very good, Eva Rae. We're more than that. We're perfect. Right now, in this moment, everything is just perfect."

I kissed him again and closed my eyes when I heard loud voices coming from the hallway. Voices I knew a little too well. Matt chuckled, and I held his face between my hands.

"At least it was perfect," he mumbled, "for a few seconds."

"You brought the kids with you, didn't you?"

"Of course. They insisted. I didn't really have a choice."

"You never do with them," I said with a wry smile and let go of him as my youngest stormed inside the room.

"Mo-o-o-om!" Alex shrieked and ran to me. He jumped onto the bed and sat on top of me. "You got hurt again, Mommy."

"That's because she caught a very dangerous domestic terrorist, you doofus," Olivia said, coming up behind him. "Don't you watch the news? It's all they talk about. Now, be careful with her. She's in a lot of pain."

"Well, actually, I think I'm on a lot of pain medication right now," I said. "But as soon as that wears off, I'm sure to be."

"The doctor said you'll be fine," Matt said. "Two broken ribs and a lot of bruises, but other than that, you should be all right."

"I feel great," I said as Christine grabbed my hand in hers. I sent her a smile and took a deep breath, enjoying this rare moment, feeling more blessed than ever. For just a second, I wished this moment would last forever and that there would never be any more evil in this world that I needed to protect my loved ones from.

Maybe one day. In a perfect world.

THE END

Afterword

Dear Reader,

Thank you for purchasing *Let me Go (Eva Rae Thomas #5)*. The idea for this story came from an article I read about a woman who had been swatted as a form of harassment. Her teenage son was home alone when it happened, and she was terrified that he might be killed by the police entering her home, thinking he might be armed. He wasn't, but the thought of it stirred up something inside of me, and I began researching the phenomenon. I found a lot written about it and found out it was very common in the gaming world. Some YouTubers are being swatted regularly while doing their videos. Luckily, it's rare that it ends in fatalities or even people getting hurt. But I did find one story where it went terribly wrong. That was the story I used as the inspiration for the "Then" story. Tyler Barriss was actually a serial swatter, and he called in bomb threats regularly and was making money off of people wanting him to swat someone for them. He bragged about it online, and one day, he and someone else decided to swat a guy that they had a dispute with in a *Call of Duty* game. They called in a hostage situation to an address, and when the police arrived, the man living in the house at the address they had given walked out on the porch and was shot because the police thought he was armed and reaching for a gun. The man died. But that's not all of it. It turned out it was the wrong address. It wasn't even the guy they wanted to harass; it was some complete stranger, a 28-year-old man and a father of two who lost his life that day. The guy who made the call was later found, and he got twenty years in jail. His friend got fifteen months.

Now, the story about a mother holding down a kid so her child could beat someone up is also taken from real life, incredible as it sounds. It is quite insane. You can read more here and also see the video that was recorded of the attack at a bus stop. The woman was later arrested.

https://www.wsmv.com/news/police-mother-and-daughter-beat-girl-waiting-for-school-bus/article_325cd646-dee9-11e9-a4c2-67c2f3877b6c.html

I will end this with a couple of fun facts that surprised me when researching for this book. I can tell you that there are more than twenty-three million YouTube channels, and more than eight-thousand of them have more than a million subscribers. They estimate that two out of five of these are gaming related. The live streaming platform Twitch has more than two million broadcasters and fifteen million daily viewers.

It makes sense that there is a lot of money involved in this world.

Thank you for all your support. Don't forget to leave a review if you can; it means so much to me.

Take care,

Willow

About the Author

Willow Rose is a multi-million-copy best-selling Author and an Amazon ALL-star Author of more than 80 novels. Her books are sold all over the world.

She writes Mystery, Thriller, Paranormal, Romance, Suspense, Horror, Supernatural thrillers, and Fantasy.

Willow's books are fast-paced, nail-biting page-turners with twists you won't see coming. That's why her fans call her The Queen of Plot Twists.

Several of her books have reached the Kindle top 10 of ALL books in the US, UK, and Canada. She has sold more than three million books all over the world.

Willow lives on Florida's Space Coast with her husband and two daughters. When she is not writing or reading, you will find her surfing and watch the dolphins play in the waves of the Atlantic Ocean.

CPSIA information can be obtained
at www.ICGtesting.com
Printed in the USA
LVHW110018211120
672143LV00006B/58